Praise for *Th*

A *Real Simple*

A *Marie Claire* Ultimate Summer Beach Read

A *New York Post* Best Book on Our Summer Reading List

A *Country Living* Can't-Miss Beach Read for This Summer

A *Cosmopolitan* New Book to Feed Your Wanderlust

A *Parade* Book You'll Want to Read This Sizzling Season

A *Fortune* Entertaining New Book to Read This Summer

—

"With a gorgeously picturesque setting, an utterly charming cast, and a hilarious protagonist, Lizzy Dent's *The Summer Job* is my perfect summer read! Sure to be one of the sweetest, funniest, and sexiest books of the year. As soon as I finished it, I wanted to read it again. Do not miss this one!"

—Emily Henry, #1 *New York Times* bestselling author of *Happy Place*

"This novel is what happens when you combine *Sweetbitter* with *The Princess Switch*, place it in the Scottish Highlands, and throw in a whole lot of wine." —*Entertainment Weekly*

"A rom-com-esque adventure in which a girl steals her best friend's identity to spend the season at a luxury Scottish Highlands resort. Lol, same." —*Cosmopolitan*

"Funny, romantic, hilariously chaotic, and full to the brim with Scottish charm." —*Parade*

"The secluded Scotland setting makes it easy to immerse yourself in Birdy's world. . . . Plenty of bad decisions and dramatic disasters, a cast of supporting characters to love and hate, and a sweet and tender romance despite all odds. But through it all, you can't help but root for Birdy!" —*PopSugar*

"If you're a fan of *Outlander* but want an adventure in the Scottish Highlands with a little more Wi-Fi, this is the read for you." —Shondaland

"Dent hits a home run with her first novel. . . . This witty, banter-filled novel seems frothy at first, but aptly balances the humor with darker subjects. Lovely descriptions of Scotland, quirky supporting characters, and a thoroughly lovable heroine make this a sure bet for fans of Jenny Colgan." —*Library Journal* (starred review)

"Dent's debut is a frothy story reminiscent of late 1990s chick lit, complete with unexpected friendships, offbeat situations, and a relatable protagonist whose inner journey will charm and delight readers. It's escapist fun with surprising emotional depth; fans of Emily Henry and Katie Fforde should add this to their summer-read list." —*Booklist*

"This book is fun with a capital F. It made me want to go to Scotland, drink wine, and kiss hot chefs, IMMEDIATELY. Dent has such a fresh voice, and so many of us will identify with Birdy Finch. If you've ever felt you're getting left behind in life, or don't have everything worked out quite yet, this is the book for you." —Sophie Cousens, author of *This Time Next Year*

"What a welcome escape from lockdown. It's witty and funny and it packs an emotional punch, too, which is really tricky to pull off. I was willing Birdy/Heather on, knowing all along that her ticking-bomb secret was going to have to blow at some point. Which of course it did, in a spectacularly satisfying way! Loved it, I'm in the queue for more Lizzy Dent."

—Josie Silver, author of *One Day in December*

"*The Summer Job* is a great read—fresh, funny, and filled with delicious food and wine. It made me long for a summer in Scotland with Birdy and all the team at Loch Dorn."

—Beth O'Leary, author of *The Flatshare*

"Funny and heartwarming, *The Summer Job* is a delightful summer escape. . . . The Scottish setting is pure magic, and fans of Emily Henry or Sophie Kinsella will fall for debut novelist Lizzy Dent."

—*Shelf Awareness*

Praise for *The Setup*

—

A *PopSugar* Best New Book
A Motherly Buzziest Book
A Love to Know Must-Read Book

—

"An adorable rom-com packed full of nostalgia and Dent's trademark wit." —Sophie Cousens, author of *This Time Next Year*

"I fell in love with Lizzy Dent's writing with *The Summer Job* and have been waiting with bated breath to see what she does next.

This book is everything I wanted and then some. With Dent's usual humor, wit, and warmth, and a spectacularly charming cast of weirdos, *The Setup* is exactly the kind of summer read I'm constantly on the hunt for. I love astrology-obsessed, hot-mess Mara, I love the crumbling little Broadgate lido she's out to save, and I love, love, love Lizzy Dent."

—Emily Henry, #1 *New York Times* bestselling author of *Happy Place*

"Lizzy Dent, known for her bestselling novel *The Summer Job*, is back once again with another witty story filled with love and lighthearted humor."
—*PopSugar*

"[A] sweet and funny tale of a woman who has been barely scraping by as she opens herself up to new friends and new experiences. For fans of Abbi Waxman and Emily Henry."
—*Booklist*

"Perfect."
—Motherly

"Grab your SPF and your carry-on because we have the ultimate beach read for your summer getaway. *The Setup* is a laugh-out-loud story. . . . You can't imagine the twists and turns [it] takes."
—Love to Know

"The perfect storm of a rom-com—the chaotic, hilarious entanglement of a kickass heroine, her hot AF neighbor, and a very unwelcome ex. As intoxicating as a cocktail on a summer's day."
—Beth Morrey, author of *The Love Story of Missy Carmichael*

"A gleefully over-the-top plot, but anyone who's ever been screwed over at work will empathize with Amy's plight. In the end, justice is served most deliciously. This is pure popcorn."
—*Publishers Weekly*

JUST ONE TASTE

Lizzy Dent

G. P. PUTNAM'S SONS
NEW YORK

PUTNAM
— EST. 1838 —

G. P. PUTNAM'S SONS
Publishers Since 1838
An imprint of Penguin Random House LLC
penguinrandomhouse.com

LIBRARY OF CONGRESS CATALOGING-IN-PUBLICATION DATA

Names: Dent, Lizzy, author.
Title: Just one taste / Lizzy Dent.
Description: New York : G. P. Putnam's Sons, 2024.
Identifiers: LCCN 2024011299 (print) | LCCN 2024011300 (ebook) |
ISBN 9780593716038 (trade paperback) | ISBN 9780593716045 (ebook)
Subjects: LCGFT: Romance fiction. | Humorous fiction. | Novels.
Classification: LCC PR9639.4.D45 J87 2024 (print) |
LCC PR9639.4.D45 (ebook) | DDC 823/.92—dc23/eng/20240315
LC record available at https://lccn.loc.gov/2024011299
LC ebook record available at https://lccn.loc.gov/2024011300

Interior art by logoheroman / Shutterstock

Printed in the United States of America
1st Printing

Book design by Ashley Tucker

For Bernie xx

1

London

FROM BEHIND THE front window of London's most pretentious bar, I watch as my late father's restaurant, Nicky's, starts to stir for the evening shift across the street. The head chef, Leo Ricci, spins the handle to extend the black canvas awning across the eight outside tables. The little neon door sign my mother gifted my father for Christmas twenty-five years ago blinks intermittently beside the black front door. I feel a stab of deep regret and sadness. And wonder why the hell no one got the damn sign fixed.

"Here you are, madam. The whiskey is served at a precise 65.35 degrees Fahrenheit," says the sulky waiter as he hands me a double malt in cut crystal, elegantly withdrawing a stylish metal thermometer from my glass. He then slides a small bowl of smoked almonds with powdered Himalayan salt on the window bar in front of me. I paint on a smile before I briefly look up from under my baseball cap to thank him.

His mouth sags. "Oh. It's *you*." He's so deliciously bitchy, I laugh.

"I'm not barred, am I?" I ask, raising an eyebrow playfully. "They haven't got a mug shot of me hanging behind the bar?"

"Just don't let my manager see you," the waiter replies, shrugging with indifference. "You're public enemy number one round here."

I chuckle as he leaves. I'm a food journalist at *The London Times*, a free but very widely read paper that circulates on the Underground. About three issues ago, I wrote a several-paragraphs-long hit piece targeting this place—Temp—in a story entitled "Is This Effing Satire?" I'd hated the self-consciously gimmicky idea that all drinks must be served at a particular temperature with a bespoke thermometer. So, you get your Chardonnay at 48.1 degrees, your rosé at 51.8, and your Chablis Grand Cru at 55.4. And everyone can *really* taste the difference, apparently.

Don't get me wrong, it is nice to do things "properly," but can we please be serious? This bar is frequented by bankers who only appreciate the quality of wine by its price. I also hated the way the proprietor, a software engineer turned bar owner, had talked down to my friend Ginny when she requested a cube of ice in her Sauv Blanc. *We are not a dive bar, darling.*

"Olive!" Ginny and Kate arrive in a flurry of kisses and hugs. Ginny, an excellent interior architect with bouncy black curls, wide brown eyes, and a chic tan suit, and Kate, an ice-blond relationship therapist who exudes Scandi chic in wide-leg jeans and a designer sweatshirt.

"Why on earth did you choose this place?" Kate asks. "Didn't you call it a Tesla for oenophiles?" She drops her voice. "This *is* the tech-bro bar, right?"

"It's disruptive drinking for the biohack generation," I reply, mockingly serious. "Kendall Roy would love it."

"Sweet returns, bro," Kate snarls playfully.

"I hope that awful owner isn't here," Ginny says, glancing around the restaurant.

"I've not seen him. Yet," I say, tugging down my cap, just in case. Ginny eyes the cap, somewhat despairingly.

"You look . . . cute," Ginny says, touching my slouchy gray hoodie and attempting to admire the ends of my fuzzy outgrown bob. Ginny is the friend who cannot lie.

"It's grief-core," I say, laughing at her. "I look like shit, but I'm fine with it."

They pause, glancing at each other with concern.

"I'm fine! Sit, I'll explain," I say.

I wait for them to settle in their seats on either side of me, so we are three in a row, peering out the darkened window into the daylight like barn owls.

"So, I went to the estate attorney's office today and you're seriously not going to believe it," I say, pointing across the road to Nicky's, where chef Leo Ricci has taken a seat at one of the outside tables and is going through paperwork. A cute red-haired waitress with a sleeve of tattoos comes out and slides a coffee in front of him.

"Oh my goodness, Nicky's! That's why we're here?" Ginny asks, mouth open.

"He left you the restaurant?" Kate asks in breathless awe.

"He left me the restaurant," I confirm, still in shock myself.

"Do you get that hot chef with it?" Ginny asks, pointing at Leo, who at that very moment looks up in our direction. He can't possibly see us with the evening sun so low and bright in his eyes, so I indulge myself, staring as he runs his hands up through his dark hair, biceps popping as he rests them on his head for a moment before breathing out, eyes to the sky, and then returning to his paperwork.

"All of it, yes," I say, a strange sort of prickly feeling going up my spine before I pull my eyes from Leo.

My father died suddenly almost two months ago. I emerged from an underground bar and my phone sprang to life with seven missed calls and several text messages from both my father and a number I later learned was Leo Ricci's. When I saw the sheer volume of calls, I just knew. But the speed at which he went downhill was dizzying. Some run-of-the-mill infection one day, sepsis and death the next.

I feel as though I've been stuck in a state of shock, moving like a marionette through the responsibilities of being his only living relative. Go here. Sign this. Cancel that. Send this letter. Call the energy company. Call the energy company again. And *again*. Mum offered to help, but it felt weird having her reading through his personal effects; she'd just remarried, and Dad and she were divorced so long ago. I also felt it was right to try to protect his privacy, especially since he died alone.

Dry, sardonic humor is one way to get through the sudden death of a parent. Booze is another. I lift my whiskey to my lips and tip it back like I'm taking a shot.

"He *left* you Nicky's?" Kate says again.

"My god, Olive, when did you last even go in there?" Ginny says as her wine arrives, and she accepts it graciously.

"I mean, maybe ten years ago?" I say, feeling the heat of shame creeping up my neck as I say it. "Longer?"

It was definitely longer. I remember walking away and dramatically announcing I was never coming back. I was seventeen years old. That's just about fifteen years ago. I'd seen my dad since for a birthday here, a Christmas there. We messaged. But it was Mum whom I stuck with when things fell apart. She was the wounded party, leaving when she could take no more of coming second to Dad's obsession with Nicky's. I still bristle at the memory of Mum crying at the bottom of the escalators at Angel station as we stood there with our bags, heading to live with my aunt until Mum found another job and we found another home. It was hard to love him after that.

"Holy shit," says Ginny, eyes wide, face grimacing. After a long period of silence, she perks up. "But also, I mean, what an opportunity. It's yours?"

"Mine," I confirm.

"You *were* kind of born for this, Olive."

I sink into my seat, deflated by Ginny's misplaced excitement.

People romanticize hospitality. It often shows up in books or movies as a cutesy job for creative, homely types. It looks like freshly baked croissants in mouthwatering piles on a table covered with homemade jam in a pretty shop on a sweet high street with plenty of middle-class foot traffic. It looks like chalkboard menus and handsome staff in stiff linen aprons with leather ties, and bench seating decorated with thyme and rosemary in tiny silver pots. And always, a tired but tenacious owner who is busy—yes—but deliriously fulfilled and with plenty of time to fall in love.

What it *actually* looks like? Carnage. Like the scene of a crime. Bloody, sometimes. Chaos, always. Meeting the booze delivery truck at 6:30 a.m. and calling the rat guy and sneaking him in and out during lunch service. It's sticky kitchen floors and hungover chefs who are fucking the waitstaff and waitstaff who are stealing from the till. It's a mild coke habit if you're under thirty and a mild drinking problem after that. It looks like high blood pressure, heart disease, couch-surfing exhaustion. It's sixteen-hour days with no one in your life but the people you work with.

Don't get me wrong. My parents had it good for a long while. Nicky's was a classic family restaurant, a simple and easy-to-execute Italian menu with a modest but comfortable turnover. A very good turnover for a time, when my dad's TV cooking show aired. They had a rotation of competent chefs and enough staff who could steer the ship so we could go on an annual family summer holiday to Italy. A week in Sicily, staying with Dad's friend and mentor Rocco in Catania, and another week somewhere on the north Riviera with his best friend, Roger. We'd see Rapallo. Cinque Terre. Portofino. Sunshine, sunscreen, and of course, plenty of eating.

They also owned the property outright. Dad bought it long before the real estate boom in East London. And the restaurant was never just a workplace. It was our second home. I would sit at table 7 doing my homework while Mum ran the restaurant and Dad made slabs of olive focaccia in the wood-fired pizza oven. At our real home around the corner, I ate utilitarian cornflakes for breakfast, but in the evenings, I sat at the bar at Nicky's eating truffle linguine with sparkling water in a wine goblet. And my parents? They were happy. Really fucking busy. But happy. *And* in love.

It *was* pretty perfect, actually.

Until it wasn't.

"I'm going to sell it," I say. "Please don't hate me, but that building is freehold."

"Holy shit," says Ginny.

"Wait. What's freehold?" Kate asks.

"She owns the actual building as well as the business," Ginny explains, her eyes wide. "Christ, what's it's worth?"

"I'd pay a lot of tax, but still, it's a life-changing amount of money," I say, feeling my cheeks redden. I'm really *that bitch* with an inheritance. The one time being an only child pays out.

"You really don't want to keep it?" Ginny asks, frowning.

"The estate attorney says it's practically a teardown. I'd have to mortgage it to renovate. The turnover is terrible, so it would be hand-to-mouth paying *that* back. I'd have to move in upstairs to avoid it being taxed as a second home. It's complicated. Plus, there's the small but obvious problem that I've not worked in a restaurant since I was sixteen years old." I try to laugh, desperate to keep the conversation upbeat, but the girls are more subdued, nothing but a simple *ha* from Kate.

"I think you'd be good at it," presses Ginny. "You've worked in *food* for your whole adult life, Olive. It's your literal job to know what makes a good restaurant. Plus, you're very warm, when you can be bothered." She nudges me in the ribs, and I smile, nudging her back.

"I could sell it and finally help my mum out, and still have enough to buy my own home, Ginny," I say, trying to get her on board. "That I'd own. Maybe even *outright*."

"*That* would be life-changing indeed," says Kate, nodding.

"The stuff of dreams," Ginny says, wide-eyed.

"Everything would be the same, but I'd be rent-free. Living in London. Can you imagine?"

"Yeah. You can, like, keep doing the job you hate," Kate says wryly.

"But rent-free," I say. I tip my head toward Kate. "Come on."

"You *do* hate your job," Ginny agrees. "You spent most of the last year complaining about it. Like a shitty boyfriend you wouldn't dump." I catch the look of agreement on Kate's face and realize I've been the subject of some *breakout* discussions.

"But look at it this way, I'd have a lot of freedom to find something else. Maybe I'll write a novel or something?" I say wistfully, as the girls both *Mm-hmm*, nodding in unison. "Which leads me to the catch."

"The catch?" Kate says, straightening up.

"Oh boy," says Ginny, reaching for her wine. I pause briefly to take a sip of my whiskey.

"My dad was in the middle of writing a cookbook, and he wanted me to finish it."

"Ohhhhh," Kate says thoughtfully. "I think that's sweet."

"I didn't know he was writing one," I say, and then stare across at the Nicky's sign again. "He always wanted to, you know. More than TV, he wanted to make a cookbook that sat on everyone's shelf between *The Joy of Cooking* and *Mastering the Art of French Cooking*."

"Aw, that's really sad he never got to finish it," says Ginny. "No matter how you felt about him, Olive, you *have* to do it."

"I know. He was due to go to Italy for a few weeks next month to do the final push. So, the accommodation is booked and paid for and I'd just need to get the flight."

"Well, this is like the perfect way to say good-bye to him," says Ginny; then she leans in, nudging me. "Perhaps you can put some of those regrets to rest?"

I nod. So many regrets. I regret missing those last seven phone calls, for one.

"Where in Italy?"

"Back to Sicily for the first time in more than fifteen years, then somewhere in Tuscany, and finally Liguria," I say.

"Oh Jesus. Can I come with?" Ginny says, clasping her hands together.

I spin the whiskey glass on the table as I analyze my feelings for the hundredth time. There are so many conflicting emotions I can't yet communicate to my friends. But the one I feel overwhelmingly right now is that I do not deserve this huge gift from my father. I feel shame at his generosity. I hardly saw him in the last ten years, tucking myself away on the other side of the river, blaming him and resenting this restaurant for the end of my parents' marriage.

I look up from my drink and across to Leo.

I should be where Leo is right now. I should have gone to culinary school just as we'd planned. Then I would have trained under my dad, preparing to eventually take over Nicky's when he was too old to descend the wine cellar stairs or too forgetful to take an order. A quiet part of me thought I'd eventually come back. The child in me also thought my dad would live forever. But he didn't.

When I walked away, Leo Ricci stepped into my place. Dad poured all that love and attention into him. They even went on holiday together, I'd learned. Leo worked beside him for nearly fifteen years, and now I'm supposed to swoop in and take the spoils? Be Leo's boss?

Does Leo even know?

I grimace into my empty glass. I *have* to sell it, and sell quickly.

"*Duck!*" Ginny shouts as she spots Temp's owner arriving in his three-piece suit with bright-white trainers and a trilby.

We sink our heads in unison; Ginny arranges the wine list

(which is irritatingly sorted by fucking temperature) to hide our faces.

"Well. A lot to process, Olive. But I think a few weeks in Italy doing this for your father will really be a good thing for you," Kate whispers from behind the menu, in her practical way.

"Sun. Sex. Sangria," Ginny begins.

"Sangria is Spain," Kate interjects.

"I'm sure you can get sangria in Italy," whispers Ginny stubbornly.

"We have to get out of here," says Kate, craning her neck. "Let's go sit in the Book Bar instead."

"Yes, let's go," I say, throwing a twenty-pound note on the table just as the owner spots me. "*Quick.*"

As we spill out onto the street, I pull them down the road and between two parked vans, out of the glaring view of the owner, who is waving a fist and yelling down the street. "You suck, Olive fucking Stone!"

"Oh my *god*," I say, cringing.

I glance at Leo, who is on the phone now but looks up to see what the commotion is about. Ginny starts to laugh, but my heart beats hard in my chest, and I hold a finger up to my mouth to shush her.

"Tech bro is gone," whispers Kate as she peers around the van.

"Damn," I reply, panting. "I'm a serious liability."

"You're a very rich liability," Ginny reminds me, pointing back at Nicky's.

"Shit. I haven't finished explaining the catch," I say, following her gaze, and we all turn to get a better look back at the restaurant.

"He's a catch, all right," says Ginny, swooning at Leo.

"The thing is," I say, putting a hand on both of their arms as we peer around the van like a trio of comedy government spies. "Because I'm not a chef myself, and can't really do the recipe part of the book . . ." I take a deep breath and point across to Leo, who is about to head back inside Nicky's and begin the evening shift. "Part of the deal is that the hot chef over there—Leo Ricci—he has to come and do it with me."

"You have to spend a month in Italy with *him*?"

"My nemesis," I say.

2

FEEL LIKE THIS is illegal. Or it should be. Like I'm breaking the law just standing here. And if not illegal, it certainly feels immoral to be holding the keys to my father's restaurant.

My restaurant.

My heart has kicked up and my palms are sweaty. It's been a week since I heard the news from the estate attorney, but it's barely sunk in. And so here I am, at almost 1 a.m., the full legal owner and yet too afraid to step in. Not just afraid, if I'm honest: *unworthy*.

I gaze up at the flickering neon sign, irritated to see the *N* barely glows, making the name of the restaurant appear to read ICKY'S. Which—and I cannot stress this enough—is a terrible name for a place where anyone might want to eat food.

"Here we go," I say under my breath.

And then I slide in the key.

It's dark inside, but the familiar smell of garlicky earthiness with a nose-tingling hit of lemony floor cleaner hits me like a punch to the nose. Smell is the most visceral of senses, and I am transported back in time. I catch a glimpse of my mother twisting her hair into a bun. I hear flashes of my father shouting *"Order up!"* while he winks at her. Rowdy, drunken laughter at table 5. Glasses clinking. Later, tempers flaring between my parents over a forgotten order. Mum crying on the back steps after a particularly grueling shift. I breathe through the memories, which flash before me like an old photo carousel, until I can ground myself here in the present.

"Hello?" I say, the sound echoing into darkness. But there is no reply.

I reach, instinctively fumbling for the light switch. But then I stop myself, allowing my eyes to adjust and the yellow-orange light of the streetlamps outside to guide me. Better to keep on the down-low.

I move through the tables, sliding my body left and right, gently touching the plastic lamination on the red-and-white cloths covering the chipped Formica. *The same tables.* I touch the chrome frame of one of the chairs with its red-leather cushioned seat. *The same chairs.* I look ahead to the bar, its long oak-topped counter with the rounded carved edging, and I place both hands on the cool wood, resting my bum against one of the fixed round stools that sit underneath.

I feel an ache in my heart as I picture my father there behind the bar. I lean into the memory as though it were yesterday.

Afternoon light fills the restaurant.

Dad has thick brown hair, which always looks a bit wet from the cream he uses in it. He is handsome, and very expressive—a twinkle in his big brown eyes and a wide, welcoming smile. He loves sun, shown in fine lines everywhere on his face, but he looks jolly with it, rather than weathered. He wears the same thing to every shift: black suit pants and a black chef's jacket.

The memory is so real, I hear him.

"Up you get, sweetheart," my dad says as he pats the bar.

I scramble up. I must be nine years old, the bar still too tall for me to peer over without climbing onto one of those stools.

Dad is watching Jamie Oliver on the TV behind the bar, and he's teaching me how to make tortellini.

"It's called *The Naked Chef*. I'm checking out the competition."

Dad always wanted to be like those TV chefs, but Jamie Oliver wound him up because he was successful so young.

"Though look at him using mascarpone. He's not even Italian."

"He trained at the River Café and that's Italian food." *My mother.*

I remember her smoothing her spaghetti-strap dress and fixing an apron around her middle. I thought Mum was the most beautiful woman in the world. But in this memory, I see a jittery anxiety I didn't recognize back then.

Mum was trying to keep the restaurant viable because all their money was tied up in it, and Dad never took her concerns seriously. I don't want to pretend Dad was some kind of creative airhead, or that Mum was some all-business robot, but it was clear where their strengths lay: Dad was the cook and Mum was the coin.

Dad shows me how to fill and fold tortellini, but my young fingers are clumsy and the results are misshapen.

"It's perfect," I hear my dad say. "Non tutte le ciambelle riescono col buco."

"Not all doughnuts come out with a hole," I say, giggling, as I roll another collapsing tortellini.

Mum fills out the specials board, and they haggle over the prices. Then Mum leans over the bar and they kiss.

"So, what do you reckon, Olive, darling?" Dad says. "Reckon your old dad could be on TV like Jamie Oliver?"

"More like Gary Rhodes," says my mum with a laugh, as she slides in the till tray full of change, before opening the reservations folder and double-checking the table settings. "Isn't it more like a *travel* show they want you to do, Nicky? Gone six weeks at a time?"

"Papa?" I gasp. But not at him being gone. About the excitement of him being on television.

"It's time, Nicky," Mum says with a soft smile.

She always said that just before opening. *It's time.*

"This is going to be the start of something big, Olive," Dad says, starting to clear up. "A little six-part series, then a guest spot on morning television, a string of new restaurants, and then, hopefully, that cookbook!" Dad beams in a slightly unhinged way, which makes me giggle.

I smile at the memory, as a warm feeling wraps around my heart. *There were good times*, I think.

"I'm sorry. I'm sorry I took so long to come back," I say softly, eyes closed, the sound echoing into darkness.

"Hello?" A man's voice.

My eyes shoot open, heart racing.

"Hello?" the voice says again. "Olive?"

I snap my head around, and there, standing in the dimly lit kitchen entrance, is Leonardo Ricci. He takes a step forward and his movement triggers a motion sensor light in the back so his tall body falls into silhouette, and I cannot make out the features on his face. I hold my hand up to shield my eyes from the light.

"Yes," I say. "Leo?"

"Yeah. Hi. Sorry to give you a fright. What . . . what are you doing here?" he says. "It's after one."

"What are *you* doing here?" I shoot back, sliding a hand up to my heart as if to slow it. As my fingers graze the cotton of my sweatshirt, I realize the state I'm in. A hastily tugged-on outfit after a fitful attempt at sleep. There have been many sleepless nights lately.

"I forgot my house keys," he says, moving out of the light and walking behind the bar to retrieve them. I step backward from the bar, creating even more distance between us. Leo pauses, holding his keys aloft as evidence. "I'm sorry to disturb you, I didn't expect . . ."

His voice trails off. *Does he know yet?*

"I picked up the keys today," I say, feeling him out.

"Right. Of course," he says, nodding slowly.

Maybe he does know.

"Just wanted to take a look," I explain, turning my head toward the dining area. "I see nothing's changed."

I don't mean to sound disparaging; it just comes out that way. But it really hasn't. In fact, the only change is the clear degradation of the fittings. The little nicks I could feel on the once high-polished bar top, the scuffed floor, the chipped paint I can clearly see with the light on in the kitchen.

"Oh," he says, shoving his keys into his pocket.

The motion light snaps off and we are plunged back into darkness; it takes a moment for our eyes to adjust. When they do, Leo leans forward and rests his elbows on the bar, his arms crossed. His T-shirt pulls tight at his biceps, his shoulders round with muscle and wide. He looks so completely at home behind that bar, his black hair falling forward into his eyes from a cresting cowlick, his eyes framed by long lashes and his jaw strong, but not overly so. In fact, he's incredibly sexy in this light.

"Can I get you a drink or something?" Leo says, nodding toward the pint glasses stacked up high next to the beer taps. "Although I'm not sure if it feels right to *celebrate* as such." I see a muscle tick in his jaw.

"No drink," I say quickly.

Leo nods, biting the inside of his cheek, as he considers his next words.

"Well, this is strange," he says finally.

"I know," I reply, balling my hands together, rubbing them nervously. "Hopefully not for long."

"What do you mean *not for long*?" he asks, tipping his head to the side.

"Well. I'm selling," I blurt out. I don't mean to say it, and I cringe at how callous it sounds, but I can't take it back now. Ginny warned me that in the ranking of awful conversations to have with a person, telling Leo I was going to sell fell somewhere between "We're restructuring, and we don't see a position for you in the new org chart" and "I stole your boyfriend, and then I shot him in the nuts."

I sigh. *At least it's done.*

"What?" he says.

"*Selling.* I mean, you understand, right?"

"Why?" Leo's body tenses in the dim light, and he stands up, his arms falling back against his chest, still folded. He's elevated behind there, just enough to feel towering in the dynamic of this conversation. "Why would you sell?"

"What do you mean *why*?" I ask, straightening up a little myself.

"You don't mean it," he says, tipping his head slightly.

I let out a small laugh. "I *do* mean it," I say, my tone challenging.

"You can't sell!" he says, throwing his arms open. "No. *What?* You can't do that. After all these years, after everything. This is his legacy. This place is all that's left of your dad."

My mind flickers to the urn I am supposed to pick up from the funeral home. *"Miss Stone, could you please come and collect your father,"* as if he's had one too many at the local wine bar.

"It's not *all* that's left of him," I mutter.

"What?" Leo leans in, stretching his neck to hear me.

"Nothing. Sorry. I *have* to sell," I say, lifting a hand to pinch the bridge of my nose. I didn't want to do this, this way. I wish Leo wasn't here. Fuck him for being here.

"No, you don't," he snaps, taking a moment to settle his breathing.

"Excuse me?"

I narrow my eyes a little at Leo, standing there behind the bar, just like my father used to. Just like *he* owns the place. A stab of anger passes through me, but it's quickly replaced by guilt at what my decision means for him, and then finally embarrassment that I'm even in this position for no deserving reason. *Only blood.* Truly, a whirlwind of emotions have been swamping my brain since Dad died.

"I have to," I say again, my voice small but steady. "Sorry."

"You don't want your own restaurant?" Leo asks, almost confused, as if it must be every single human being's lifelong dream. It's clearly Leo's dream.

Oh god, this is a nightmare.

"I don't understand," he says, incredulous. "How can you just sell it? Without talking about it?"

"Talking to who?" I shoot back, frowning. He can't mean I should run the decision by him.

Leo shakes his head, his mouth open.

"I don't want to own a restaurant," I say, spelling it out for him. "I didn't ask for it. I don't want it."

Leo's eyes fix on me, hard.

"Why *would* I want it?" I challenge. "I've seen the books. The estate attorney shared them. This place is a fucking sinkhole."

I shouldn't have said that either. It's true, but I should *not* have said that. Leo has put his whole adult life into Nicky's. He started here not long after I last stepped out the door. Dad, by all accounts, loved him like a son. He was the apprentice I might once have been and I've just said the worst thing I could about the place he obviously loves. I want to take it back. I want to grab the words like they're on a length of rope and tug them back in.

"*Olive* . . . ," Leo says, almost in a whisper. He stops himself from continuing. Then he turns, looking at the back wall of the bar, where dozens of Italian aperitifs and digestifs line the mirrored shelves. Another jolt of heady nostalgia rockets through me as I see my dad reaching for a bottle above the shelf. *"On the house,"* I hear him shout over his shoulder.

Leo lifts a hand to his face, and I watch as he slowly drags it from his forehead to his mouth, dropping it as he tilts his head back and stares up at the ceiling. His broad shoulders rise and fall and he remains still for what feels like minutes.

The guilt returns. The shame follows.

He can get another job. Kate's counsel is on repeat in my head like a mantra. *You didn't ask for this. And what are you going to do? Give him a whole fucking restaurant? No.*

I take a step back in anticipation of his . . . anger? I don't know what's coming.

Leo turns, hands on his narrow hips where his jeans hang a little low.

"And if it wasn't a sinkhole?" he says slowly.

"I'd still sell," I say, hearing the crack in my voice as I say it.

"Please reconsider," he says, more firmly.

"*No*," I hit back sharply, teetering very close to tears. The tiredness. The just . . . not wanting this important conversation to happen like this. *Now.*

Leo flinches, a crease appearing between his brows as he leans forward and pulls a beer out of the fridge, knocking the top off on the edge of the bar.

He glances at me and then back at the beer. "I always pay for them," he says quickly. "There's a list under the till and we . . ."

I hold my hand up, shaking my head. "I really don't need to know."

"We're going to Sicily in seven days," he says. "Could you keep an open mind? Could we talk about it on the trip?"

No. It isn't fair on anyone to drag this out.

"No expectations," he says. "Just. *Wow.* I can't quite bear the idea this is over without so much as a discussion."

I feel annoyed. I drag my eyes from Leo toward the dark kitchen. I wanted to go to Dad's office. I wanted to see if he kept his gelato in the freezer at the perfect height for a kid to sneak in and scoop it out into a paper cup without Mum noticing. I wanted to see if I felt anything other than the years of resentment I'd carried for this place. Although . . . I already have that answer.

"I'm selling," I say, exhausted by the questioning. "Sorry. I didn't ask for this."

I see a glimpse of something like disgust in Leo's eyes. And I stiffen, my anger sharpening as I feel a bit like a criminal giving a statement under duress.

"I'm going," I say. "Sorry. I shouldn't have come. I should have waited until . . ."

My voice drifts off and I frown at Leo, who watches me intensely. Too intensely. I turn quickly and walk out the door.

3

CAN'T BELIEVE I have to be there for four fucking weeks with *him*," I call out to Ginny.

Worse still, in Tuscany I'm supposed to be staying at his family's home—there will be no escape from Leo.

"You can book a hotel in Florence if you're still mortal enemies by the time you get to Tuscany," Ginny calls out, as if she's heard my thoughts.

"I have not packed for Italy in fifteen years," I call back to Ginny as she finishes putting away the dishes from our boozy good-bye lunch. "And now I'm doing it after a glass of wine."

"Beach clothes," Ginny calls back, the clatter of cutlery startling me as it's tossed back into the drawer. I'm so on edge: a heady mix of anxiety and excitement.

"But I'm not sure I'll be at the beach much," I reply, holding a strapless silk dress before tossing it into the *maybe* pile. I glance at my phone, wondering if I should just grow the hell up and call Leo back, but the idea of another confrontation with him makes my palms sweat. The tone of his text messages has gotten increasingly impatient.

LEO: Olive. I think it's important we have a plan ahead of the trip, don't you? Shall we meet for coffee?

The next day.

LEO: Or a call if it's easier?

And yesterday.

LEO: We can just arrive and try to figure it out, but that sounds like the least sensible option.

Dad's unfinished manuscript and the urn carrying his ashes are sitting on my bedside table. I only just collected them yesterday, a job I'd put off until the very last minute. I haven't read the manuscript yet—another reason I wasn't ready to see Leo. The mere thought of it feels like tearing open a crusty wound. I want to feel calm when I read it, in control. I will feel much more mentally prepared once I've touched down and checked in and have a glass of wine in my hand. Or maybe I'll never feel ready.

"It feels wrong to put Dad in the luggage hold," I call out, lifting the polished silver urn, which is surprisingly heavy. "I can't put him in the hold, can I?"

"Carry-on for sure," Ginny calls back.

"Carry-on for sure," I repeat, placing the urn in my tote. I frown seeing the bulk of it; there won't be room for much else.

I hesitate, then put the manuscript in my check-in suitcase, along with a beach towel, a red bikini, a green one-piece, a pair of espadrilles, several T-shirts, my running shoes, and then a couple of fancy going-out dresses.

"Just in case," I say quietly, imagining Leo and me sitting down to dinner together. Not an entirely unpleasant vision, so long as we don't talk much.

"In case of what?" Ginny asks, shooting a damp tea towel into the laundry basket in the corner as she enters my room.

"A couple of going-out dresses," I say, grimacing. "In case I go out, I suppose."

Ginny looks at me with a mixture of love and pity.

"You're going to be fine, Olive," she says, glancing at her watch. "Don't let this guy unsettle you. Focus on the job. You really don't have to spend twenty-four seven in each other's laps." Ginny looks at me and grimaces. "Although it's a very attractive lap—"

"Ginny!" I shake my head, tapping her gently on the arm. "He's not just *some guy*, though, is he? He's spent over a decade with Dad. God knows what Dad's said about me. *She never calls. She abandoned me. She's an awful person.*"

"You had your reasons. He could have called *you* more. And besides"—she waves at the keys to the restaurant sitting on my dresser—"he obviously still cared, Olive."

I look at the bikini in my suitcase and then back to Ginny. I throw my arms around her. "I *will* be fine," I say. "Thanks for being here."

Earlier, Kate and Ginny pep-talked me over lunch, which I'd prepared for them as a distraction from the stress of tomorrow. I'd needed my friends; also, the meditative nature of cooking for other people has always been my happy place.

Ginny requested "something vegetarian" and I had delightedly obliged.

"You know where you can be vegetarian and still eat like a king?" I'd asked.

"Italy," they'd replied, eye-rolling back at me in unison.

Cringe. My dad used to say that all the time, and now, apparently, so did I.

I'd prepared burrata with a sweet onion and cherry tomato salad, my signature overnight focaccia, and a risotto with wild mushrooms and in-season wild garlic, and finished it all off with lemon, almond, and ricotta cake for dessert.

Kate called it "three courses of delicious responsibility avoidance" before she hugged me good-bye, scolded me for not speaking to Leo yet, and headed back to work.

"At least you'll know people in Sicily," Ginny replies, pulling back so she's holding both my shoulders.

I nod. I'll know my dad's old mentor, Rocco; his wife, Isabella; maybe even their grandson Luca if he's still around. I'll know their restaurant. Their family home. And as awkward as it feels to be "the estranged daughter," at least they've invited me for lunch. I feel a wave of anxiety at the thought of seeing them. *It will be fine.* Who knows what memories will be roused by the smells, the tastes, and the views of that beautiful southeastern coastline.

"I want to do a great job," I say, biting on my lower lip.

"Dude," Ginny says, frowning. "You're going to be writing about food. It's what you do."

My phone buzzes and I glance at it as it vibrates against the pale floral bedsheets. *Mum.*

"I better take this. She's jittery as hell about everything," I say apologetically.

"I have to go, anyway," Ginny says, grabbing her handbag from the floor as I reach for my phone. "Call me. Anytime. Any. Time."

"I love you," I say, as I take Mum's call and Ginny disappears into the hall and out the front door.

"Have you got everything you need? *Put the chèvre down over there, darling, on the cheese board. No, the other one. The smaller one. That's it. With the honey.*" She's having a two-way conversation between me and her lovely new husband, George.

"Olive?" she says back into the phone.

Mum remarried last year and it was a weight off my shoulders. She has rebuilt her life in a small rural village in Yorkshire. After a decade of unfulfilling jobs, she finally found her place as a buyer at a local farm shop five years ago, before meeting George, the sweetest beekeeper and all-round good egg. It took a long time, but I think she's really happy again.

"Is the honey still sweet in Yorkshire?" I say, with enough sass to make my mum laugh.

"We've got friends coming over and it's a whole thing," she says. "George is in a tizz and I'm trying to keep him calm. *I know you're not used to entertaining, George, but I can do this with both hands tied behind my back. Oh goodness, George, you're wicked.*" She cackles at what must be an off-screen sexy gag between them.

"Ewwwww," I say.

"Are you ready, Olive?"

"I'm just finishing packing," I say, tossing a cardigan into the suitcase. Although Sicily in July can be a furnace, there can be cool nights by the sea, and up in the hills of Mount Etna. I allow myself to feel a tantalizing hope we might head up there. There is something thrilling about the pull of the volcano towering over the Sicilian coastline, constantly puffing steam and fiery red ash like a sleeping dragon, while farmers and villagers quietly live and work, aware that she can wake at any moment.

"You've always been a terrible packer," Mum says with a weary chuckle. "Did you make a list?"

"I made a list!"

Mum is a days-long packer and list writer. Dad was a throw-it-all-in-an-hour-before-we-leave kind of guy. It drove her mad. He'd frequently arrive without basic things like underwear and a toothbrush, and we'd have to dash to the shops to the sound of Mum tutting and Dad telling her to *relax*. God, it infuriated Mum, even if the memory of it makes me smile.

"It's going to be quite a trip down memory lane for you," she says. "Are you okay? I think of you all the time, Olive."

"I'm fine. I'm nearly done," I say, plonking down on the bed next to my suitcase and staring at myself in the mirrored door of my wardrobe. I touch my hair and wonder if I should go to the salon at the end of the street before it closes. Ginny suggested it. *"No need to go to Italy with a man that handsome looking like the Unabomber,"* she'd said.

"I'm nervous about all of this," Mum says quietly.

"It's okay, I want to do this book for him," I say.

"I know . . . but I feel like I've let you down, Olive—"

I sit up a little straighter and cut her off. "Mum, please. For the last time, it isn't *your* fault I saw so little of Dad. I made those decisions, not you."

"I should have made more of an effort to let you see his side of things," she says.

Since Mum remarried, her once-bitter recollections of Dad have noticeably softened to wistful memories. But in a way, that's what happens with the parents when they meet someone else, isn't it? She's been able to finally move on and start a new life and leave the past behind her.

Whereas Dad will always be the father who prioritized a restaurant over me.

I chastise myself for thinking about it again, but there has been a lot of recalibrating going on in my head lately. Reexamining what happened all those years ago. Kate suggested it's part of trying to make sense of the inheritance. She thinks I'll only feel truly happy about it once I feel worthy of it.

"I just have regrets, that's all," Mum says.

"I *know* how he used to override you, Mum. Dad shouldn't have sold our home to fund that bloody restaurant. And he should have found a way to pay you out properly when you divorced."

I'm going to right that wrong when I sell it. I stare at myself in the mirror hard. I need to keep my eyes on *that* prize.

"I couldn't ask him to sell Nicky's, even then," she says.

"He still should have."

"He sent money," she reminds me.

I think of the pokey flat in Burnt Oak we shared and shake my head at the memory of me announcing to Mum I'd be going to study journalism instead of catering college as I'd always planned—my last act of revenge against my dad. She was proud of me, and that felt good.

"Mum, please," I say, putting my head in my hand.

"Not now. Fine," she says. "*Oh, how sweet, thank you.* George's put a cuppa in front of me. *Thank you, darling.*"

"Mum, I'm going to finish packing. I don't want you to worry. I'm nervous but excited to finish this cookbook off, and Leo seems really nice."

Okay, that last part isn't true, but I have enough complicated emotions without worrying about how my mum is feeling.

"Well, great," she says. "Wear sunblock. And don't go hiking in the middle of the day; there's another heat wave due next week. And have you done your international driver's license? Make sure you always have coins on you in case you need the bathroom. Especially in the train stations, okay?" She covers the phone, listening to George. "Olive, George says to remember to switch your phone off roaming or you'll come back to a disastrous bill."

"I'm not going to Peru," I say, laughing.

After I hang up, I zip the suitcase, triple-check my passport and cards are all neatly packed, and then head into the kitchen.

I pull out what's left of my lemon and ricotta cake from the fridge and dig in without bothering to cut a slice. I sit, wondering if I could have added more lemon rind, or perhaps a pinch of salt to draw out the taste of the ricotta more, and then with each mouthful, I slowly and gently allow myself to feel the excitement.

Because, the truth is, while Nicky's might have had a dark cloud over it, the recollections of my family holidays in Italy do not. They are sepia, sun-drenched snapshots of a perfect, privileged childhood that I have reveled in my whole life.

My phone buzzes and it's Leo. Appearing as if summoned like a demon to dispel my happy family memories once again.

LEO: I guess I'll see you there then?

It's nearly five. I'm going to go get that haircut.

4

Catania

"MIA SUITCASE," I whimper to the man collecting trolleys in the baggage reclaim area.

He shrugs and points wearily to a queue by the lost-baggage counter. An hour later, no suitcase in hand, I finally exit the airport with the crushing news that my bag is likely en route back to London.

But I'm unable to dwell on this for long, the heat hitting me like a blow dryer to the face, allowing me only one thought. *I'm here.* I can hardly believe it.

I stretch my sore neck and heave my tote with the urn onto my shoulder and slowly breathe out.

Sicily. I feel a little tingle in my toes, and a wistfulness that makes me smile.

As a taxi takes me toward the city center, we pass the white weeping trunks of eucalypts and tall, breezy palm trees lining the busy road. The blue sky stretches for miles out ahead of us toward the sloping sides of Mount Etna. There she is, towering in the distance, a little puff of cloud hovering above her mouth.

"There's a coast road, right? La strada . . . erm . . . al mare," I call out in my best Italian.

"Sì," the driver replies. "It's longer."

"That's okay. Va bene," I reply.

We turn right and, after a back-road detour, hit a long, straight avenue, the city to our left, and between the beach houses, restaurants, and shops on our right I catch glimpses of a broad sandy shore, and beyond that the Strait of Messina, the long blue stretch of the Mediterranean Sea that separates the mainland of Italy from Sicily. Glorious.

After we hit the main port, we turn left and into the city center, navigating a string of narrow one-way streets, until finally he's driven as far as he can go. He points down an alley filled with restaurants.

"Ecco il suo hotel," he says.

Torrisi Boutique Hotel. I feel an intense wave of déjà vu as I haul myself out of the taxi. I remember it. I remember arriving just like this, at the end of this little street, hauling ourselves out of the taxi, Dad beaming, Mum fanning herself with a magazine, me a spoiled teenager wishing that for one summer we went to Ibiza instead.

But we never did. Our holidays began here in Catania, this loud, bustling city pulsing with memories. I know these scenes, like a movie once adored and now almost forgotten. I know the large square lava-stone pavers that line the footpaths. I can smell salty, fishy air coming from the fish market I think is just down the far end of the square. I remember this intense heat, the sea breeze flowing like water between the buildings, down the alleyways, never quite cooling enough.

Inside, the hotel owner, Antonia, with her fiercely pulled black bun and smoky eyes, moves quickly from behind the reception desk to welcome me. *Clip-clop*, her sky-high heels echo as they hit the tiled floor of the reception. The lines of her face pull upward with her delight at seeing me, before sagging into sorrow as she gets closer.

"Mia bella," she says, pulling me in tight. "Your father. I'm so sorry."

"Oh. We're hugging?" I mutter, as I reluctantly lean into her embrace, all deep floral perfume and hairspray. I hear her sniff slightly and I stiffen in embarrassment. It ain't deep floral perfume I smell of; it's travel funk, and I need a shower and a change of clothes.

Ergh. I don't *have* a change of clothes. Damn bags.

"Olive, it has been too long since we've seen you here," she says, her hand flat across her heart. "Welcome back. Come."

I follow her through a white-plaster-and-exposed-stone reception, with huge vases of bright pink bougainvillea cascading out and trailing from tabletops to the stone floor.

"This way," Antonia says again, as I move slowly, taking everything in; she's leading me upstairs to room 13. She glances over her shoulder at me. "Shall I tell Leonardo you're here? He was looking for you."

"No, no. It's okay," I say quickly. "Maybe later."

"Oh," she says, looking slightly pleased. "A handsome man, no?"

I swallow a surprised smile. Antonia clearly finds Leo *fine*.

"Yes," I say, nodding as earnestly as I can, adding what I think she wants to hear. "Practically Dolce and Gabbana handsome."

Antonia narrows her eyes a little, and I realize she's trying to figure out if there is anything between Leo and me, romantically.

"If you like that kind of thing," I add with a nonchalant sigh.

"Bene, bene," she says merrily, pushing open the door.

The suite is beautiful. A sumptuously made-up bed dressed in soft white linen sits in a large white room with patchy exposed gray stone and a sky-blue ceiling with hand-painted clouds and a cherub with a bow and arrow in each corner. Thin white drapes frame the balcony doors, which are open, the afternoon breeze gently calling hotel guests out to the most darling view: stairs leading up to an ancient monastery in one direction, and a small, paved street lined with restaurants in the other.

I love the sounds of the city. There's traditional Sicilian music jostling to be heard over the lively chatter of diners, their voices rising and falling between the intermittent *broooom* and honk of scooters weaving between the cars. I watch a tour group follow a woman with a raised yellow umbrella speaking loudly in Spanish; a man in a white singlet unloads heavy polystyrene boxes, likely laden with seafood, from the back of a small van; a young couple walks arm in arm, lazily; and the smells of hot concrete and seafood waft in through the windows.

I drop the tote-bag-with-urn onto a midnight-blue velvet chair and look around, eased by the calming feeling of the room.

"Air-conditioning!" I exclaim.

"And a minibar, cotton waffle robes, a big bathtub, and of course . . . the city at your fingertips," Antonia says proudly, clapping her hands in delight. "Your father always took this room these last years. We are sorry that we won't see him again. But we are very happy to have you back, Olive."

"It's beautiful," I say, turning around to face Antonia.

"Allora," she says. "I will go. You will relax. And if you need anything, you call."

Then I'm pulled in for another uninvited hug. "I'm sorry, Olive. It was never the same without you here," she says into my ear, so soothingly I wonder if I'm going to cry. I am emotionally spent. It is difficult to know how to grieve for a father you felt estranged from. Whom you had decided to hate when you were a teenager and with whom you never really reconciled. A father who inspires so many regrets.

Antonia pulls back abruptly.

"Tesoro. You should have a shower."

"I know, I know," I say. "A nap. A wash. And then . . ."

"You eat!" she says enthusiastically. "Shall I book you and Leo a table for dinner? There are many—"

"Oh, no," I say quickly. "Really. We can sort all that. But I'll shout if we need some recommendations."

"Perfetto," she says, frowning a little. "Allora. I go."

And then she is gone. I sit down on the edge of the bed and feel too small for it.

It's strange. All of it. Not just the ghostwriting of my father's cookbook, but also being on this trip he should have been on, staying in the place he would have stayed, on the working holiday he would have enjoyed. For the next few weeks, I will be surrounded by the memory of my father in the company of the one person who was there when he died.

Whom I'm putting out of a job.

God. I really don't want to see him.

I feel alone.

I glance toward the urn.

Mostly alone.

5

"ITS," I SHOUT, as Ginny and Kate both freeze on the screen again and I hold the phone out of my bathroom window. "Can you hear me?"

"*I* can hear you," replies Ginny.

"Stand still, Olive, for god's sake! Give the wi-fi a chance to catch you," Kate shouts, as if the volume of her voice alone will frighten my wi-fi into action. I laugh. I can so imagine Kate as a parent.

"Here. Three bars," I yelp. "It's the best I can do, I think. Fuck it, let me try in the hall."

I grab the key and go sit on the stairs next to the ice machine and a wine-bottle vending machine, which I eye thirstily. This hotel really is divine, in a way I never appreciated when I was younger. I take in the beautifully ornate baroque detailing in the carved wood of the banister, the walls and carpets all pale blues and green tiles cool to the touch. On the landing just outside my room hangs a vaguely erotic and highly relatable painting of a naked man being simultaneously kissed and stabbed by a woman.

I glance at my phone. Five bars! Bingo.

The girls spring back into high-resolution full motion.

"Thank god for that," I say.

"The hotel sounds *dreamy*," says Kate. "And how are you feeling?"

"Adrift. Lost at sea."

"You'll find your feet," says Kate firmly.

"It's hot, the airline lost my fucking bag, and all I have is the heavy denim jumpsuit I'm wearing. And my lavender Crocs," I moan.

"Oh dear," says Ginny, grimacing.

"But you have the ashes with you?" Kate says, momentarily horrified.

"Yes. Although I'm terrified of leaving them behind somewhere," I reply wearily. "Can you imagine?"

Both the girls laugh gently, and I feel warmed by their voices, as though they really are here with me, holding my hand.

"I don't know what to do first. It's only four. I can't just stay in and—?"

"No! You *must* go out," says Ginny. "Go to the bar, flirt with some hot strangers, and try to relax. You're a single woman traveling mostly alone. You've practically got *hit me up* written on your back."

"That's terrible, emotionally destabilizing advice. Also incredibly slutty," Kate chastises, before tilting her head from side to side in careful consideration. "Still. You should probably do it."

"Speaking of *doing it* . . . have you contacted the hot chef yet?" Ginny asks.

"Leo?" I ask, as though there are a gaggle of other hot chefs.

"Oh, please tell me you've at least called him and made friends now," she pleads. "I have visions of you under the Tuscan *son*," Ginny adds wistfully.

Kate and I snort-laugh and I try to contain myself, as two guests squeeze past me on the stairs. "You're not going to get a transformational journey out of me, I'm afraid. I can't think of a cliché any more tired."

"Come on, this could be your *Eat, Pray, Love* era," Ginny says.

"I'm more Eat, Play, *Run*," I whisper to more laughter, as flashes of Leo's dark eyes staring intensely threaten to unsettle me for a moment. I clear my throat.

"One day, Olive, you'll fall in love, and there will be no more running," says Kate, who thinks I reject men because I don't wish to be rejected. Whereas *I* think the problem is simply that most men eventually have an insurmountable fault. Like clapping when a plane lands, or pronouncing David Bowie's name wrong, or over-using exclamation marks.

Ginny thinks I could find fault in a sunset.

"The only thing I'm falling into is a bath," I say firmly.

"Fair," says Kate.

"Then I'm going to ask to meet him over a drink and plan the work stuff."

"Do it," says Kate.

"Good idea," agrees Ginny.

"Eyes on the prize," Kate says, nodding. "If he makes you feel guilty or pressures you about the restaurant, you can walk away. You have zero obligation to spend any more time with him than is absolutely necessary."

"I don't know what I'd do without you girls," I say wistfully. "Okay. Done. I'm going to go get into holiday mode and have a drink."

"First things first, though. What are you going to wear?" asks Ginny.

I sniff the armpit of my denim jumpsuit. "This?"

"No," comes the firm response in stereo.

"Well, I've got time to nip out and get some basics, I think."

"Good. Shop. A little shower and then out you go," Ginny says. "Tell your plan to Leo, and then at least you can pass out in bed half-drunk and day one will be done."

"I reluctantly concur," says Kate.

I AM TWO drinks in and sitting at a bar underneath a canopy of twisted vines and fairy lights a few hours later when Leo finally shows up. I spot him in the reflection of the bar mirror. He's impossible to miss: tall, dark-haired, well put together, with a confident swagger. He's kept me waiting, which I suppose is a little payback, but the result is I'm on to my second glass of wine and already feeling a little floaty.

"Hi, Leo," I say nervously, holding up a clammy hand to shake his, as he slides up next to me at the bar, placing a small notebook, phone, and his room key down. He takes my hand and gives it a cursory shake. I get wafts of woody tones and citrus from his cologne, and something else? Scotch, I think. *Curious.* He had a straightener before he met me. Maybe he's not so confident after all.

"Hello again," he says, glancing at the flimsy neckline of my hastily purchased, thin-as-cheesecloth red cotton beach dress, which looked just fine in the store but now, next to Leo, feels cheap. "Finally."

I didn't get around to messaging him until 6:20 p.m. Or

maybe it's fairer to say *I put off messaging him*. I glance at him as he pushes back his dark hair, still damp from the shower. His dark brown eyes are serious, and he narrows them on me curiously.

"Yeah, sorry. I had to go out and pick up some things," I say wearily. "The airline lost my bag."

Leo nods, and his eyes flicker back to my neckline. "Annoying," he sympathizes. "Where did you go?"

"Valentino," I say flippantly, wrapping my thumbs around the spaghetti straps on the dress. I'm tipsy, and even if it's patently obvious, I will not sit next to an Italian, even one raised in London, and admit I paid nine ninety-nine at a back-street store called Coochi Beach Wear.

"If that's Valentino, then I'm head-to-toe Armani," he says with a wry smile.

I take in Leo's look and casual stance—foot on the gilded footrest beneath the bar, leaning in, the lights giving his face a warm, healthy glow. He's in tan chinos with brown leather loafers and no socks, and a loose-fit black linen shirt rolled up at the sleeves. He *could* be in fucking Armani.

"Oh. I didn't know Primark did an Armani line," I say cheekily, raising an eyebrow.

Leo half chuckles. He manages to do this without fully smiling, which is remarkable, frankly. Still, I relax a little. Maybe this will be okay. Maybe this is just what we need. Two colleagues having a drink on a work trip.

"Grazie," Leo says to the bartender, who has appeared with a beer. "Well, thanks for meeting me. I have ideas we can go through."

"What? No small talk?"

"We can do that after," he says with a cheeky lift of a brow. "You're kinda hard to pin down, Olive."

I glance at Leo, feeling instantly prickly, but decide not to bite. I *was* hard to pin down. "You should probably sit," I say, waving a hand at the stool next to me.

"How can I refuse such a warm invitation?"

"If you could see the sweat dripping down my back to my butt, you'd know I'm about as warm as I get right now," I moan. It is *so* hot, and it's nearly 8 p.m.

I see a slight narrowing of his gaze on me before he pulls his eyes away and looks down to his drink. He lifts it and taps it once on the bar before taking a large sip.

"Yeah. Well. It's about to get hotter," he says, clearing his throat, eyes on his drink as he slides onto the stool next to me.

I know he's talking about the pending heat wave, but his comment hangs in the air, making it sound a little foreboding. I glance at our reflection in the bar mirror and wonder for a moment what Leo is thinking. How much resentment does he feel?

Eyes on the prize. Focus on the book.

"Right. Well. Talk of the weather complete. Shall we devise our plan, then?" I say, rubbing the stem of my wineglass between my thumb and forefinger.

"Yes," he says, a look of relief on his face. He puts his hand on top of his notebook. "I have a ton of ideas."

"Okay," I say, sitting up a little straighter. "Fire away."

Leo says nothing and then narrows his eyes. "You first," he says.

"First?"

"Yes. *You* must have thoughts on execution. Ingredients you've short-listed. Places you want to visit?" he says, his tone a little challenging.

"Oh. Okay . . . ," I stammer, taking a breadstick and munching on it to buy myself time as I feel the heat creeping up my neck to my cheeks. I don't know where to start. My copy of the book is currently somewhere over continental Europe, and I have not read a single page. I am not at all clear on what we're supposed to do.

Damn it. This is *not* who I am.

I glance at Leo, who is waiting patiently for my reply. I really, really want to lie. Can I lie?

"No. *You're the chef.* You go first. Why don't you pretend I'm just now coming to it as a reader," I say, clearing my throat. "Give me the elevator pitch."

Leo looks down at his drink and then shrugs.

"Fine. It's called *Nicky Stone's Journey through Regional Italian Cooking*," he begins, his voice catching slightly so that he has to clear his throat again. The title hits me hard, hearing Leo say it aloud. A wave of sadness washes over me like a mist, and I pick up my drink, focusing hard on holding back tears and hoping like hell Leo doesn't notice.

"Go on," I say, as evenly as I can.

"It's twenty chapters about the twenty regions. And we need to finish the last three: Sicily, Tuscany, and Liguria," Leo continues as I nod along. I do know this much.

"So. There's a key ingredient for each region, like, say, Calabria is pork. And then there are three recipes from that region. Each region has a short introduction, usually your dad telling some crazy story about the first time he tried ravioli or when he went out looking for truffles and lost the prize pig."

"Oh my god, that story!" I say delightedly. *I know that story!*

"A great story," he says, and smiles into his drink. The first time I've seen him smile properly; it transforms his face into something beautiful. "He lost the pig and then was served it for dinner a few days later at a knockdown trattoria. The prize fucking truffle pig."

"Twenty grand worth of hog, stewed in a fairly average ragù," I say, biting my lip. Leo also tries but fails not to laugh, until we finally come together in mutual horrified laughter.

The laughter relaxes me, and I finish my wine in one large sip, nodding to the bartender for another. My third. It must be my last. I am starting to feel it.

"So," says Leo as the laughter subsides, "that region was—"

"Umbria," I interject, nodding, finding myself smiling at Leo for the first time. We hold each other's eyes for a moment as the volume of the music suddenly rises, and the overhead lights dim so that now it's just strung fairy lights around us. The scene becomes annoyingly intimate.

Leo pulls his eyes away first and picks up his drink, a little smile on his face again. He's made for this place, I think. This bar. The Italian jazz, the murmur of guests, and the gentle clink of glasses creating an atmosphere that feels as entrancing as he looks.

"Yes. Beautiful Umbria," he says.

"Truffle country," I say, nodding. "The only landlocked region on the Apennine Peninsula. I could honestly write about Umbria without even going there."

Leo laughs again. "Not really," he counters. "Not for this book at least."

"I *could*," I say, my tone sharpening.

"The way your dad writes in the book is different to what you write."

"Oh yeah? How do you know what I write?" I say, brows raised in challenge.

Leo turns his head and shakes it slowly. "Olive. Please. Of course I've read your reviews. Anyone who owns so much as an ice-cream stand has. You're Stone Cold Olive Stone."

Stone Cold Olive Stone?

"No one . . . no one calls me that, do they?"

"It's one name," he says, grinning, before he presses on and I'm left with my jaw on the floor, mortified. "Anyway, stories like the truffle pig? It's not just reviewing the region and critiquing it. It's telling a *story*."

"Don't worry about my part of the job," I say. *Stone cold*? All I feel is hot under the collar, simultaneously irritated with Leo and annoyed that my irritation does nothing to stop me from eyeing his gorgeous lips against the rim of his beer. Leo looks pensive as he puts his glass down, and I follow his tongue as it licks the foam from his lips.

I clear my throat. *Eyes on the prize.* "You worry about getting the recipes right, and whether they can be reproduced easily. I'll worry about the writing."

Leo's brows furrow deeply. "Is that how you want to do it?"

"I think so," I say, not daring to make eye contact for more than a cursory glance. "Isn't that the best use of our skills?"

"I think we should work together. Two palates, one mission," he says firmly.

"Together?" I blurt out.

Leo looks at his beer and, after a moment's awkward silence, says, "I'm sorry the idea of spending time together is so awful for you."

"It's not about *you*," I say quickly, my heart picking up. "I'm trying to be efficient."

"Get it over with?"

"No, be *efficient*," I say again.

"You don't want to be here," he says in a tone that suggests *he knew it*.

"No. I do," I say steadily. "I'm here to do a good job."

Leo nods, though he's clearly unconvinced.

Part of me wants to blurt it all out, explain everything about my relationship with my father. But it's so complicated, and I don't know Leo, or what he thinks *he* knows about me. The idea of thrashing that out right now feels an impossible, emotionally fraught task.

"We should go out together. Experience the food together," he presses. "If it doesn't work, we can do it your way."

"Fine," I say quietly. I wish I'd been ready to read the manuscript in London. That I didn't feel so unprepared for whatever shots Leo is going to sling at me.

"Great," he says, sighing, before turning to me, putting his elbow on the bar counter. He's closer now, and I get a hit of that woody cologne. I don't like the flutter I feel in his presence, not one bit.

"One more thing, though?" he says.

"Fire away."

"The publisher said our section will be noted as finished by us posthumously, right?"

"Yes. I think so."

"So, while we *could* just continue as is, we could also try to bring a little of ourselves in, you know? Differentiate it. Elevate it. Modernize the last few sections."

"*Elevate it?*" I snap my head toward him.

"Yes, elevate it," he continues, and then he flicks through the little leather notebook he put on the table. I catch pages of sketches and tiny notes before he settles on a page: *Topinambour Foam*. I recoil, looking at the sketch of torn toasted bread, thinly sliced Jerusalem artichoke, and some kind of pooled oil.

"What is that?" It isn't a question, really.

"Foam," says Leo.

"Foam?" I repeat.

"Don't think of it as a foam. It's lukewarm soup, really," he says, then flicks the page to show a tightly rolled pile of linguine covered in what looks like an upside-down cage.

"Why is that pasta in prison?" I ask.

He tuts in frustration. "It's a Parmesan basket," he says quickly, closing the book. "You crack it." I nod, amused, but Leo sighs. "They're just ideas. For refining the dishes a little. Still simple and traditional, but elegant. Your dad's section is traditional, and ours could be . . . the future?"

I grimace as I imagine some over-the-top recipe with sous vide, gel balls, and porcini foams. It's the last thing I want. And then I'm wondering how Leo can think Dad wanted a Jerusalem artichoke foam anywhere near this book. I've seen a copy of the latest Nicky's menu, and topinambour foam it was not.

"A chance for you and me to show a little of ourselves. Our own brands," he continues.

Brands? Did he just say our *brands*? I narrow my eyes on him in the mirror. Suddenly, I'm picturing Leo trying to launch an Instagram channel off the back of a few awful, pretentious recipes in my dad's book. Then I feel a stab of compassion. I'm about to put him out of a job. Of course he's thinking about his future. But this isn't the way to do it.

"I don't think so," I say softly.

"No?"

"Leo," I say. "Can we not overcomplicate this?"

"It doesn't need to be complicated," he counters.

"It sounds pretentious."

"Why is elevating something pretentious?"

"Have you seen that bar opposite Nicky's?"

"Temp? You think that's pretentious?"

"Pretentious *nonsense*."

"What? At least it's *creative*. What's wrong with drinking something at its perfect temperature?"

"It's pretentious and gimmicky."

"You know, reverse snobbery is a thing, Olive."

"Ha. Wrong. I'm keeping it real." I place my wineglass on the bar and fold my arms.

"I'm all for simple food, but there are worse human traits than the desire to try something new," he says.

"But Dad's food is decidedly *not* new." This feels like an insult to my father, so I quickly add, "It's classic. It's *traditional*."

"And there's nothing *wrong* with it," Leo says slowly, his voice low and controlled, laced with frustration. "You ate at the Chambers in St. Pauls, right?"

"Yes," I reply, still slightly taken aback that he's been reading my reviews. Had Dad been reading them too?

"And you *liked* it. The Chambers is *elevated* British classics. You said it was *banging*. You gave it a rare four and a half forks out of five. Which I think is your highest ever."

"I never give five."

"Why not?"

"You always need room to improve."

Leo tuts. "Well, anyway. That's the level I'm talking about."

"Don't use my reviews against me," I say, my knee starting to jiggle. "And that's different. This is Dad's last good-bye; we need to do it his way. No Parmesan baskets. No fucking foam."

We sit in a silence so thick you could insulate a nightclub with it.

"Look. I can see you care about doing a good job," I say eventually. "I do too. But please. It's what *he* wanted."

Leo's eyes narrow, and for a split second I can hear the words, *And how would you know what your dad wanted? You barely set foot in Nicky's before last week.* But he doesn't say it. He doesn't have to.

Instead, he sighs, shakes his head, and says, "Fine. So, still nothing changes."

"What does that mean?"

Leo takes a huge breath, then turns to me.

"Let's just keep things the way they've always been," he says, with a tone so deflated it makes me wince.

"So, tomorrow," he says, his voice clipped. "We do what?"

"We meet for lunch?" I suggest cautiously.

"Great," he says.

"Let's be as focused as we can so we can have some time to do our own thing and enjoy Sicily," I say, and then because I'm afraid I've suggested we enjoy that time together, I add, "*Separately.*"

"I get it, Olive," he says, scoffing as he shakes his head. "Finish his book. Sell his restaurant. Get on with your life."

Ouch. *Fucking ouch.* Leo glances at me; a fleeting look of concern crosses his face like he knows that was too much.

"Sorry. I just wish you'd reconsider selling," he says, his frustration palpable. "Or at least have a conversation about it."

"I'm sorry you'll need to look for work—"

"It's not about a job," he snaps, frowning at me. "I can get another fucking job."

I flinch. He seems *furious*.

"You know what?" I say, standing up and pushing my drink away. "I'm going to bed. I'll message you tomorrow."

"See ya," he says, eyes focused on his drink. At least now I know what he really thinks.

Just before I leave I turn to Leo.

"That bar, Temp?" I say, as gently as I can. "The place opposite Nicky's?"

"What about it?" he says, eyes still on his drink.

"I bet you five bucks it's closed by the end of the summer."

"Let's make it ten," he says, a wry smile returning to his face as he looks up and reaches out his hand. When we shake, his hand feels cool and dry and strong around my own smaller one, and an unexpected zing of electricity travels down my spine. I pull my hand back as quickly as I can, muttering a polite good night. As I walk away I look back across the twinkling lights of the bar and catch Leo watching me in the mirror's reflection.

6

TWO PEOPLE? BENE. This one?" the very nice waiter at lunch says, holding his hand toward a table under a citrus tree with a picture-perfect view of the cobbled street below. "It's romantic, no?"

"Yes, lovely," I reply, looking around the balcony bustling with diners, trying to see if Leo has arrived yet. "But, ah, we won't need the *romantic* table."

"Per favore?" he says, holding his hand out, insisting.

"Ah. Save it for a nice couple. We're not a couple," I explain. *We're barely even friends.* "We're working."

The waiter looks bemused. "You're working or you're eating?" he says.

"Oh, both," I say quickly.

"You're a food writer?" the waiter says suspiciously. "A reviewer?"

"*No!*" I fire back quickly. *Shit.* "I mean *yes*, I am. But not today. The table is fine. It's wonderful. I'll take it. We'll take the table."

Damn it.

I spot Leo walking toward us, a hand up, and I wave back meekly.

You got this, Olive, I tell myself, breathing slowly out as Leo moves toward me through the busy balcony tables. I try not to stare, but I keep thinking of the zing of electricity I felt last night when we shook hands. Objectively, he is attractive, I reason with myself, as my eyes scan his jaw and the broad curve of his shoulders. Like a nice painting. Or a sculpture. One of those particularly well-cut and very naked marble ones. *Of course you're attracted to him.* He's a good-looking guy with a confident swagger and he loves the business of food as much as I do.

"Nice table," says Leo, immediately endearing himself to the waiter.

"Prego," says the waiter, handing us menus, beaming at Leo and then frowning at me. I watch him go and curse myself. *Damn it.*

"What did you say to him?" Leo asks as he slides into his seat.

"He kind of knows I'm a critic," I mutter, shamefaced.

"You *told* him you're a critic?" scoffs Leo. "Do you always do that when you go out for lunch?"

"Of course not," I say quickly, pulling my napkin off the table and laying it in my lap. "It was an accidental slip."

Leo laughs as though he doesn't believe me. "Well, you chose a good spot, at any rate. The Crazy Octopus. Should be a good lunch."

I recalled Dad loving it here, eating under the citrus trees in the warm midday sun. Mussels. Fish. Pasta. I managed to find it online, following my hazy memories and using Google Maps.

You know Sicily, I'd reminded myself over breakfast that morning. Even if it's been a hot minute since I've been here. I crammed all morning like a disorganized teenager before exams, reading up on the history, the eclectic cuisine, thousands of years of evolving culture. Unearthing memories and so much rusty knowledge.

I'm ready.

The waiter returns with menus and offers us two Sicilian sparkling wines. "It's a beautiful aperitif," he says, presenting two already filled glasses.

Here we go. We're going to get the special treatment because I'm a critic. I shoot Leo an eye roll, but he misses it. Unfortunately, the waiter does not. I hate making waitstaff feel on edge. I hate being this person who just judges everything all the damn time.

"I'll take one," Leo says, rubbing his hands together with delight.

"Bene," he replies, smiling sweetly, then turning to me with barely masked contempt.

"I will too," I say meekly.

When we're alone, I point at a dish on the menu. "Let's start here."

"Alla Norma?"

"Yes. I think we should start with all the obvious dishes, if only to disregard them. We can't be here and not at least consider alla Norma."

Leo raises an eyebrow. "Named after Bellini's most famous opera."

"The greatest son of Catania."

He looks pleased, and it buoys me.

"I also think it's worth trying some basic seafood, even if it's simply grilled with pepper and lemon. It's not Sicily without it."

Leo nods. "Have you got an idea for a key ingredient?"

"A few. We've so many to choose from," I say, my confidence growing.

"Yep. Hard to settle on one. I've thought about almonds, red prawns, pistachios, sardines, blood oranges, sea urchins. I do have my front-runner," Leo says, tipping his glass at me.

I grin at him. "So do I."

The waiter returns with a notepad and pen, smiling at us both.

Leo flicks his menu closed. "May I?"

"Go ahead. But don't forget the caponata. And the grilled aubergine," I say.

Leo turns to the waiter with a dazzling smile, orders a bunch of starters and sides, and then a couple of glasses of rosé from a local vineyard. Then he lifts his glass of bubbles in my direction.

"To finishing this," he says, his eyes round and hopeful.

I lift my glass and we let the edges touch gently, tentatively.

"And . . . I'm sorry about last night," he says. "I was . . . well. A bit out of line."

"Let's forget it," I say, shaking my head. "I wasn't at my best either."

"As long as we both want to do a good job of it."

"We do," I say firmly.

And for the next forty-five minutes, it feels like we both might just be able to. The caponata arrives, a delicious aubergine, pine nut, and raisin dish, slow-cooked and served with crusty semolina bread. I feel transported back to summers long gone. My dad used to make this.

"So good," I say, moaning into my fork. "Could tone down the vinegar, though. A few too many raisins probably."

Leo laughs into his mouthful of aubergine. "Ever the critic," he says.

"If we're not here to critique, I don't know what we're here to do," I say, glancing around, making sure the waiter is out of earshot.

"True," he replies.

We eat mussels stuffed with breadcrumbs and swordfish carpaccio with lemon and orange zest. When my alla Norma arrives, I plunge my fork into a slice of meltingly soft aubergine smothered in grated hard ricotta, and then I smile confidently at Leo. "You want to know my front-runner?"

"I'm on tenterhooks, Olive," he says, grinning. A very nice grin. Boyish, with one side of his mouth slightly higher than the other.

"I'm thinking aubergine," I say, pointing to the alla Norma, the grilled aubergine, and what's left of the caponata.

"Aubergine?" he says, putting down his fork and sitting back again in his chair, his arms folding.

"Yes," I reply, nodding. "This pasta is a classic for a reason. And the caponata? I mean, it's just classic Sicily. And the history is fascinating. Brought here in the ninth century during the Arabic rule of the island. I can see a story where we ..."

Leo holds both his hands up for me to stop, and I stare at him, picking up my drink. "Just to be clear, you want to do *aubergine* as the key ingredient?" Leo says, folding his arms again in a way that makes me feel a little unsettled.

"Yes. Aubergine. Melanzani. Eggplant. What do you think?"

"What do I *think*?" he asks. "I think you need to read your dad's manuscript."

My heart sinks.

"Shit," I say, rubbing my forehead with my hand and glancing at Leo through my fingers. *Aubergine is taken*. And I'd have known that if I'd read the book. I'm such an idiot.

"It's the key ingredient for Puglia," he goes on, his voice frustrated. "You haven't even read it, have you?" he says slowly, examining me.

"It was in my baggage. The *lost* baggage," I confess.

"Right."

"I didn't pick it up until the day before we flew," I say quickly. I'm frustrated with myself. And now, perhaps unfairly, with Leo. I feel the heat rising in my neck all the way up to my cheeks.

"I see," he says, as though the only thing he's *seen* is that I'm ridiculous. "How can you not have read the book we're here to finish? Your father's book?" he says, dropping his fork down with a clatter. "It feels like you don't want to be here."

"I don't," I say, then I slump. "I mean I *do*. Of course I do. It's just . . ." My voice trails off as the waiter chooses this moment to clear away our meal. I barely notice him, my humiliation turning to frustration and then to anger as we sit in tense silence until the waiter scuttles away.

I turn to Leo. "It's hard for me, okay?" My voice is loud enough that the other diners turn to look at us. "Don't you get that?"

"Of course it's fucking hard," he says, throwing his hands up in frustration.

"You will *never* understand my relationship with my father," I say, feeling tears start to well. I swallow hard, forcing them back down. "I'm doing my fucking best." My voice cracks and I can't look at him. I can't look at him sitting there judging me. "When I open that book, it's the last of him."

That silences Leo.

The waiter returns, fussing with the plates and looking anxiously between the two of us. "Do either of you want gelato?" he asks, as though he were offering an aspirin.

"No," Leo and I say in unison.

I stare out at the postcard-perfect view as the waiter leaves.

"I just want to do a good job," Leo says finally. More gently. "If you need me to lead, I can. I have ideas . . ."

I look up at him. "No," I say. "You'll just turn the caponata into a jelly ball."

It's supposed to be a joke, but it comes out flat.

"I'll bring you my copy of the manuscript," he says as the waiter presents him with the bill and the card reader.

"It's okay. I already emailed the publisher for a digital copy."

"Take mine," he insists. "Why don't you take the day tomorrow, read the book. Find your feet. Then we can meet in the afternoon."

I nod gratefully. Then I fish in my purse and pull out a twenty-euro note, which I slide under my untouched drink, thinking of the special treatment I eye-rolled and the waiter's anxious gaze.

"I already left a tip," says Leo.

"It won't be enough," I say, and then I pick up my phone and start typing furiously.

"What are you doing?"

"Giving my first-ever five-star review," I say sheepishly.

7

THE NEXT MORNING, I exit my room frantically messaging Kate and Ginny on yesterday's Leo shitstorm. With my head down, completely engrossed in my phone, I turn the corner toward the stairs and run straight into him. Chest to chest, our bodies smack together and I fly toward the floor, but Leo moves with lightning speed, grabbing a flailing hand and sliding his other hand behind my back along the bare skin at my waist, catching me just before I hit the floor. Then we are frozen as though he's dipped me in a tango.

I look into Leo's eyes, which are searching mine from above. "Are you okay?" he asks, and I nod frantically. I'm acutely aware of his warm hand on my bare lower back, and the fizzing feeling spreading through my body as he slowly pulls me up, his touch crackling against my skin like popping candy.

As soon as I'm on my feet, I pull away as quickly as I can, and Leo rubs that hand with his other as if massaging away a cramp.

"Sorry," he replies, as we crouch at the same time to clear up the mess. I start laughing as I scramble to gather my lipstick, wallet, pens, notebook, tissues, tampons, and gum into my bag, wondering if this is what hysteria feels like. "Are you hurt?"

"Only my ego," I reply, hiccuping the last of my laughter. As he hands me my phone, a message on the lit-up screen reads:

KATE: He doesn't sound very nice

"Who's *he*?" he says, an eyebrow raised.

I snatch it from him.

"No one," I say quickly, standing up, smoothing my hair, and lifting my chin. Leo looks sympathetic. My body still fizzes from his touch, and I hate the uncomfortable pleasure it brings. Am I so desperate for human touch?

"I brought you the manuscript. And I took the liberty of writing a list of the ingredients that are already taken on the front."

He taps at a scribbled list stuck to the dog-eared, ring-bound manuscript.

"Thanks," I say, taking it quickly from him and shoving it into my bag.

"What are *your* plans today?" I note a towel poking out of his messenger bag and get a vision of Leo in swim trunks, chest bare, like some kind of Beach Ken walking out of the sea, and I have to work hard to push the image away.

"Oh, don't worry. Just a quick dip," he says, making his way toward the stairwell. "But then I'll go and check out a food market, I think."

"Just give me a few hours," I call as he disappears down the stairs. "I'll call you."

———

BOTH KATE AND Ginny suggested getting out of Catania and exploring the coast. And so I visit a small car-hire place adjacent to the hotel. What I want is a cheap little thing to zip about in and what they have is a black Fiat 500C convertible.

My instinct is to find something less fancy, but then I remind myself if I was ever going to hire a black convertible, now is the time. As I drive out, the attendant comes running out of the store, I think to wave me off, until I hear him shouting, "Destra! Destra!"

Right. Drive on the right, Olive. I quickly course correct.

I am crawling in traffic for a good hour on the coastal road, listening to an audiobook called *Forgiving the Dead*, a self-help book given to me by Kate that I reluctantly decided to give a go.

Step one, I'm told, is to audit the behavior and decide how bad it *really* was. Step two is to talk to an empty chair. As the traffic comes to a complete standstill, two nuns in black-and-white habits pull up beside me in an old Lancia with the windows rolled down. We turn and smile at each other, while the booming voice of my audiobook continues.

"Step seven," says the California therapist loudly. "Open your heart to loving the good parts. If it was your lover, then try to remember a time when you made love. Sink into the feeling of sexual connection and romantic bonding."

"Shit." I hit stop very quickly and crouch down as low as I can in the driver's seat without disappearing altogether, not daring to look over.

"Sorry, God," I say, looking skyward. And then: "I have given this my best go," I whisper to an imaginary Kate, quickly turning on some Lou Reed and pretending to stall the automatic until the nuns are well ahead of me.

Taormina sits on a natural platform above the coast, its small streets and tiny staircases climbing to the summit of Mount Tauro, where an ancient Greek theater looks out across the sea. Stunning views aside, its coral-colored stone houses with wrought-iron balconies climb above elegant piazzas lined with cafés and filled with people. Deep green bushes with their bright pink flowers seem to grow everywhere, straight from the baking-hot stone. The town is beautiful, the pearl of the Ionian Sea, recently made famous by the show *The White Lotus*.

I pass by a little bookshop and grab a copy of *The Flavors of Sicily*, and then I decide to have a coffee, right on Piazza IX Aprile, the main piazza, with bold checkerboard paving. I glance at the price on the plastic menu. *Ten euros!* I cannot help but laugh; the price of sitting in this slice of paradise has been firmly baked into the bill.

As I gaze out, drinking my coffee, I have a flash of a memory of waiting with a cardboard cake box, over by the wrought-iron railing that looks over the sea. Mum posing for a photo in a broad-brimmed hat and a floor-length lemon-print sundress. Dad making her redo the pose a hundred times while I waited, *bored*. Mum, finally throwing her hands up, exasperated.

"Nicky, this is the only face of mine you're going to get. What should I do different?"

"Nothing," he'd replied, laughing. "I'm just enjoying the view."

Mum and her coquettish giggle. Dad and his charming chuckle. A warm embrace. A heartrending memory that makes me immediately miss them.

Miss how they *were*.

I glance around. Wasn't there a cake shop here that served a cake my mother loved? I search the depths of my memory, but it is only her delight and my teenage indifference to it that I can recall, not the cake itself.

"Un momento," I say, as the waiter approaches, pen aloft, breaking me from my thoughts.

I flick open the menu and scan for something light to eat, and my eyes fall on insalata di finocchi e arance. Fennel salad with oranges. I'm intrigued, but then my eyes scan to the arancini al ragù. A little fried rice ball? Yes, please.

I have to be smart about this. I only have one stomach and I can't eat everything. But then again, I kind of need to.

"I'll have the arancini, the seafood with couscous. And . . ." I tut as I scan the menu. "The spaghetti al pesto alla trapanese. That's with almonds, right?"

The waiter nods, looking around for another person.

"It's just me," I say, grinning. "I'm hungry."

He laughs, scribbling my order on his pad. "Sì," he says, collecting my menu and gliding off.

Right. I take a deep breath, and then I pull the manuscript out, flicking my thumb down the pages, guilt rising at how much attention Leo has paid to it. Brightly colored Post-its with scribbled notes stick out of the edges.

The manuscript feels like a precious artifact. And in a way it is. It's the culmination of all my dad's years of hard work. I get a small chill down my spine looking at it. In some ways, I feel like when I open the book, it will be my last conversation with my dad. Perhaps that's truly why I've put it off for so long.

I run my fingers down the title page, my dad's name in black. *Nicolò Stone.* With a breath I open up to a random page, scanning across the introduction to Bologna, but then my eyes catch on my name, and I close the book quickly. I feel a wave of something like vertigo. I'm not ready. *Will I ever be ready?*

I know for sure I cannot do this here. *Not surrounded by people.* I need to read this somewhere alone.

I slide the manuscript back into my bag. I don't need to read it right now, anyway. I have the list of ingredients, with a few notes from Leo written in parentheses. I scan it: *garlic, mushrooms (covering porcini and truffles), olive oil, Parmesan, rice, pork (cured and cooked), balsamic vinegar, capers, aubergine, polenta & other grains, bread, eggs.*

When the waiter brings the dishes, all at once, I fork through them slowly. The arancini is delicious, but rice is already taken, so we'd have to focus on the black-squid-ink filling, but, although it's to die for, I'm not sure squid ink can maintain us for three whole recipes.

The second dish is so inviting. I plunge my fork into a piece of soft squid, devouring too much of the North African–influenced couscous dish. There are so many potential key ingredients in here: any one of the different seafoods, even the flecks of marigold-orange zest that add a hit of tangy citrus.

But then I try the pesto pasta and it feels like the best of the three. It's rich and unctuous. I only wish I had room for more.

Didn't Leo mention almonds in his short list of potential ingredients yesterday?

ME: I just had a very nice dish with almonds.

LEO: I'm all ears.

ME: Pesto alla Trapanese—do you know it?

LEO: Oh yeah. I know it.

ME: Shall we meet around 5?

LEO: 👍

I cruise back toward Catania on the autostrada, allowing myself to feel a little better.

I stop halfway down the coast for a first plunge into the Mediterranean. I park in a small verge covered with shrubs, and climb across rocks until I get to a set of metal stairs and a railing, which leads down into the turquoise-blue sea. There are only two other people here, men in matching red trunks, lying across the rocks, their bronzed chests to the sun. And so I peel off my clothes and head in, in my underwear; the water is cool, but only for a second. I lie back, starfishing in the water, the sun beating down on me.

After I've sunk myself into the water, my heart slows, my breath too.

I start to feel somehow a little less adrift and more at home. I wonder, as I trail my hands through the gently lapping waves, if I will ever find peace with my relationship with my father. Is there a way to forgive the past and move on from this guilt and sadness I feel? I wish I'd called him more. I wish I'd asked him what happened one more time, to see if I understood as an adult what was so confusing as a teenager.

Maybe all that's needed is time. *"Time and bravery will get you through anything,"* my mother used to say.

But there is no time right now. There is a book to finish. And there is Leo, with his lopsided smile, waiting for me.

8

WHEN I ARRIVE back from Taormina, Antonia is standing at reception and points me toward the kitchen entrance.

"He's waiting for you in there," she says, a perfect eyebrow raised in disapproval.

"In the *kitchen*?"

"Sì," she says, looking down at her bookings.

Confused, I push open the door to the hotel kitchen to find Leo standing there with four bowls of neatly presented pasta waiting for me under the heating lamp. What the hell?

"What have you been doing?" I ask. "Are you cooking?" I am still wet from my swim and I clutch at my ratty ponytail nervously and slide onto the seat opposite him.

"Of course," he says, shooting me a look of faux laid-back chill. "I made four different pestos and two types of pasta."

"The pesto alla trapanese?" I say, and he nods, then I glance around at this small, modern space, nothing but trays of nibbles ready to go out when the bar opens. "I guess they don't need the kitchen after breakfast."

"Yep. Antonia's always very happy to lend a hand, for some reason."

For some reason. I roll my eyes internally. *I'm sure she is happy to help you out, Leo.*

Leo leans on the counter and slides forward the first dish.

"This one is the straight-up version you probably had today. Almonds, tomato, garlic, basil, pecorino, and cherry tomatoes. Egg pasta."

He pushes bowl number two toward me. "This one, I've used a little mint, and something else surprising—see if you can guess.

"Here we have a version with red prawns stirred through, left slightly raw. An homage to the raw red prawns they love here. I tried a version of this in this little place in Trapani. I've left the almonds a little more coarsely ground. For crunch."

I stare at him, a little speechless, as he pushes forward the fourth bowl.

"And this one, forgive me, but I've swapped out the almonds for pistachios. It's the other traditional island pesto: pasta al pesto di pistacchi. And I made these cute little pasta worms. Busiate, they're called." He flips the tea towel he's been holding over his shoulder.

"Pistachios?"

"Well, I figured that if you liked the almond one, you'd love this one. Personally, I think there's more going on with pistachios in Sicily."

"I . . . um." I look between the bowls and feel impressed.

"I resisted the urge to create a prison out of Parmesan cheese for dish number one," he says, grinning.

I shoot him a look. "You did all this in four hours?"

"Less. I had to buy everything first," he says, folding his arms triumphantly.

Oh boy, if I wasn't so utterly amazed, I'd want to smack that smug look off his face.

I take a moment, picking up the fork from the first dish. *This is what you do.* You know good food. Taste the dishes and then give feedback. *This is your lane.*

I twist my fork around in dish number one and take a bite. It's creamy, but . . . I take my time to allow the layers of flavor to come through. Leo slides me a glass of water, which I take a large gulp of, before moving on to do the same with dishes two, three, and four. I watch Leo get increasingly more fidgety as I move slowly, going back and forth, considering tastes.

Then I place the fork down on the stainless-steel surface. Okay, Leo Ricci can cook. I mean, these are all *so good*, I'm a little taken aback.

"Well?" Leo says. "Which one shall we go for?"

I clear my throat and decide I can only answer honestly. "They're all great. *Delicious.*"

"But?" he says warily.

I squeeze my lips together and take a breath.

"Honestly, a little fussy," I say, grimacing. "Compared to the dish I had today, which was rustic and simple."

"*Fussy?*"

"Yes. Number one is so wonderfully creamy, but you roasted the almonds, right? They should be blanched, I think. It's too overpowering. And can I taste seaweed in there?"

Leo nods sheepishly. "You can use any store-bought kind," he says, quickly.

"Number two, I can't really taste the mint, and I think you've added fennel? It doesn't work in my opinion. The third, with the prawns? It's nice, but fiddly, and I'm not sure about a raw prawn dish. Can we skin and devein them, and cook them through? And number four is good. You're right, the pistachio is an improvement on the others, but it doesn't contain almonds."

Leo looks instantly deflated.

"They're all *delicious*," I say, reaching for the glass of water and glugging it down. I don't want to eat any more pesto today. I feel a little queasy. "I'm just giving you the hard feedback. We're professionals, no?"

"No kidding," he says, shaking his head at me. "You seriously think those dishes are too fussy?"

"For a cookbook," I say, carefully.

"But for a restaurant?"

"This is for the cookbook, Leo," I say, feeling a creeping dread.

He's talking about Nicky's. I realize this exercise was only partially about the cookbook. Leo wants to show me he can cook.

"Which was your favorite?" I ask, steering the conversation quickly back.

"Well," he says, shaking his head. "Honestly, maybe the fourth? But I have to say, Olive . . ." He puts both his hands flat on the surface and leans in. "I think it's probably too soon to be making dish selections."

"Hang on a minute," I say, laughing in disbelief. "My text just asked if you knew the dish. I didn't ask for all this." I wave my hand over the multiple dishes.

"I'm trying to *help*," he says, like he's talking to a toddler who needs a Band-Aid ripped off.

"You *are* helping," I say, exasperated. "This, all this cooking, was amazing."

He looks across the kitchen, staring into the middle distance for a moment.

"Olive. Are you actually going to listen to me? To accept any of my ideas?"

I narrow my eyes on him, confused. "Yes. Of course I am. You're a chef, and I am not. Plus, Dad wanted you here."

"He did," he says with a nod.

I can see the depth of his frustration, and I wonder if he's bringing some serious baggage to this conversation. I know I am. A thought penetrates, just for a moment.

Is he comparing me to Dad here? Did Dad shut Leo down like he shut Mum down? Does Leo think I'm going to do the same to him? I feel my heart start to race and the heat rising in my cheeks. Then Leo leans back against the sink and folds his arms. I know what's coming. It's been in the subtext of the last thirty minutes.

"I don't get it," he says. "He said you'd come back to Nicky's. He said, over and over again, Olive will be back and she'll run this place one day. But you never came back, and now you're selling it. Do you hate him? What did he do?"

"Please stop," I say, shaking my head.

Do you hate him? How can I defend myself? How can I answer such a horrible charge?

"I just don't understand," he says. "I know it's not my place to ask, but I wish you'd tell me."

I take a breath, looking hard at a tear in the linoleum on the floor. I imagine explaining it all to Leo, the feelings of rejection, the hurt he caused my mother, the confusion I feel now. But like the pages of Dad's book, which are too painful to read, it is too painful to speak. All I can do is stare at the floor and wish he would stop asking.

"Let's just meet tomorrow for lunch."

"Tomorrow we're going for lunch at Rocco's house," he says impatiently.

"Oh yes, Rocco's," I say, biting my lip nervously. Another anxiety I can't share with him is seeing my dad's beloved mentor and admitting that I'm selling the restaurant. "Shall we talk afterward, then?"

"You're the boss," he says, sighing as he turns, clears the first plate of pasta away, and drops it into the bin.

9

"GUESS WHERE I went yesterday," I say into my phone as I take one last look in the full-length mirror. I'm readying myself to join Leo downstairs. We're going to meet Rocco outside his restaurant, and then he's driving us to his home for our planned lunch. I used to love going to Rocco's home, but it's been fifteen years, and now I'm dreading every moment of it. I look good, though, in one of my hasty new purchases: a summery full-length cornflower-blue skirt and white T-shirt. At least there is that.

"Where?" Mum's voice sounds hopeful.

"Taormina. Do you remember? You used to make Dad take you shopping there every holiday. And we went to a cake shop you loved?"

"Oh yes. The little pastel-yellow one on the corner with the canvas chairs. So pretty, underneath that pink bougainvillea. I remember," she says wistfully.

"In my head you hated it there. 'Forced to bloody Sicily every year for our five minutes of summer respite.'" I mimic her Yorkshire accent. "And then I remembered you had a favorite cake shop, and some other nice memories." I fish through my new makeup bag. "There *were* happy times here, right?"

My mum laughs. "Well," she says, her voice tensing a little. "There were happy days there, yes. Very happy. How are things with Leo?"

I know a motherly subject change when I hear one.

"Well. Leo thinks I'm useless. That I abandoned my father. I don't care about Dad's restaurant or his cookbook and shouldn't be here." My makeup is not going on well, I think, staring at the mirror. I'm like a toddler with a Magic Marker, clumsy hands, heat-induced insomnia, high anxiety, and stress.

"'I just want to elevate the dishes, probably include some fucking smoked kumquat jerky and pig semen jus,'" I say, mimicking Leo's deep voice.

"Who cares what he thinks? And anyway, you did *not* abandon your father," my mother chides, without offering an alternative perspective. "I ate fish semen in Nagasaki," she adds wistfully. "It went down surprisingly easy."

"*Mother!*" I shriek, clutching imaginary pearls as she giggles.

I attempt to make the cat-eye flick longer to hide its imperfections, but the makeup just smudges further in the humidity. I use my fingers to try to blend it into a smoky eye and then I pull back from the mirror and examine my face.

"I look like a Goth. I'm now firmly back in my fourteen-year-old My Chemical Romance era. Still. It's how Rocco probably remembers me."

"Your *what* era?"

"Nothing, don't worry. Mum, do you think Rocco knows I'm selling?"

"How could he?"

I wonder if Leo has told him.

"I just really, really don't want to tell him. If I thought it was bad telling Leo, imagine having to tell Rocco, who trained and mentored Dad, that I'm cashing out."

"It's yours to sell," she says.

I glance up at the time. Eleven thirty.

"Mum, I have to go face them."

"Olive, Rocco was like family to your father; he will be thrilled to see you."

After we hang up, I look hard at myself in the mirror.

"None of this is your fault, Olive," I say firmly to myself. "Except that eye makeup."

LEO IS ALREADY in reception when I get down, reading an actual physical newspaper, in Italian, with his legs crossed, an espresso on the glass coffee table alongside his phone and a stylish straw hat. He'd look like a scene out of some 1940s European art house film if it weren't for his burnt-orange shorts and casual black tee.

"Morning, Olive," he says, sending an apprehensive smile in my direction as he folds his newspaper and slides it onto the coffee table. Then his brows lower a little as he's slightly taken aback by the eye makeup.

"I know I look like Robert Smith," I say before he has a chance.

"I wasn't going to—"

"It was my thing once upon a time. Didn't you have a teenage subculture? LARPing or whatever?"

"You look at me and think Dungeons and Dragons?" he says, smirking.

No, Leo Ricci, that is not what I think when I look at you.

Our eyes connect for a split second, and I look away.

"We should get going," he says, standing, slipping his hat and sunglasses on, so we are both wearing our very intentional physical barriers. "I'll show you the way."

"I *know* the way," I blurt out, and without a word Leo stops, holding his hand out to let me lead. I brace myself for the furnace-like blast of air that awaits us as we leave the cool reception.

"Jeez, that's some heat," I say, removing my hat and fanning myself with it.

"Yup," he replies.

"This way, right?" I point down the little paved street, past a row of restaurants with their tables spilling out onto the sidewalk, to where the street snakes around a vine-engulfed church.

"Yup," he says again.

Scooters weave in and out of the one-way street, horns honk intermittently, and in the distance, the dampened sound of music comes from inside a bar as it readies itself for the lunch rush. Tables are being set with paper place mats and little baskets of oil and vinegar; the smell of baking concrete mixes with the earthy scent of the greenery that weaves around streetlamps and crawls up the plastered stone. A couple kisses against a stone pillar, pulls apart, searching each other's faces before falling back together again, and I'm fascinated to see Leo watching them with a certain longing. I know that feeling. I find myself wondering if Leo has ever been in love.

We spill out onto a piazza and my mouth waters as we pass a café filled with tourists, shading under the canvas canopy, spooning huge mouthfuls of sweet granita into their mouths. I dream of a creamy ice coffee with a floating vanilla gelato scoop. Sugar. Caffeine. Cold. Anything cold.

"It will be cooler up the volcano," he says. *All we've done is comment on the weather*, I think as our walk continues down toward the sea in a relentlessly frosty silence.

"That's kinda how altitude works," I say back, before spotting the swinging sign saying ROCCO'S. It never occurred to me until just now that Nicky's is named the same way. After the chef.

"There it is!" I say, rushing forward with a gasp, momentarily forgetting to be cool as I peer into the window and spot a lone cleaner mopping the floors underneath tables with mismatched wooden chairs stacked on top. I can see the little hanging fishing baskets on the ceiling and dim light coming from the open kitchen at the back.

"It hasn't changed at all," I say in wonder.

The spell breaks as we hear the honking of a tinny car horn coming up behind us. The sound is dreamily familiar, a friendly staccato playing out a rhythm. *Da-da-da-da-da . . . da da!* I swing around to see Rocco leaning out the side of a vintage ice-cream van, waving madly. My heart starts to thump as I nervously raise a hand back. Oh goodness. I remember the van. And I remember Rocco. He's *exactly* the same. Thick black hair graying at the sides; kind, round eyes framed by big, bushy brows. His slight belly is covered by a too-tight short-sleeved shirt, his slender legs in a pair of loose chinos, and he's wearing box-fresh white Nikes on his feet. He is pure warmth. Next to him appears a handsome young man in a blue singlet and aviators who is strikingly familiar, but I can't place him.

"Olive!" Rocco's voice calls from the ice-cream truck, a hand waving frantically out the window.

I instinctively turn to Leo to share my nervous delight and find he's studying me already. He looks mildly sentimental, but as our eyes meet, the emotion fades as though he's remembered he's in a mood with me.

After Rocco yanks the hand brake up and jumps out, I instinctively fall into his big open arms, and for a split second I worry that I'm going to cry.

"Olive. Olive. Olive. Where the hell have you been?" he says, pulling back to take a good look at me and muss my hair like I'm ten years old. "We thought we'd never see you again!"

"Hi, Rocco," I say, feeling myself blushing wildly. I remove my sunglasses and he beams with delight, patting me on the back as I allow myself to be held. I marvel at how normal and real it feels.

"Bene, bene! You remember the restaurant?" he says, beaming full of pride as he holds his hand to the sign. "You eat here whenever you want. Sì?"

"Sì," I reply.

"And you remember my grandson and now my terrible sous chef, Luca?" he says, pulling back, pointing to the Adonis next to him. Luca grins at me, a couple of deep dimples appearing in his tanned cheeks.

"Oh god, it's *you*, Luca," I say, shaking my head as I hold my hand out at waist height. "Last time I saw you, you were like this high."

Luca grins harder. "It's the Sicilian sun," he says bashfully, as he lifts his fist toward Leo for a fist bump, which Leo returns enthusiastically. They know each other well, clearly.

Rocco holds out both his hands, palms up, his face falling slightly. I brace myself for the moment I know has to come.

"Olive. We are all very sorry for your loss," Rocco says, before turning to Leo. "And to you, Leo, too."

"Thank you, Rocco," I reply, eyeing Leo, who absorbs Rocco's sympathy with a manly nod, his lips squeezed together.

"We all loved him. He was a good man," Rocco continues.

Before I can steel myself for what feels like a long, emotional eulogy, he clicks his fingers and points to Leo, breaking into a huge grin. "But a *terrible* cook."

He slaps Leo on his shoulder, and Leo, for the first time this morning, laughs. Leo self-consciously moves in for a half man-hug, throwing one arm around Rocco's shoulders and shoving his head into Rocco's neck briefly, like a small, shy boy. It's the first time I've seen him look vulnerable and it warms my stone-cold heart for a split second.

"I'm kidding, I'm kidding," Rocco says, looking at me as he pulls back from Leo. "He was an excellent cook. *I* trained him! Oh, bella. Always such a serious kid. And still with all the black makeup." He points to my eyes, grinning.

Luca shoots me a sympathetic eye roll as we clamber into the van, Leo and me in the back. Rocco struggles to get the engine of his old silver ice-cream truck running. I wonder how the hell this thing is going to get us halfway up Mount Etna. *Clutch, gas, ignition. Brrrrrrrr. Cut.* This routine is repeated a couple of times until finally, its loud diesel engine roars into gear and the van jerks forward, slamming me into Leo, who is perched on one of the two fixed white stools in front of me.

"Shit," I shout, pulling backward, removing my elbow from his thigh. "Shit. Sorry."

"It's fine," he says, steadying me with a strong hand and helping me to the seat next to him.

I fail to find a seat belt, instead clutching the sides of the stool as we chug around a corner and up the narrow lane, past Rocco's and north, taking back roads to avoid the motorway, toward the slopes of Mount Etna. Leo and I sit about six inches from each other in tense silence.

"Isabella has the other car," Rocco says loudly, as I grab the old chrome counter to steady myself around a particularly tight turn. We climb slowly through olive trees, native forest, and wild fennel, the sea appearing out of the small serving window on our right. I want to lean across Leo and peer out at the view but think better of it. Instead, I nudge him, trying to break the ice, pointing to an old peg letter board above the serving window.

"A thousand bucks for a cone is a bit steep. What do they put in the gelato, diamonds?" I quip. Leo looks at me with a withering combination of confusion and concern.

"For god's sake, it's a joke," I say. "I *know* it's in lira."

"It's not always easy to tell when you're joking," he replies.

Urgh. I'm going to have to call some kind of truce or lunch is going to be an awkward nightmare.

We turn down a dirt lane toward a cute two-story stone house in a faded dusty peach color. On one side, thick vines threaten to swallow the house; on the other, a gnarled olive tree shades a stony front porch. I see the faded plastic swing still hanging from one of the branches, and my eyes move instinctively to find the old wood basin under the outside faucet, but it's gone. *Fifteen years*, I think. *Of course it's gone.*

In the distance I can see the misty cloud that often clings to the top of the curved crater of the volcano. I stop for a moment and stare up at it in wonder, listening to the slight breeze rustle the leaves and the intermittent chirp of a nearby cricket.

As we slow to a stop in the patchy brown grass by a crumbling brick wall, Rocco and Luca jump out of the truck and hurry ahead of us, Rocco carrying a box of glasses, and for a moment Leo and I are alone.

"Hey, Leo," I say carefully. "Maybe we should talk?"

"Talk?" he replies stubbornly. I try to suppress my frustration, but Leo catches me balling my hands into fists. I release them, my heart thumping so hard I can feel it in my right temple.

"Yes, *talk*. Please. You're still very upset with me about yesterday," I say. "I really don't want you to feel sidelined or whatever it is you're feeling."

"It's fine," he replies, staring past me.

"It's obviously not fine," I say, exasperated. I want to shout at him. I want to remind him that I've not seen these people in fifteen years and that I'm incredibly anxious. The trouble is, Leo thinks this is a problem of my own creation, a result of my abandoning Dad.

"Please don't hate me today." It's all I can whimper, my vulnerability tumbling out.

Leo looks at me and his face softens.

"I don't hate you, Olive," he replies, shaking his head, his eyes flickering to mine and then to the floor. "Of course I don't. I'm frustrated. Come on. We have to go."

Leo puts out his hand to indicate I should disembark the ice-cream truck first, and I do, the midday sun hitting my face. Despite the altitude, it's still hot in the sun and I feel sweat start to trickle down my back as Rocco appears around the side of the house.

"Olive! Leo!" he calls, and Leo paints on a big smile and waves back to indicate we're coming.

Then he turns toward me, takes a deep breath, and says, "Let's enjoy lunch and talk about the cookbook later. We'll sort it out. I'm sure."

I nod. It's a white flag of sorts. "Thanks."

10

R OCCO'S FAMILY STAND and move toward me as we approach. I absorb waves of hugs and kisses and pinched cheeks, remembering some people more than others, but all of them are warm and welcoming and full of sympathy.

Rocco's handsome son Michael and daughter-in-law Maria are here; they are Luca's parents. Rocco's other son, Sal, is also here, visiting from Naples with his two younger children, who, after a shy hello, resume running about the garden trying to catch a tiny orange butterfly. Rocco's dad, who must be in his nineties, sits with his wine wearing a corduroy coppola, beside two old women: one squat and round, obviously Rocco's mother, and the other tall and elegant like Rocco's wife, Isabella, a graying goddess with bangles up her arms and a floating green kaftan.

The long wooden table is set with delicate white bone china, and small mismatched vases with handpicked flowers are strewn throughout the center runner. It's a classic spread. A small bowl of fresh green olives. Fried artichokes. Sardines with a little oil and salt. Plates of hams, a hard ricotta, and to my joy, caponata—that aubergine dish—served in a colorful ceramic bowl hand-painted with citrus fruits. It is to die for, and I feel the flush of a memory. This could be my childhood family table at home.

Isabella kisses me on my forehead and says, "Bellissima! Finalmente ti rivedo! You're alive!"

"At least someone is alive," Rocco bellows from the head of the table, winking at me.

"*Rocco!*" scolds Isabella, clutching the cross around her neck before turning to me. "He jokes because he hurts."

"I can relate," I say to Rocco, before turning to Isabella, smiling. "Mi piace scherz—" I stammer. *Damn my Italian.*

"Scherzare? You like to joke to make it easier? Like this one," she says, nodding back at Rocco.

"Thanks. Yes. Gah. My Italian," I say, shaking my head.

"Your papà didn't speak the mother tongue at home?"

"He did. I just . . . stopped . . . learning," I reply, feeling the heat creep up my neck. Truth is, I have barely spoken Italian in fifteen years.

"Ma figurati!" she says, waving her hands. "You pick it up again fast."

We take our seats. Leo and I are placed next to each other, so close I can smell his zesty shampoo. I watch him stiffen as he glances at the distance between us on the bench; the tension starts to burn like radioactive fallout.

"Welcome," says Isabella raising her glass. "Oh, this is such a treat, Olive."

"We are absolutely delighted," Rocco agrees, waving for Leo and me to pour ourselves a drink. I shudder at the thought of drinking today, looking for the pitcher of water.

"It's Sicilian," says the petite nonna opposite me, whose eyebrows are identical to Rocco's but pure silver to match the wisps of hair that escape her messy bun. She swipes the bottle from the table and pours me a generous glass of pale-pink wine.

"If you insist," I say, taking a sip. It is cold and delicate and my spirits lift a little in the way that they always do when I'm enjoying the ceremony of dining in a group. Nonna nods, pleased, burps loudly, and leans forward to pinch Leo on the cheek. I'm amused to watch him submit to the gesture, after which she fills his glass to the rim.

"Feels rude not to," I say to Leo.

"It's an economic duty round here," he replies dryly, clearly feeling the same queasiness I am.

Rocco stands and taps his knife on his glass. "Allora. A toast!" he says. "But in Italian, I'm sorry, Olive."

"Go ahead," I say, waving a hand at him, smiling.

"Alla famiglia. Al cibo. E Leonardo. Benvenuto a casa. Eri come un figlio di Nicky."

You were like a son to Nicky. I know Rocco doesn't mean to belittle me with this, but still, the shame weighs me down instantly, my shoulders rolling forward in fear of what's next.

"E Olive. La bambina di Nicky. Benvenuto a casa," he says, before grinning at me again. "Meglio tardi che mai."

Nicky's baby. Welcome home. Better late than never. I chuckle along with everyone, though my heart is aching.

"Thank you for having me back," I say, raising my glass.

"Sempre." *Always.* Our glasses touch with an enthusiastic clink.

"Eat. *Eat!*" Rocco says loudly, waving his hands, and we dive into bowls of sumptuously dressed vegetables, meats, breads and cheese, and heavy pots of sardines with pasta, which are all being handed around under my nose. I am unable to refuse any of it.

"God. *Drool*," I say to Isabella, dishing a massive helping of everything onto my plate. "I'm gonna be rolling home down that volcano and straight into bed."

"The best food in the world," Luca says, grinning like the Sicilian chef he is.

"The cookbook!" Rocco says suddenly. "How are you two getting on with the recipes? All this choice." He waves his hand across the simple, delicious table spread and I nod in agreement. If only Leo didn't want to fancy it all up.

"Well . . . ," I say, pausing to rack my brain for an appropriate answer.

"We're working on the approach . . . ," Leo cuts in gallantly.

"Approach?" Rocco says, confused.

"We're at the planning stage," I explain.

"Mamma mia," says Rocco, doing the Italian pinched fingers. "Can I help? How many recipes do you need?"

"Three," I say quickly, feeling Leo next to me sit a little straighter in his chair. Why didn't we think of speaking to Rocco?

"Sì. Sì. We can make something with seafood," he begins. "Your father loved all the classics. Pasta con le sarde. Bottarga."

"Narrowing down to three dishes? Oddio!" Isabella says, clutching her forehead dramatically. "And one special ingredient?"

"Arance," says Luca quickly.

"No! Pinoli!" says Nonna. "Olio. Limone."

"Mandorle, per favore!" shouts another.

"That's another vote for almonds," I whisper to Leo.

And then the conversation runs away from us as everyone begins to argue in colorful Italian over what the quintessential Sicilian ingredient is, and the dishes that ingredient serves best.

I lean toward Leo. "Con le sarde? One of the Sicilian classics," I say quietly.

"Indeed," he replies.

"No elevation required," I cannot help but add.

Leo leans in toward me now, lowering his voice further, and I feel his breath hot against my ear as he says, "You got it all wrong, Olive."

I move my head to escape the fizzing feeling I'm getting from his mouth's proximity to my ear. "Exactly *what* did I get wrong?" I shoot back.

"Me," he says, tearing some bread so roughly he almost topples a wine bottle.

As the conversation on Sicilian food turns more heated, Nonna stands, throwing her arms in the air as she stomps off back toward the house calling Rocco "un idiota!" as she leaves.

"They are arguing about rice again," explains Isabella. "Arancino or arancina. She comes from Palermo. In Sicily, we can't even agree on what to call something."

"This is not going to be easy," I whisper to Leo. "Not even this table of Sicilian foodies can come up with an agreed approach." I see the corners of his mouth curl up into half a grin.

Isabella then holds her arms out to quiet the table. "The answer is *food*," Isabella says, unhelpfully.

"Very good food," I reply, feeling my belly start to stretch with the sheer volume of food I've virtually inhaled.

"What I mean is, you two need to get out and eat. I can give you a list of places to visit. You have so much to try."

"We're doing that," I say quickly, feeling my cheeks burn.

"She means *together*," says Leo. "And she's right."

"I'm *always* right," Isabella says.

"What is she right about now?" Rocco says, throwing his hands up.

I can't help but giggle at the two of them as I reach forward to take more bread, tear it between my teeth, and dunk it into the vinegary oil at the bottom of a plate of anchovies.

I turn to Leo. "She *is* right," I say. "I got it wrong, Leo. I thought we could do this quickly and easily, and it's going to take time and a lot of working together to get the best result."

Leo nods. "Yup," he says, turning to me, a smug smile on his face. "I knew you'd get there eventually, Olive."

I ignore the jibe. Leo *was* right too. I've been fooling myself. I was determined to protect my heart by keeping my distance from Leo and by avoiding reading the manuscript, but it's no use. To do this properly we have to work together.

The wine flows, the heat bears down, the lively debates continue, the constant chirping of crickets fills the air, and I feel a sense of familiar comfort. I spot a bird in the distance, its wings large and still as it glides. I start to relax.

"How have you been since Nicky passed?" Isabella asks gently, leaning in to keep the conversation between us.

"Oh. Um. It's been difficult," I say, clearing my throat. I reach for my wineglass and take a sip, in the hope that she doesn't press for more.

"Of course," she says. "And Rocco says that he left you Nicky's?"

"He . . . did," I say, instantly stiffening.

"Well, that must be exciting. I know you were off doing your own thing, but Nicky always thought you'd come back . . ." She looks wistfully across at Rocco. "Isn't that right, Rocco?"

"What?"

"I'm talking about Olive coming back to work at Nicky's."

My heart starts to pick up. No. *Not this.*

Not with Leo right here.

"What will you do with it?" she asks. "Big changes, little changes? New menu?"

I sit there, my mouth half-open, willing myself to say something, anything, to shut the line of questioning down.

"Leo, you had some ideas for modernizing, didn't you?" Isabella says, turning her attention to him. I wait in a kind of cold horror for him to tell them I'm selling, but he shrugs and reaches for more wine.

"But you must have some ideas?" Isabella presses me, leaning in, smiling eagerly. I feel heat rising through my body, every cell starting to vibrate as my chest tightens.

And that's when I feel the weight of Leo's hand on my arm below the table, and then a gentle, reassuring squeeze. I look down at his fingers, momentarily stunned, processing the feeling of comfort, but also a fizzing feeling at all the points where our skin touches. My breath catches in my throat, all the sounds around me dim, and there is only his hot touch on my bare skin. Then Leo moves his hand away as fast as it arrived, and lifts the bowl of caponata, handing it to Luca.

I realize: *He's not going to tell them I'm selling.*

Does Leo actually understand? I look across at him and he briefly meets my eyes, making a soft grimace. *This must be hard,* his face tells me.

I close my eyes as warmth blossoms inside me. I analyze every edge of the moment before it disintegrates like smoke into the breeze and am able to come back to Isabella's question about my intentions with more calm.

"You know, I'm still trying to process everything," I say, and it feels truthful.

"Of course you are, darling. Running a restaurant is a big new challenge."

I cringe, grateful once again that Leo has my back on this.

"Do you love it, Isabella?" I ask her now. "Running a restaurant?"

She laughs lightly. "With him?"

"She loves it," Rocco booms.

"If you don't mind the long hours, I love it," she replies.

"Nonna, you *never* do long hours anymore," Luca says, laughing.

"It is all about *family* first," she says, shooting Luca a wide, toothy smile. "Rocco and I make sure there is time for this." She holds a hand out to the table, indicating the family sitting around it. "But it helps to have a very busy restaurant, which is not too big for the family to handle." She smiles. She knows she is lucky; in hospitality, this is a dream.

I think about how Dad engineered a trip here every year. I wonder why the importance of family first didn't stick with my restaurant-obsessed dad, who allowed his own family to fall apart. It feels utterly incongruous. Maybe he *was* just plain selfish.

Luca raises another toast. "To family!" he says, smiling.

"To family," I repeat, lost in the tangle of memories.

"Family is family. No matter how you all come together," says Rocco. It's so minor, but think I see Isabella fire Rocco a *look*.

"What? I didn't say anything," he says, before shooting me a big grin.

What was that about?

"Allora," Isabella says brightly, and the thought vanishes from my mind. "More caponata, please, Luca?"

In the thin shade of an ancient Saracen olive tree on one side, and the thicker, more cooling shade of an orange tree behind us, we eat. And eat. The talk is loud and fast and in Italian, and people don't always stop to explain, but I don't care. I can follow, mostly. I am enjoying sitting back and letting this large, loud family eat and love and shout across the table until espressos arrive, and sweet cannoli dipped in pistachios are devoured by the children, and I am ready to head back to the hotel to rest.

"At least have some cut oranges," says Rocco to me as I clutch my stomach and groan. He slides a plate of chilled, segmented bloodred oranges right in front of me. "The orange growing is fading because people make so much money from the nuts. But we keep it going here on the farm. This is the Moro."

"Oh god," I say, unable to refuse. It is, without a doubt, the most delicious orange I've ever eaten. Notes of raspberry give it a tartness and complexity that leave the classic supermarket navel orange in the dust.

"It's sunshine. It's bittersweet. It's perfect. My god," I say, gasping. "I think I just fell in love. I'm going to have a civil partnership with an orange."

Leo, who has been fairly quiet for the last half hour, leans forward onto his elbows. "They're not for everyone," he says, taking a segment. "Very fleshy, delicately juicy, and not obscenely sweet."

"Fleshy?" Luca says, tipping his glass toward us, playing with his mustache.

"Delicately juicy?" I say, raising an eyebrow. I expect Leo to feel embarrassed, but instead he shoots Luca a cheeky grin, eyes buzzing with mischief.

"Seriously, Olive," Luca says. "For me, the orange is so special to Sicily. We juice it, we ice it, we bake it, we zest it. It's an aperitif, a pasta dish, a dessert. It's the color of sunset on the outside, and a bleeding heart inside."

"That's poetry right there. You should write that down, Olive," Leo says playfully, and I narrow my eyes at him.

"And *you* should reflect on the simplicity of this delicious home cooking," I retort, to a wry smile from him.

Later, after I've taken a final mouthful of my drink, allowing the warming flush of Marsala to hit the back of my throat like a full stop on the lunch, I clutch my stomach and groan again.

Leo agrees. "Enough."

"I need a nap," I say, yawning.

"Luca can drop you back," says Rocco.

After more hugs and promises to return soon, we head back to the ice-cream truck, walking slowly. As I feel the prickle of hot sun on my skin, a part of me hopes that the day doesn't end here. I watch as Leo loiters by the edge of the lava stone wall, just out of Luca's eyeline.

"So, do we have a new plan?" he says, hand to his chin, deep in thought.

"We go out together," I say. "Find the dishes that spark something in both of us. And I need to find my Sicilian story for the introduction."

"Shall we hit the street food, fish markets, tomorrow? It's a fast way to try a lot," he says. "And see a lot."

Tomorrow. I gaze across the stone wall to an orange tree and a part of me wants to run. A part of me is still too afraid to open my heart and my mind and throw myself completely into this with him. I sit with this feeling for a moment. Is it because getting to know Leo, getting to like Leo, will lead to further pain? Because it's easier, isn't it, to hate someone you think replaced you. It's much harder to find them worthy.

I look back at him. Leo is reaching across the aisle and I need to take his hand.

"Sure. I hope I'll have room tomorrow," I say, holding my stomach like a pregnant belly to emphasize the point. Leo smiles, then glances away and then back at me like he's got more to say.

"We got off to a bad start." He turns his head away again, staring into the middle distance, struggling, it seems, to find words. "I'm sorry I complicated things with my ideas for the book. I want to . . . do the best for Nicky. For your dad."

"I know you do," I say, drawing in the dirt with the edge of my sandal. I look up at Leo, and his face is shadowed with grief. Our eyes meet and his lips squeeze together. A fleeting moment of shared loss.

"I'm sorry I have been difficult, and wanting to work alone. It's just . . ." I feel a very small prickle of tears, which I push away with a deep breath. "You know. The restaurant sale. Your obvious closeness to my dad. It's hard being . . ."

"Around me," he says.

Leo seems to be considering something, but then he shakes his head. "I'll happily execute this the way Nicky would have wanted. My very last job for him," he says, his eyes flickering to me. I look back down at the dirt until my eyes start to lose focus. It hits me hard, to realize how much Leo must have loved Dad, like a father. And Dad loved this man like a son. Any feelings of jealousy or shame or whatever I might have, I need to bury them.

"Thanks for not telling them I'm selling," I say quietly, as we make our way back toward Luca.

"It okay," he says. The smallest hint of a shoulder shrug. "I won't tell them."

"I'm grateful," I reply.

"But it wasn't completely altruistic," he says, slowing once again, turning to me, grinning.

"It wasn't?" I say, distracted by the shape of his arms as he rubs the back of his neck. I look at him in his black T-shirt with his black sunglasses and his smile and think once again how attractive he is. Objectively.

"I figure if you're too nervous to tell Rocco you're selling," he says, as I find my eyes locked on the curve of his shoulders, "then some part of you cares. And if some part of you cares, then the window of opportunity is not quite shut."

"Ha ha," I say, smiling nervously. *I hope he's kidding.*

11

L EO AND I meet first thing at the famous Catania fish market, a busy, loud, industry-and-locals-only affair, until the area transforms into a tourist trap later in the day. Shouting men covered in fish guts sell their wares from huge crates of the day's catch destined for restaurants all across Catania and the surrounding villages, including Rocco's. I spot his grandson Luca in a pair of blue-striped swimming shorts and a white T-shirt, cigarette dangling out of his mouth as he barters with comical indignation.

We stand at the railing above, looking down, a line of old men in flat caps stretching out on either side next to us, all of us watching the action below. Huge swordfish are cut into slices. Snails try to escape their baskets. Cuttlefish and octopus are held aloft, their prices shouted out to the buyers.

Luca finally sees us from under the arched bridge and waves. "Leo! Olive!" he shouts, and we wave back, but within seconds he's back aggressively bartering. This is pure street theater, and I could stand here all day.

"Coffee?" Leo asks, turning to me, looking as apprehensive at the prospect of the day together as I feel.

"Yes, thanks," I reply, pushing my hair behind my ears. *I have to make this work*, I think to myself. *Focus on the eating.*

We wander to a small café on the corner and Leo orders two macchiatos.

"What if I wanted an almond latte?" I say, laughing as I take the coffee from him.

"You didn't," he says, handing me the small coffee. "I read your review of the Roasted Bean, on Bond Street. Four stars. And you hate lattes. Just like your dad."

I blush. Fully. I don't know why, but the mix of Leo referencing a fairly obscure review of mine and comparing me and Dad warms my heart.

After coffee, we eat raw prawns with a beer behind a monastery. Then, down a small alley, we share spaghetti al nero di seppia—squid ink pasta—and a plate of sardines simply fried in oil with ice-cold white wine. We both work hard to keep the conversation friendly and focused on the job.

By two o'clock I ram my fingertips into the palm of my other hand. "Time out!" I say, exhausted from walking and eating. "I need a break. I need sleep and water and nothing but iceberg lettuce for a week."

Leo laughs. "We've covered a lot already, and there's still dinner," he says, grinning.

"Can we not mention food for, like, the next two hours? In fact, I definitely need a nap."

He leans across and points at some of the scribblings in my book. "Anything stand out for you so far?"

It's as physically close as we've been all day, and I feel the heat of his breath catch the back of my ear. He moves closer still, turning the page of my notebook, and the smell of wine and that woody cologne overwhelms me. I gently inhale, breathing him in, closing my eyes for a moment. But when I open them, Leo is looking at me. He quickly moves, making exaggerated space between us by leaning back in his chair. I mirror him, terrified suddenly that he's sensed my attraction.

"Perhaps it *is* time for a break," he says, looking at his notebook.

ME: It's going better
KATE: Glad to hear it!
GINNY: You're getting on now?
ME: We eat, we talk about the food. We write in our notebooks. We stick to the job. I wouldn't call us Frodo and Samwise quite yet, but at least we're not fighting.
KATE: "At least we're not fighting" is better
GINNY: But Lord of the Flings is what we want
ME: 😠 I have to go. I have to eat. More eating.

The next day, Leo and I take appetizers in one place, then walk twenty minutes across town for secondi. Our palates feel alive with fleshy seafood, fresh grilled vegetables, sumptuous pasta. We eat Greek-influenced dishes, learning it was they who brought the pistachios and inspired a love of seafood when they settled the east of the island.

"I like the way the smoke has permeated the flesh here but hasn't charred the edges," Leo says.

"Try this," I say. "I love the way the little flecks of orange zest set off the creamy pistachio in the squid ball. This is incredible."

"Five out of five?" he asks.

"No. That was one time and only because I felt terrible."

"I swear to god," he says, laughing. "What's a person got to do to get full marks out of Olive Stone?"

"I like to keep my grading a mystery," I reply haughtily. "Otherwise, people stop trying to impress me."

Leo laughs. There is more laughter now, less tense quiet. If we can keep this up, by the time we get to Tuscany, maybe I won't be quite so nervous to spend time in his world, with his family. My feelings are softening toward him. And occasionally, I'm feeling other things. Thrilling things about Leo that I shouldn't be. I clear my throat.

"Does any part of you get excited about this?" Leo asks, eyeing me carefully. "All the weirdness aside, on a professional level. Are you excited about working on a cookbook?"

"Yes," I say thoughtfully. "It's obviously a loaded job." I glance at Leo, who nods, his lip curled up slightly as though he's waiting for me to say it. "But yeah. Part of me is excited. Of course. And nervous. Nervous excited."

Leo nods again. "Finding that perfect recipe."

"Finding and penning a warm, heartfelt story," I add. "Really making people excited about the food and the area. Oh god, the *irony*." I can't help but laugh at my own admission. I, a food critic, who has spent her whole life intentionally looking for fault in other people's food, now wanting to create something for once.

Leo nods again, looking smug, and then leans forward, resting his forearms on the table. He raises his eyebrows, fixing his smile on me. "Want out of the critiquing business, Olive?"

Olive. The way he says my name unsettles me. I like the way it comes out of his mouth, with his London accent, the *v* pronounced almost as an *f*. I feel the air in my lungs thin and a tightness in my chest.

"Come on, let's keep going," I say, pointing toward a sign that says CANNOLI.

We continue our journey, stopping only to break for afternoon digestive recovery and escape from the sun. We make progress. Gently share thoughts. Carefully consider each other's ideas.

By midafternoon Leo suggests we try a little place in the south of Catania by the sea. I'm happy to follow his lead, and we walk in something close to companionable silence until we arrive at an unassuming little place that sits between the port and the beach.

"Want some cake?" he says, grinning.

"Sure," I say, smiling wryly. "I'm sure there's a corner of my stomach that has room for some Italian cake."

"Sicilian," he says in a deadpan tone. "And I think you'll like this cake, Olive."

When said cake arrives, it's rather plain to look at, with its terra-cotta crumb and simple dusting of icing sugar on top. "Torta all'arancia," says Leo. "Orange cake."

"It looks deliziosa," I say, holding my fork aloft.

"Your dad loved that cake," says Leo. It is the first direct mention of him in ages, and my eyes flicker up at Leo. I nod once, unable to find a way to reply. Even in this simplest of comments, *your dad loved that cake*, I read a thousand tiny, painful things. The warm nostalgia with which the words are delivered, the sense of loss that I didn't know about a cake he loved. I picture him, sitting here with Leo, raving about the cake, his hands waving around with excitement and gusto.

"Grazie," I say finally.

"Prego," Leo replies, smiling as he also picks up a fork.

Ninety seconds and four forkfuls later, I look up at Leo. "My god. I am actually dying . . . the orange flavor. It's so good."

"I knew you'd like the cake," he says simply.

"I do," I say, grinning as he holds my gaze. Our eyes connect again over the little square table. I don't look away. I hold his intense, dark gaze as his hand reaches forward to take my fork and try a mouthful. I watch the fork as he slides the cake off the end, and I find myself wanting to moan on his behalf. At the cake. At his lips. At him. All I can hear is David Bowie's "Modern Love" on the café radio, the sound of frothing milk, and my heart pounding in my ears.

And then, I realize, there is something more to this cake.

"This was my mum's favorite cake," I say suddenly. "She loved it. We went up the coast for her favorite version of it."

"Your dad's too. That's kind of sweet," he says.

"I hated it back then," I say, staring down at what's left on my plate. "God. I'm amazed. How can an opinion change so much?"

"No one thinks the same way they did as a teenager," says Leo. "Not really."

"I hated it," I say again, thinking of my father.

"Well, you don't hate it now," he says, laughing.

I'm a little quiet on the walk back, thinking of Dad and Mum and how tastes and feelings and perspectives grow and change. Leo is lively and excited by our progress and wants to agree on the key ingredient so we can start to narrow down the dishes.

"It's not almonds, is it?" I say, grinning.

Leo's lip curls slightly. "No," he says, clearing his throat.

"Oranges?" We both say it in unison.

"Oranges," he confirms, nodding. "The blood orange is so unique. They even have a festival each year, right here in the city."

"It's the right ingredient," I reply, meeting his eyes. "Orange granita. Orange zest in those delicious little squid balls from the market."

"And that orange cake," he says.

"The *cake*!" I reply.

"That orange and fennel salad with the anchovies?"

"That *salad*. Salty and sweet and with those plump black olives," I say, moaning.

"And oil," he says.

"And crusty bread," I add, ducking into the shadow of a tall building.

"Have we had a breakthrough?" he asks.

"Yes," I say, nodding, "I supposed we have."

"We need to celebrate," he says.

"Okay, but can we celebrate with gelato? I need a day off the wine."

"You have room for gelato? You know we have dinner tonight," he says, laughing.

"I have room," I protest.

"Let's go to Rocco's restaurant."

"Does Rocco have gelato?" I ask, frowning.

"Does Rocco have gelato?" he says, laughing. "Where do you think your dad got his famous recipe from?"

12

ROCCO IS PREPPING for dinner and beams when he sees us, calling us back toward the kitchen. The restaurant is dark and cool, though there are still a few lunch customers sitting on the ends of bottles of wine, chattering lazily. A child lies on the ground with a coloring book and a jar of pencils. I feel a strong sense of nostalgia in these dark walls; it is so familiar, from the little painting of the boat on the wall to the sound of the chairs scraping across the floor.

"We fancied a gelato," says Leo.

"Bene, bene," Rocco says, grinning. "Stracciatella is the best."

When Dad trained here, long ago, he lived a few doors down with my nonna and nonno, who owned a fishing charter business. In many ways, he grew up here and I see its influence on him. In many ways, it feels like Nicky's used to feel to me. A home away from home.

I lean against the wall, staring at the huge corkboard opposite, covered in photos. Dad had one like this too, and I wonder if it's still there. If there are photos of me still pinned to it.

I scan the images: fading photos, Polaroids and prints, decades of happy, sun-burnished customers of all ages holding their gelato, grinning. And then my eyes catch on one. It's the two-tone trunks, red on one side, blue on the other, that draw me in. I know those trunks. The image's colors are a little washed out, but the picture is crystal clear. I feel a strong wave of sensory memory fill me as I walk slowly toward it, peering in closer. *Dad*. Dad and his handlebar mustache, his wide smile. Dad looking handsome and happy, with me on his hip, holding out an ice cream. He is looking at me like he just won an Oscar.

"It's me," I say, breathless. My hair is that young, wispy blond that fades as you grow, my skin milky and pink next to Dad's deep tan. I'm wearing a little cotton sundress, white with red cherries.

"It *is* you," says Rocco, coming back with two towering cones of ice cream. "Che bellissima bambina."

I unpin the photo. "Can I make a copy?"

"Sì, sì," he says. "Take it."

I clutch the photo to my heart for a moment, then slip it into my handbag and take the cone from Rocco.

"He loved your name. Olive," he says, smiling. "Era il destino."

"It's not really destiny if you chose the name yourself," I say, laughing.

Rocco shakes his head. "Ah. Yes," he replies. "My English. Sì, sì."

"Olive," says Leo, taking his cone from Rocco. "I'm going to head off and put my head down before dinner tonight."

I nod, looking back at Rocco. "Do you mind if I hang out for a bit and watch you guys get the dinner service ready? I have some work to do.

"See you at five?" I say to Leo, who nods and disappears out the door.

I sit at a little table by the window and transfer the notes in my notebook to my laptop, readying myself to start writing the introduction. I watch as Isabella glides in to check that everything is running smoothly, look over the books, and correct the specials on the blackboard.

I notice so many similarities with how Nicky's was run. It is so clear watching the way they move that Dad trained here and then tried to re-create Rocco's in London. It had really worked for a while, until it didn't. Where did Dad go wrong? Was Leo right? Was it simply that it needed to modernize? Why then does Rocco's still work so well?

Rocco asks if I want to help shuck oysters, and I do. "You can't get good oysters in London."

I want to correct him, to tell him that Whitstable Bay is one of the great wild-oyster locations in Europe. But instead, I just smile.

There is something to the rhythm of this place that makes me terribly homesick for my childhood, watching the way Isabella and Rocco banter with each other as they work. They make it look easy.

The afternoon passes like the breeze, and suddenly it is time to go and get ready to meet Leo for dinner. As I pack my bag and say good-bye to Rocco, I realize I have butterflies in my stomach. And this time, it isn't anxiety. It's anticipation.

13

I STOP AT A little boutique and pick up a new cocktail dress with a very low square neck and puffy sleeves. It's black and very short, like halfway-down-my-thigh short. It's kind of racy, especially with the heeled black espadrilles.

Sensible Olive is telling me to be chill. Put on the new green pants and the little white tank. But instead I'm wearing lacy knickers, styling my hair with soft curls, and applying a red lipstick.

I look in the mirror and tell myself I'm not dressing for Leo. *Liar.*

When I get downstairs, Leo glances up at me, and then back to his phone, but then his head snaps up again and, as I walk across the small lobby, his eyes drop slowly from my face down to my ankles.

He's also dressed up, I note with some pleasure. He greets me as evenly as a bank manager about to consider an application for an overdraft, but I see the twitch in his jaw as we shake hands.

"Well," he says, raising an eyebrow.

"Yes. Very well, thank you," I say.

He stands and fixes the cuffs on his loose charcoal shirt, grabs his wallet off the table, and slides it into the pocket of his khaki trousers. His movements are agonizingly slow, as though he's in conversation with himself.

"It's a beautiful evening," he says as we head out of the hotel lobby and into the twilight. He stops walking and faces me, the sky that delicious golden just before the sun goes down, and it catches his skin and the slight flecks of dark caramel in his otherwise dark hair. Good god, he's handsome.

"How far do you reckon you can walk in heels the height of a brandy snap?" he asks.

"I could wait tables in these babies," I say defiantly.

Leo's mouth moves to the side as he considers something. A witty comeback, perhaps? But as I turn to walk ahead, he grabs my arm and pulls me gently back toward him.

"One sec"—he points at the back of the dress—"the, um . . . Here. Let me."

He reaches behind me, his fingers brushing the back of my neck, his breath near my ear, and for just a moment he looks down at me, our eyes connect, and I feel everything in my body flicker with desire.

Then he hands me the sale tag that I forgot to remove from the dress, with a mortifyingly huge orange fifty percent off sticker on it.

"The sale tag," he says apologetically.

"Right," I mutter, smoothing the front of my skirt. The corner of Leo's mouth twitches, but his eyes follow my hands and linger on my hips.

"Come on. I know a bar."

Leo leads me down a lane, and, behind him, I try not to drag my high heels, still embarrassed. Leo points to a sign, almost hidden behind overgrown vines, that reads LA CASA BLANCA. Inside, its Catanian bones have been newly furnished in dark wood, pin-striped wallpaper, and leather sofas, and both an American and an Italian flag sit behind the bar, which is filled with a huge selection of American whiskey.

"La Casa Blanca. The White House," I say, understanding, as Bruce Springsteen's "Born to Run" blasts through the room. "I usually think dive bars when I think of American bars."

"Yes, this is giving us more Baroque Obama," says Leo.

I erupt into spontaneous laughter, bursting the tension with my throaty cackle. Leo just sits there at our little round table looking smug.

"I didn't know you had such wit," I tease as my laughter subsides.

"You don't really know me at all," he replies with an eyebrow raised as he looks for the waiter.

He tugs at the cuffs on his shirt again. A sharply dressed non-American waiter appears. Black vest, crisp white shirt. "Cosa vorreste bere?" he says, grinning. His voice is deep and rich, and he's oh so handsome.

"I feel like I should be ordering whiskey rocks," I say, waving around at the American interior. "But I'd love a glass of rosé from the Gambino vineyard—do you have it?"

"Sì, sì," he says, smiling.

"And for you, sir?" he says, switching to English.

"I'll take an old-fashioned," says Leo, smiling.

"I brought your manuscript," I say, pulling it out of my bag and setting it on the table. "I thought we could check over the recipes for the other regions together and see how we can make oranges work," I say.

Leo nods, watching me as I look back down at the cover again and open to a random page. *Puglia.*

"This looks amazing," I begin, just as our drinks arrive. "And here's the aubergine," I add sheepishly, turning the page to Leo's laughter.

"So good," he says, nodding. "Did you read the stories?" I can feel his eyes intent on me as I turn the pages, and I become hyper-aware of the scrape of the paper against my fingers, the tickle of my hair against my neck, the light flow of air against the bare skin of my shoulders, as though his eyes on me have heightened each of my senses . . . *Stop it, Olive.*

"I promise I'll read the stories before we leave Sicily," I say quickly, before looking at Leo and putting my hand over my heart.

Leo nods. "Fine. Let's focus on the recipes."

He pulls the manuscript across to him. "Okay. You'll see he usually does something like an antipasto or starter-type dish. Or maybe a salad. And then a secondo or a pasta dish. Then sometimes dessert, but not always."

"Ooh, pasta alla norcina," I say, pointing to a recipe that catches my eye. "Ooh, Venetian prawns with polenta?" I look up at Leo, my tongue hanging out. He screws his mouth up to try to contain a laugh.

"Look at the clam risotto," he says, touching the edge of the page. "How good does that sound?" I pass a single picture of my dad standing over a pan of steaming muscles. It's a candid photo, and old. Maybe early nineties. It captures him so completely as the father of my childhood. I reach across to turn the page, quickly.

"So we've got two recipes, right?"

"Cake is number one. Orange and fennel salad is number two?" he says, nodding.

"Yes to the salad. We should try a version with capers. And that second version we tried at the market was cut lovely and thin, which really gave the fennel a softness."

"Done," he says, scribbling down notes.

"And that cake was . . . everything in Sicilian life together in one bite . . ." I stop for a moment, looking around for the words to describe it. "It was perfect."

Leo smiles. "Perfect?"

"You know," I say, shrugging. "As perfect as it gets."

Leo laughs. "Can't let the critic in you go, can you?"

"Shut up," I say, grinning.

Leo smiles back at me, and I am not prepared for the electric pulse that fizzes through my body when it reaches his eyes and he shakes his head slowly.

"What?" I say, folding my arms.

"It's nice to see you so into it," he says, grinning. "It's like you've come alive."

"It's easy to talk to you about food," I say, without adding that my worries about the restaurant, about putting him out of a job and disappointing my father—all of it falls away when we're working.

"I have a suggestion for the third dish," Leo says suddenly. "Since we're in Catania, we *have* to do seafood. One salad, one cake, one seafood dish."

"I agree. Something with sardines, please?"

"Well," he says, looking extremely satisfied. "I've made us a reservation for a place that does the best pasta con le sarde in Catania."

LEO LEADS ME back toward the fish market and turns down a street filled with colorful open umbrellas outside a row of restaurants. The tables spill so far out onto the street that there is just a small walking lane between them. He points to a place with fairy lights across the salmon-pink facade and just a few full and lively tables outside.

"Gosh this place is cute," I say, getting jabbed in the side by a passing group. The interior is illuminated by soft lighting and candles. In the moody low light I can just make out mostly naked frescoes covering the walls. It's romantic. It's *dangerously* romantic.

It's research, Olive.

We're given a seat at a small round table with a crisp white tablecloth in a dark corner of the already dark restaurant. It's quiet in here, given the carnival atmosphere of the street outside. I feel like I've stepped into a Caravaggio, dark and red with yellow light. The single candle gently illuminates Leo's face, catching the flecks of lightness in his eyes.

Leo swiftly takes care of the food ordering.

"Seafood antipasto? Then the pasta con le sarde? Oh, and let's try this roe and spaghetti with orange." Leo looks up and smiles at me. "Since orange is our theme."

"All sounds good to me," I say.

The waiter brings a bottle of Feu D'o Bianco, a crisp white, and a volcanic charcoal plate bearing crusty ciabatta and olive oil with some kind of herby vinegar pooling through it. I look up at Leo.

"Do you like the presentation?" Leo asks.

"Yes, but as you know, with me it's about the taste," I reply wryly. The bread delivers a heavenly crunch as I bite into it, and the soft, chewy crumb holds the herbed oil beautifully.

"It's good," I murmur. "All this bread and oil. I might need to start running. You know what I really like? A good hike."

"I think Tuscany is going to be the place for that," he says, reminding me that I'm supposed to be staying with his aunt in a few days. "You know, you should do the Etna crater."

"Yes indeed. There is something so thrilling about the idea of standing on the edge of an active volcano," I say sarcastically.

"The view is great." He smiles. "We should go sometime."

The way my pulse jumps at Leo's invitation is more terrifying than the active volcano.

"Your dad liked that walk," he continues.

I ignore the mention of Dad and take a sip of my wine, enjoying the feeling of relaxation it gives me as the alcohol hits my veins.

Leo studies my face. "You hate it when I mention him."

My eyes flicker up to his. "It's hard. We have different feelings toward him," I say, reaching for my wine again immediately. Leo watches me as I hold the glass to my lips for a moment, contemplating whether to elaborate. I don't.

"Why? I don't understand it. Why did you fall out?" Leo presses.

I breathe out loudly, then squeeze my lips together, looking across the restaurant. Fuck it. He may as well know.

"He's not the big, amazing, perfect demigod you think he is," I say.

"He wasn't perfect," says Leo, pointing his fork toward me. "I'll give you that."

I narrow my eyes at him. I'm surprised to hear him say those words. "How so?" I say.

"You first," he replies.

I sit back in my chair and fold my arms, and Leo watches me with some degree of suspicion. "Did he cheat on your mum? Or like . . . I don't know," he says slowly.

"Nothing like that," I say, before I take a deep breath and decide to just say it. "My dad chose the restaurant over Mum. And me, really. He got so caught up in it, ignoring my mum, belittling her advice and suggestions. He always knew best and would not listen. It started hemorrhaging money, and he was never home, fighting for the restaurant's survival rather than our family's. In the end, he secretly sold our family home to keep the restaurant afloat. It was the last straw for Mum, who left the marriage with nothing because she didn't have the heart to force him to sell it."

"I didn't know that," Leo says, holding my gaze.

"And it's hard to forgive because I watched Mum fall apart and struggle to put herself back together," I say. "While Dad's life just carried on as if we were never there."

Leo looks as though he wants to say something but glances down at his plate.

"I felt abandoned," I say, ramming it home.

Leo nods. "I can see how you would feel that. Did he send money at least?"

"Yes. Of course," I say quickly. "But that was just about all he did."

"He didn't call?"

"Sometimes. Less and less," I say, shrugging.

Leo looks across the restaurant and his eyes narrow a little as he shakes his head. "It makes no sense," he says. "He always talked about you."

My breath catches in my throat, and I feel my heart squeeze as I reach for my wine. I'm not ready to hear that. I'm certainly not ready to believe it. I clear my throat.

"When I saw the books a few weeks ago, I just thought, Jesus Christ, Dad! Nothing got better. I mean, what the hell? That's what you chose over us? Over me?" I throw both my hands up.

Leo shakes his head. "It didn't get better," he says.

"Your turn now. Why? Why did nothing change there? Those old chairs? The paintwork? What had he been doing? You had four bookings on a Friday night!"

Leo blinks, pausing momentarily.

I shrug apologetically. "I've seen everything."

"He *never* listened to anyone else," he says ruefully.

"Right."

"I really tried," he says, running a hand through his hair.

I nod, lifting my shoulders, encouraging him to go on. Leo moves in, taking an oyster and tilting it so it slides down his throat. Then he licks the edge of his lips and puts his elbows on the table, bringing both hands up to his temples.

"There's a place in Florence. L'Ortone. It's fucking modern, but still, like . . . cool. Bistro-style," he says. His voice starts to fill with excitement, his hands gesticulating as he speaks. "It's right next to a market, and the food . . . it's so great."

"Lemon foam and Parmesan tuiles?" I say teasingly.

"Maybe. But it's an ever-changing menu, totally seasonal. It's

Italian, but they don't brick themselves in. Pork belly in sake and soy. Duck with burned asparagus. But also, the best version of pici cacio e pepe I've ever had. Italian, but lots of different influences. A lot of Italian cooks think Italian food can't be improved."

He grins at me conspiratorially, and I cringe.

"I get that Nicky's is a family restaurant, but you're right that it looks the same as it did in 1995, and the world has changed. Your dad just would not *modernize*. It was an insult to his very core, the idea that what was a good idea once is now out of date. And Jesus. The same fucking *Trattoria Italiana* CD every night. The same everything. And the people that come? They're that age, like, where they can only eat one course and don't really drink. I love the regulars, but Nicky's needs young London too. Sharing plates and cool Italian cocktails. Not the same old fucking Aperol spritz they sit on for two hours."

"Hey, I like an Aperol spritz," I joke, but I'm surprised to hear Leo speak so candidly about the restaurant's problems. And I'm surprised most of all that I agree with him.

Leo laughs. "Yeah. So that's my take, anyway."

"It sounds like a reasonable take," I say, as the waiter fills my glass again. "And you think Nicky's could have worked if he'd listened?"

"Yeah," he says, shrugging. "Not just worked. It had everything it needed to thrive."

"Huh," is all I can reply.

"What do you think about this?" Leo says, as I take the last oyster and let it slide down my throat.

"I *do* like the way it's presented," I say, turning the boat-shaped olive-wood platter. On the side, the initials of the restaurant are burned in.

"Modern Italian," Leo says, laughing. "See? It can be done without being too—what is that word you use in your reviews? *Overengineered.*"

I shoot him a look, and he holds my gaze for a moment. And this time, I don't look away. The intensity of the look between us is like hot breath on my neck, all my hairs standing on end. An electric pulse buzzes through me and down my spine; I fight the urge to shift in my seat. I hold still, and for the first time I think, with absolute clarity, that I am more than just attracted to Leo. I am utterly lustful for him. I've been lustful since the first day here in Catania. If I'm honest, it is probably another reason I've found it hard to be around him.

Leo's eyes seem to darken as we hold each other's gaze.

The pull is so strong, and more alarming still, it's mutual.

The waiter returns, and with that, the tension breaks. I take a moment to look at the flickering candle and try to calm my galloping heart.

The waiter removes the seafood antipasto, and we both sit back to make room as two wide-rimmed bowls of the most delicately presented pasta are laid in front of us. I get an immediate hit of orange and strong, earthy fish notes.

Leo watches me as I stab my fork into the linguine and roll it round, lifting it with my spoon and sliding it into my mouth. My face must say *heaven*, because Leo grins.

"Now, I could write a good story about this," I say, nodding, unable to remove the childish look of pleasure from my face. "A love story."

"Want to try mine?" he says.

"It's the same," I say. He plunges his fork into his dish and holds it up.

"Nope. I ordered mine with a couple of changes. I have lemon. You have orange. I have parsley, you have none," he says, and again our eyes connect. I lean forward, aware I'm giving him an eyeful of cleavage as I do.

"Okay then," I say. His eyes narrow ever so slightly.

He holds out the fork and places it just in front of my lips, so that I have to lean a little closer to put my mouth around it. I feel my cheeks burn as I pull the pasta slowly back off the fork, and Leo looks down at my mouth.

"Delicious," I say.

"It is," he agrees, his eyes on me, his voice deep and husky.

Oh boy. *What am I doing?* I'm selling his livelihood; I can't get involved with him.

We are interrupted by a man with an armful of red roses, going table to table in the restaurant. "Cinque euro," he says to Leo.

"No, thank you," I say.

"No, grazie," Leo says, also shaking his head. As the man moves away, there's a beat of silence between us. Leo picks up his glass and takes a sip. I take the last of the bread and scrape it across my plate to pick up some of the sauce. The moment of awkwardness knocks us both a little off beat.

Leo waves the waiter over and asks for more wine, since we've already finished the bottle.

"*Have* we figured this out, then?" I say, dragging a napkin across my mouth.

"I think we have," he says.

"We need to test all three dishes."

"Antonia says we can use their kitchen after breakfast again. We did it," he says, shaking his head with almost disbelief. Then he pushes his plate forward. "I'm done."

"Same," I say reluctantly. I don't want tonight to end. "You know, when I was a kid, I used to think the word *sous* was actually *Sue*, as in the girl's name. I thought Dominic's name was Sue."

"Big old Dom?"

"Yep," I reply, grinning. "I used to call him Sue, and they never corrected me. I only figured it out when I was, like, fifteen, when I was helping Mum with the pay slips. I was like, *Who is Dominic Forelle?*"

Leo howls at this. "That's really fucking cute," he says, smiling at me with such a sweet, unguarded smile that I bite my lip.

"Limoncello?" he says.

"You know it," I say, sitting back and sighing heavily. I want to sit here with Leo and talk long into the night, despite its being a terrible idea.

Two Limoncellos arrive, and as soon as the waiter is out of sight I knock mine back. It's hard, lemony, and sweet and goes down extremely well. I find that I'm struggling a little to hold on to my thoughts.

"You know it's for sipping, right?" says Leo, laughing.

"Says who?" I say, laughing.

"Careful. You'll get wasted," he says, but he cannot resist the challenge to knock his own back at almost the same speed. I take that as an invitation to get another, waving my hand at the waiter.

"Un altro," I say, holding Leo's steely gaze across the table.

I knock back the next one, not losing eye contact, and he does the same.

I raise my hand once more, but Leo sits back and folds his arms. "No more for me. I'm done. *Bloody hell.*"

I offer a smug grin. "Well, *that's* no fun."

"I can't get wasted," he says. "I have to cook tomorrow."

"Yes, you do," I say teasingly. "But nothing fancy, got it?"

"No freeze-dried caviar?"

"Absolutely not," I say, laughing.

"Raisin and grappa crumb?" he tries.

"A bit better," I say, smiling.

We stand, and I realize I'm very drunk and wearing a short skirt and very high heels. A lethal combination.

"Come on," he says, holding open the door and catching my elbow as I stumble slightly on the stone step down onto the road. Catania at night is *busy*. I shoot Leo a broad grin, and he shakes his head.

"Now I *gotta* see you wait tables in those," he says.

THIS IS A city made for the night. In the distance music swells, accordions and jaunty Italian music for tourists. A car honks as it passes me.

"Let's get you back to the hotel," he says, as he pulls me out of the way of a couple walking a small dog.

"Ciao," mutters the man, rolling his eyes at me.

"Oh no. I'm *that* tourist. The drunk one," I whisper to Leo, and he nods in agreement.

"You are."

"Hey, you've been drinking too."

"I'm not attempting the Viennese waltz on the main street, though, am I?" he says, as I step backward and almost into the path of an oncoming Vespa, whose driver swerves and honks.

"Olive," he says grumpily. He grabs my hand and pulls me across the street and back down the alleyway toward the hotel.

I'm glad he's walking me, but it doesn't stop me from wanting to taunt him the entire way.

"Come on," he says, tugging on my hand.

"Come on," I say mimicking his tone.

"Shut up," he says, laughing.

"Shut up," I tease.

Then he stops and turns to face me, and his look is of amused frustration. He puts his hands on his hips and shakes his head. "*You*," he says, "are trouble."

I laugh, reaching down to remove my shoes as we near the stairs down to the hotel. There's no way I'm attempting them in heels.

"Leo," I say as I clutch the rail and we descend the stairs.

"What?"

I look ahead to the lights strung up across the alleyway, the restaurants spilling out onto the street. *Don't say it, Olive. You're drunk. It's a stupid thing to say. Don't say it.*

"Is there any way you could afford it?!"

"What?" Leo says, stopping in his tracks.

"Nicky's," I say, trying to reach for his hand but missing as I sway. I focus, trying to speak clearly. "Like, could you speak to the bank? Put a business plan together. I don't know. I'd do a really good rate. A private sale?"

Leo looks taken aback.

"Kate says you should buy it if you love it so much."

"Who's Kate?" he asks, his brow furrowing at me.

"My sensible friend," I say, tapping the side of my head. "Ginny feels bad for you and thinks I shouldn't sell it at all. But if I do, couldn't you buy it?"

"*If?*" Leo stiffens, pulling his head back. "If?"

"When," I say, shaking my finger at Leo, with a kind of sobering panic. "I mean *when*."

Leo looks somewhere between frustrated and slightly embarrassed as he says, "I know what that building is worth, Olive. So, no. I can't afford it. No bank would lend me that. And I could look for partners, but I'm just a sous chef with no one to vouch for me . . ." He shakes his head. It's too big a thing.

I restart our walk toward the hotel.

"It was just an idea," I say.

"Don't think too much about me. I'll be fine," he replies evenly.

Leo bites his lip, looking ahead and then back at me, and in that moment, I hold myself together as tightly as I can, despite the booze thundering through me, despite the cocktail of feelings bubbling up inside me, despite Leo standing right here, on this beautiful street, the heat of the night willing me to fall into his arms. For comfort. For lust. For all of it.

I'm staring at him. Longingly. And I can't help myself.

I watch as Leo's eyes flicker between mine, and I catch his hand flexing as he clutches the handrail on the stairs, like if he lets go he'll fall too. His eyes drop to my lips, and for a second, I wonder if he's going to kiss me. Then he snaps his head away and stares off into the distance.

"Olive, I think I should go to bed," he says.

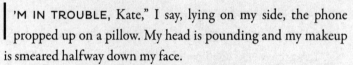

14

'M IN TROUBLE, Kate," I say, lying on my side, the phone propped up on a pillow. My head is pounding and my makeup is smeared halfway down my face.

"What's going on?" she says, closing the door to her office and sitting on the sofa. She's settling in for a long one, bless my dear friend.

"I got very drunk last night with Leo."

"Uh-oh," she says, sipping on her matcha latte. "*And?*"

I consider telling Kate I am so horny for Leo I feel like I'm a jack-in-the-box, just about ready to spring. That maybe I'm not just horny for him, but that I'm growing to quite like him too. But Kate is too practical. She will remind me that I'm about to fire him. She'll tell me to put a lid on it. She'll tell me it's wrong for me to get involved with him and terribly, terribly messy. And she'd be right.

Better to tell Ginny that part.

"Oh, no. Nothing like that. There's been what I would call some *moments* between us, but you know. Nothing's happened," I say, slowly.

"Okay," she says, pulling a face and then reaching back to put her hair in a ponytail, a sure sign Kate means business.

"I'm starting to question my hasty decision to sell Nicky's," I say.

"Right."

"I never gave *maybe* a chance. The more I think about it, the more my feelings are not what I expected."

"What did you expect?"

"I expected to hate the idea completely," I say, like she should know that. "And then Leo said some things last night that made me wonder if Nicky's could still work. He saw all the same issues I did. And it's thrown me a little."

"I thought you couldn't wait to sell," Kate reminds me.

"Yes, a few weeks ago I couldn't wait to shut the place down," I say, trying to answer as truthfully as possible. "And I resented Leo for his proximity to Dad over the years. And now those feelings have softened and I guess, naturally, I'm thinking about my decision again."

"You're back in his world. It's not surprising."

Yes. I am back in his world. And I am remembering the good things about Dad, and our family, and even the restaurant.

"Olive?" Kate says. "You've gone quiet."

"I'm just thinking how complicated it all is," I say, sighing.

"Oh, Olive," she says.

"I'm fine. It's probably just too much Limoncello. And being here. It's mixed me up. I'm sure if I was back in London and speaking to the Realtors and imagining handing Mum a check I'd feel differently."

"Well, there's no hurry, is there? Can't you just quietly remain open to the idea of keeping Nicky's? You need to be careful about how you communicate your doubts about selling with Leo, though. Like, honestly, I probably wouldn't," she says. "Not until you're sure."

"I won't," I say, not mentioning the gaffe I'd made asking Leo if he could afford it last night, saying "if" I sell. "I have to cook with him in a few hours, so I'd better pull my shit together."

"Olive. You can explore keeping Nicky's," says Kate. "Just be really clear on why you're doing it."

"PASTA CON LE sarde," says Leo, laying out an onion, a handful of plump garlic, a bunch of fresh sardines, pine nuts, and raisins.

He looks completely divine in a white T-shirt and a blue-and-white-striped kitchen apron. In the cold light of day I realize just how much trouble I am in. His hair is still damp from a shower, and his skin is more sun-kissed than when we arrived. I suddenly have an urge to see him without a T-shirt on.

When he lifts up his hand to scratch his arm, I see the tip of a tattoo I haven't noticed before peeking out from under his T-shirt sleeve. Something scrawled.

"What's that, Leo?" I ask, smirking.

"What's that, *Chef*," he says, pulling down the sleeve of his T-shirt.

"Did you get a drunk tattoo?" I say teasingly.

"I did, Olive." Leo puts both hands on the counter and leans toward me. "But I try not to do things when I'm drunk anymore," he says, raising an eyebrow at me.

Does he mean last night? Is he talking about our near kiss?

I feel a flutter in my belly. I'm teenage horny for him and I cannot ignore it. *Fuck me*, I think to myself.

"Let's cook," I say, before Leo reaches into the brown paper shopping bag and pulls out chilled fresh spaghetti.

"I figured we both know how to make pasta, so let's just cut out some of the faff."

"No faff? Who are you and what have you done with Leo?"

"Come now, Olive, stop flirting with me and let's cook," he says, tossing a pan onto the stove.

"I'm not flirting, Leo," I say, mortified to be called out.

"I'm not flirting, *Chef*," he says, as he slides a huge knife out of its leather pouch. "Show some respect," he adds, turning to grab a chopping board. I catch his grin as he turns his back, and I want to smack his butt so badly, but I refrain. Instead I reach for an apron and tie it around my neck and waist, covering most of the flirty sundress I'm wearing.

We're standing between the gas stove and a long stainless-steel bench. Leo and I have a chopping board each and we work together cutting, while Leo pulls the dish together in the pan, testing quantities as we go.

Small bowls of the dish are prepared—one with a slightly larger quantity of raisins. One with more pine nuts. A version heavy on the saffron. Breadcrumbs made with panko and lemon rind or plain ciabatta (I eye-roll at this, but Leo will not be deterred). A version with fresh fennel and one with fennel seeds. After an hour, we stand and taste from our seven versions. I have scrawled the quantities in my notebook and torn each page out, placing them under the dishes so we don't forget what is what.

"See. I told you," says Leo, pushing the fresh fennel version toward me. "It's too much. The seeds work better."

"I'd love a little fennel beard to garnish, though," I say.

"*Now* who's being fussy," says Leo.

"It's just a garnish," I say, rolling my eyes.

"Yeah, but we'd have to get people to go to Tesco's to buy a fennel bulb just to tear off the beard?"

"Yes, fine. *I agree*," I say reluctantly. "I *do* like the saffron. What if we added saffron to this version?" I tap the edge of the second dish.

He drains some bucatini, a thicker spaghettilike pasta with a hole running through the middle. And after some adjustments he plates up the dish according to both of our notes.

"Now, that," I say with a grin, "is *fine*."

"We've cracked it," he agrees, grinning too.

"Okay, let me make the final notes."

I start to scribble the final quantities in longhand in my notebook under *pasta con le sarde*, while Leo tidies up around me.

"Dad used to make this dish when he could get fresh sardines. It was a regular special from late July," I say.

"It was," he replies, stopping cleaning to listen to me.

"How would you do this dish at Nicky's?" I ask.

Leo leans back on the stainless-steel work surface and tosses his tea towel over his shoulder, raising his eyebrow. "How would I *elevate* it?"

"I'm just wondering," I say.

"Maybe with this dish I wouldn't," he says, folding his arms. "Maybe we could serve it in custom-made Nicky's Sardine Tins, and the guests have to pull back the lid to get to the meal."

I study him, my eyes narrowing.

"Or with, like, an anchovy and lemon sorbet that you spoon over the dish at the table and the guests get to watch it melt."

"I don't know if you're joking," I say, flicking my tea towel at him.

"Or maybe, Olive, we could boil the spaghetti at the table on little mini gas stoves, and the customer has to fish out their own pasta?"

"Fuck you," I say, laughing. "Although I admit I kind of liked the sardine-tin presentation idea. That was fun."

He resumes cleaning and considers the question seriously.

"I wouldn't do much to that dish," he says. "Close to this recipe, I think. But Nicky's desperately needs new crockery, and I reckon we could have worked on the presentation. It *could* use some fennel beard, since we'd be using the bulb elsewhere."

"No waste," I say.

"It's not about one dish, though; it's about the whole menu. There are thirty-four dishes on the latest menu. Your dad thought that offering everything meant that no one was disappointed. But, Jesus, that meant a lot of prep and a lot of waste."

"I read that seven mains is the lucky number. Less, and people feel they're missing out. More, and people get overwhelmed and opt for something they already know."

"I did not know that," he says.

An alarm interrupts us, and Leo pulls the orange cake out of the oven. I watch as he frees it from the springform pan, slides it onto a cooling rack, and carefully pours our prepared orange glaze over it. I move in and add our dried-blood-orange rounds.

"Looks good," I say. "But how does it taste?"

I reach over at the same time as Leo to get the knife. And he pulls back. "It's all yours," he says, holding his hands up in surrender.

The knife is heavy as it glides through the cake, and I cut a slice for us both. Leo slides a couple of forks onto the bench, and in he digs.

Leo nods approvingly, a small groan escaping his lips. "Almonds, oranges, bitter, sweet," he says with his mouth full. "It's understated. It's balanced. It's perfect."

"Whoa there, big guy," I say, as I watch Leo tuck in with the enthusiasm and the manners of a Dickensian orphan.

"When something tastes this good, you can never have enough," he says, eyes flickering up to mine.

I dig my fork in. "Well then. I better taste."

"Luca's making his version of this too, so we should save some to compare at Rocco's tomorrow," he says. "I've told him we're going to feed them our final dishes, by the way."

"Oh, that's a good idea," I say, nodding. Then I look over at Leo, who is looking as pleased as I feel. "We did it, didn't we?"

"We did."

"Sicily done," I say.

"Except for the story," he reminds me.

"Except for the story," I say, nodding nervously. "But I have some ideas."

Leo nods. "Well, today was fun," he says, smiling. A full genuine smile. Nothing hidden behind it. No playful teasing.

"Yes, Chef," I say, smiling back, removing the scarf that was holding my hair back and letting it fall. Leo watches me fix my hair, and I feel a touch of heat in my cheeks, quickly staring down at the three pages that contain the final recipes for this section of the book.

I glance across but look away when I see he's watching me.

"What are you thinking, Olive?" he asks.

"It just feels good to make some headway," I say, shrugging.

"Olive," he says, grinning as he puts the plastic hood on the cake and fixes his eyes on me. "Please consider not selling."

Everything inside me squeezes hard. I breathe slowly out.

"If there is even a shadow of doubt—"

"I need to sell it," I say, the slight hitch my voice betraying me. "I'm sorry."

"Forget about me," he says. "Just think about yourself. Because . . . I could see you there, notebook in hand, cracking the whip."

"Cracking the whip?" I say, something dark zipping through me.

Leo shakes his head slowly. "Olive. Olive. Olive," he says.

"Yes, Chef?" I reply, undoing my apron and tossing it into the laundry bin.

He glances back at me, the hint of a wicked glint on his face, and then back at the sink, and I hear a little breath squeeze out of him. "You shouldn't be a critic," he says. "It's a waste of all that joy you have for food."

I laugh lightly, a heaviness in my heart.

"Celebratory glass of Spumante?" he asks.

"Not tonight," I say. "I actually need to work tonight."

"Right," he says, nodding, disappointment flickering across his face.

"Sorry."

"It's okay. I did ask Rocco if he had time to go somewhere, drink Italian beer, and, you know . . . man talk."

"Man talk?" I ask, eyebrow raised.

"Older manly life advice?" he says, with a touch of boyish vulnerability, shoulders forward, hands in pockets. "That one might get from a father?"

What to do next. Where to go after Nicky's. Leo needs that kind of advice.

I give him a spontaneous hug, and when my body melts into his, I almost whimper. That feels very good.

Olive. Pull away now.

"See you in the morning," I say, pulling back.

"Va bene. Ci vediamo in mattinata," he says.

I CURL UP on the balcony with a half bottle of Marsala and take a deep breath. It's time to read this manuscript. My eyes sting at the dedication: FOR MY OLIVE.

I was not forgotten. I take a steadying breath and turn to the first chapter.

PUGLIA—AUBERGINE

I made the decision to become a cook the first day I was in Puglia. I was eighteen years old.

For my birthday I'd asked for a new car, but my mum gave me lire and a rail ticket around Italy. "Go see the mainland," she'd said.

As a kid, I saw this as an insult. I was too young to appreciate the magnitude of this gift, but now, as a man nearing my seventies, I am filled with gratitude for the experience that changed my life forever.

I took an old train with pull-down windows and green leather seating, striking up a conversation with a tenente in the army returning home in his fatigues. I remember vividly the carriage's stale smell of cigarette smoke and fresh coffee with a background of rusting metal. Mum had given my

*packed lunch away to a homeless boy at the train station, so
I arrived starving. A starving, scared eighteen-year-old with
no taste.*

*The stuffed aubergine with smoked scamorza and Ital-
ian sausage I ate was served in a trattoria by the main station on a paper plate by an old man who was playing scopone
with a tatty deck of cards. I had to pay six thousand lira in
advance, and the dish came with wine whether I wanted it
or not. I immediately had a second helping.*

*Later that day, I called Rocco Ragusa, an old family
friend who ran the seafood restaurant a few doors down from
my family. I started as a dishwasher in his restaurant in
Catania the following spring.*

I clutch the papers to my chest and have a long, cathartic cry.
I can hear my dad's voice. His Italian accent, which strengthens
when he's talking about food. It's like he's talking to me. He's telling me this story as I sit at the kitchen table doing homework and
he prepares dinner.

I miss my dad. I have missed him, I realize, for a long time.

IT FEELS FITTING to have our final Sicilian lunch in Rocco's restaurant, just over a week since we touched down at Catania Airport. The restaurant is open for lunch, but we sit down around
two, just as it's beginning to empty. Rocco has put a family table
together, and Leo and I prepare the meal in his kitchen. I check
my watch for the hundredth time. Our ferry to Naples leaves at
seven. We have plenty of time.

"Want me to choose the wines?" Isabella offers, but I've already chosen the pale rosé and hand her two chilled bottles from the Deepfreeze.

We serve the orange and fennel salad to coos of approval from the table, although Rocco has plenty to say about how it could be improved. *Too many olives. Not enough anchovies.* Leo and I grin at each other. People tell you there is only one way to make Italian food, but it isn't true. Some dishes vary wildly from region to region, season to season, and even family home to family home.

I can feel my story of Catania starting to form.

During the meal, I catch Leo looking at me like he is reaching inside of me, rummaging around, hunting for something long lost. I wonder what's on his mind: me or the restaurant?

"You'll come back, Olive?" Rocco asks, as we clear up the pasta and set the table for the orange cake.

"I'll come back," I say. I adore him. I adore him and his family. He's a bear of a man with an abundance of heart. Kind. *So* gracious. No wonder my father loved him. I stand up immediately and hug him, knocking the knife and fork out of his hands in the process; they clatter to the ground. I don't care.

I can feel Leo watching me, but I don't feel awkward or out of place anymore. I feel like I have a right to be here.

"Thank you for everything," I say. "There's no way Tuscany is going to be this good."

"Toscana is okay," Rocco says reluctantly. "I hope you're looked after there. Leo, will she meet your family?"

"She'll meet my aunt. And probably the rest of them," he says. "She better get ready for that."

"Okay, that's a little scary," I say.

Moments later, Luca emerges from the kitchen with the cake we made yesterday and two others balanced on three large plates.

"Taste-test time!" I squeal, clutching my hands together.

"Here is your version," Luca says, dropping the first on the table. "This is my version, with a little more almond flour. And this is Isabella's nonna's, made with the whole Moro orange from her grove—pulped into the mix and no dusting, no glaze. Plain."

"You mean *perfect*," says Isabella, scolding Luca.

There was no doubting Isabella's would win. The pulp added something even softer and more luscious to the crumb. If the cake we had yesterday, warm from the oven, was divine, this was magic.

"I told you," says Luca. "The *orange*."

LATER, AS LEO and I are putting our bags into the back of our shuttle, he notices my shoulder bag with the urn. I heave it next to the suitcase Antonia donated from her lost-property cupboard, an impractical leather case with an old strap and buckle lock, and definitely no wheels, but it will get me through the remainder of the trip.

"You didn't find the right moment . . ." His voice trails off as he nods toward the urn, leaning his arm on the car. His bare arms glisten in the sun, and I imagine how quickly I could slip into the space between him and the car. I imagine feeling pinned in place under his intense stare.

"Not yet," I say quickly.

Antonia hugs us both and insists I return.

"Promise?" she says, as I allow myself to be hugged again.

Luca, who gifts me a string bag of oranges, begs me to take

him with me. "Please, for the love of god, get me out of this one-horse town. There are only so many tourists I can take."

"Come and visit," I insist.

"I will!" he says. "I want to come to London. Maybe one day *you* need a chef?"

"Anytime, Luca," I say, laughing, kissing him on the cheek.

15

Tuscany

EVERYTHING IS FRANTIC on the ferry to the mainland. There are kids, prams, families, dogs, mountains of luggage, and very little clear information as to where we are going.

I fish in my handbag and grab my phone, pulling up the information on the booking. "We have to look for cabin 243."

I do a double take—there's only one room. Am I sharing a cabin with Leo? Shit. Of course I am. He and Dad were probably going to share.

"Leo, did you get your own cabin?" I say, calling out to him as he bustles with the other boarding passengers into the small corridors that lead toward the cabins. He doesn't hear me.

"What is your cabin number, Leo?" I try again.

"You said 243, right?" he calls back, arms full.

"Yes! *My* room is 243," I call out, my heart picking up pace a little. *We're sharing.*

We wander endless corridors until Leo stops outside a small silver door and dumps the bags, rubbing at his shoulder as he waits for me to join him. I'm dawdling. I am both terrified and thrilled at the prospect of being forced to share a room.

I push the door open, and Leo follows me in. Ahead there is a large porthole window looking out across the ocean. Beside the window are a television and a minibar, and opposite the window sits one double bed.

"How the other half live, eh?" Leo says. Then he sees my face, my cheeks scarlet. "Oh shit. Are we *both* in here?"

"What a cock-up," I reply, trying to look upset, when all I can think about are the things I could do under a blanket with Leo on a gently rocking boat.

"One way to put it," he mutters, raising an eyebrow at me.

I try to sound as outraged as him. "Absolutely terrible oversight. Who was in charge of the booking?"

"Your *dad*," he says, stating the obvious. "I was meeting him in Florence, so of course it's just one cabin."

"I'm sure he's cackling down at us," I mutter, trying hard not to laugh now. "He loved a misadventure." I glance over at Leo, who looks vaguely panicked. Better rein it in.

"Well, let's make the best of it," I say, with the cool determination of a Scout leader during a hailstorm.

"Okay," he says hesitantly.

Leo looks at me, his brows furrowed. There is a long pause. "I'll just go up on the main deck."

"No," I shoot back a little quickly. "I couldn't do that to you."

"*Olive*," he says sternly, his own cheeks taking on a pinkish tinge. "I'll just go up on the main deck. This isn't going to work, is it?"

I should agree to this.

"Just stay in here with me," I say, betraying myself, heart thumping in my chest. "We can figure something out. The bed might be two singles pushed together." I lift the blanket and am a delirious mix of concerned and excited that it is, in fact, just one bed. "We can build a blanket wall."

"A blanket wall?" he says, unconvinced.

"I'll feel so guilty, I won't sleep if you're up there," I say, cursing myself for my traitorous tongue.

"It's okay, Olive," he says, his mouth firm. "I'll be fine. I'll just crash out on one of the seats. I'm so tired I think I could sleep on a horse."

I frown at Leo and then start to second-guess myself. Would he rather spend twelve hours on the top deck, upright and rigid, than spend the night in a room with me? This is embarrassing, and I have to stop insisting.

"We're doing six hours each, then," I say firmly. "You first, then I'll swap with you. You're already hungover and exhausted and you'll be no use to anyone tomorrow if you don't get some sleep."

Leo breathes slowly out, looking across at the bed, his shoulders slumped forward. Then his eyes close in resignation.

"Blanket wall?" he says, a wry smile on his face. "Then we both get some sleep."

"I'd suggest we top and tail but I'm sure you don't want my toes in your face."

Leo's wry smile widens.

"I'm honestly offended you're worried about it," I say, pulling open the minibar fridge and fishing out a mini-bottle of wine. "Do you think I'm going to ravish you in your sleep, for fuck's sake?"

"Put that back," he says.

"You *are* afraid I'm going to ravish you in your sleep," I say.

"No," he says, shaking his head. He leans over and unzips his bag, pulling forth a bottle of champagne in a chilled sleeve. He touches it. "Ice-cold, still."

"What's that?"

"This is a Gambino Winery Spumante," he says. "I thought this might be the right moment to celebrate the end of the first chapter—so to speak."

I am touched he bought a bottle of bubbles for the ride. "Are you sure? You looked a little green around the gills today."

"I'm okay. We can rest in Tuscany."

I gaze hungrily as he strips off the foil and then unwinds the metal cage on the cork. A moment later, it's popped and he's pouring the cold, bubbly deliciousness into two glasses. I bite my lip as he pours, pausing to allow the bubbles to settle. Then he looks at me and grins.

"To us?"

"To us," I say, smiling, while I picture reaching across and slowly unbuttoning his shirt, running a finger across his bare chest. I have to steady myself slightly on the countertop.

"Better find your sea legs, Olive. We're not even moving yet," says Leo, watching me stagger.

16

LEO AND I are halfway through the Spumante when I head into the bathroom to change. What I *should* be doing is putting on a long-sleeved T-shirt and a pair of trousers, but instead I come out in a pair of very short terry-cloth shorts, red with a white stripe, and a white tank top. I have shaved my legs and applied a thin layer of tinted moisturizer and a little lip balm. It's a fine balance between ready for bed and just-in-case ready for action.

Leo takes one look at me and then looks quickly back at his book.

"You all done in there?" he asks.

"Yep. Your turn," I say, settling into the seat next to the little porthole window.

Leo emerges from the bathroom in a short-sleeved pale-blue-and-white-striped cotton PJ set, still clutching his paperback. It is ridiculously adorable.

"A present from my aunt." He laughs.

"I'm looking forward to meeting her," I say, my feet up on the round windowsill as the boat chugs its way across the sea to Rome.

The sun is setting, and the long strands of cloud are deep red and orange. I try not to be too offended when Leo rolls up the spare blanket and then arranges and rearranges it in the middle of the bed. The whole thing is a silly performance really. We're adults. When he attempts a second construction using his own pillow as reinforcement, I start to laugh.

"What?" he says. "*You* said blanket wall."

"Looks a little overengineered," I reply.

He gives up with a chuckle, tossing the pillow back down, and takes a sip of his sparkling wine.

"It's not too much for you, is it?" I say suddenly, feeling worried I've pushed him. "Be honest. We can still do shifts on the top deck."

"If it's cool with you, I'd prefer a bed," he says, the corner of his mouth quirking. "Even if it's with you."

I throw a pillow at him and he swerves to avoid it.

"Well, I don't snore much," I say, staring out the porthole window. "Somewhere between a revving chain saw and a car alarm."

Leo laughs as he glances up at me. "I haven't shared a bed in a while, but I could be sleeping next to a rocket launcher tonight and I'd still manage a few cycles of REM."

My heart picks up. He's single. I *knew* it. Leo looks up again at me and our eyes catch—there is an undeniable message passed between us. His eyes darken for a split second and my stomach starts to fizzle, heat drawing up through the insides of my thighs. *Give me strength*, I say to myself quietly. *You can't do this.*

"I also haven't shared a bed in some time," I say slowly.

Leo's eyes drop to the book in my hand, and then he turns to the light switches by the bed. "Are you reading? Or do you mind if I turn off the big light?"

"Please do," I say, dropping my book on the small table next to the window. Leo flicks the switches, and we're plunged into darkness for a moment, with only the red of the sunset casting its glow across the room. Finally, he finds the small reading lights and then the room is dim, cozy.

"What were *you* reading?" I ask. With the wooziness of the wine, and the gentle rocking of the boat against the swell, the whole atmosphere is charged.

"Oh, some spy novel," he says.

He glances at my heavily thumbed copy of *Riders*, the Jilly Cooper novel I've read a hundred times, which I swiped from Antonia's hotel give-and-take library before we left.

"I promise there was a Charles Bukowski in my suitcase," I say, grinning.

"Sure there was, Olive," he says, laying his book on the bedside table and turning to me, arms folded. "And back on my bedside table it's strictly Nietzsche and a first edition of *Naked Lunch*."

"Did you go to uni, then?" I ask, chuckling. "Nietzsche? *Naked Lunch*? I'm guessing you didn't finish your first year."

"Nah. I was singularly focused on becoming Gordon Ramsay," he says with a little smirk.

"Please find a different culinary hero," I say, rolling my eyes.

Leo puts his own book away, his gaze catching on my thighs as he looks up at me from across the cabin.

"I'm not some techno-chef; I don't get off on seven-course fine dining or Gordon fucking Ramsay," he says, laughing in exasperation. My mind has unfortunately frozen on the titillating imaginings of what exactly would get Leo off.

"I went to a Ramsay restaurant one time with my mother,

who'd saved for a year. Before that pretty much all I'd eat was tuna sandwiches and lasagna."

"I get it, I get it," I say, forcing myself out of the fantasy and back into the moment. "It's just that first night, you had that notebook with the super-fancy sketches . . ."

"I write down ideas of all sorts all the time," he says. "You didn't give me a chance to speak. You wanted to dislike me, I think."

Gah. He's right. I shake my head and look at the floor, not able to word the apology just yet. "This has been hard for me."

"I know," he says, leaning forward, his eyes serious. "I do know that. I came with my own prejudices. I said some dumb things at the bar on the first night."

"Well. I *was* being overly pretentious about food," I concede, laughing again. "Even if our tastes are different."

"Are they, though?" Leo says, as he tries to hide a yawn, and I wonder how he can be so tired when every single cell of my body is wide awake and jittery. I feel like I've had seven coffees.

"Do you want to sleep?"

"No, not yet," he says, nodding to his glass on the side table. "What I really like is more modern classic food. Do you know Osteria Mozza? That famous mozzarella bar in Los Angeles."

"Of course," I reply. *The chef is Nancy Silverton. One Michelin star. Italian. Simple.*

"I like that," he says, gesticulating with his hands. "It's all done in the very best possible way, and it's far from pretentious. From the flour she uses, the yeast, the milk for mozzarella. All in the little details of preparation. You know—"

He stops talking, shakes his head at me, laughing to himself.

"You know what? Forget it. I'm getting a little tired of trying to win you over."

"You've been trying to win me over?" I say. "You gotta work on your banter, Leo."

Leo shoots me a wicked grin. "Oh, I've got banter," he says. "Don't you worry about that."

"You do?" I say, grinning back.

I decide to leave the hard seat and join him on the bed. I sit at the foot of it, legs outstretched and crossed at the ankles, the small glass goblet cupped between my fingers.

Leo watches my every move. We are close, and when we head to sleep, we will be *very* close indeed. I wonder how the hell I'm going to relax.

"So if not uni, you must have gone to culinary school, then?" I say.

"'Fraid not," he says, stretching out his free hand to examine a fine scar on the back of it, before dropping it onto the bed, close to my ankle. It's centimeters away and yet I can feel the heat radiating off it.

Leo takes a deep breath. "My mum died of breast cancer when I was eighteen. When she got really sick, she wanted to be back in Tuscany with her sister and our extended family. We were in England because my nonevent of a father was British." He adds this with a degree of disdain, and it gives more context for his night out with Rocco and, in fact, his close relationship with Dad.

"Right," I say, nodding, feeling my body wilt with compassion.

Leo reaches down and tugs up the short sleeve of his shirt and shows me his tattoo.

"It wasn't a drunken mistake," he admits as I read the word *Mamma* in script that runs under his arm.

I feel the prickle of tears in my eyes, but Leo tugs his shirt-sleeve down quickly and moves on. "I'd finished school, and I wasn't sure what to do next.

"Though we didn't have a lot, Mum was into food, being Italian," Leo says, laughing. "I went down a rabbit hole when I was in Tuscany. Nothing to do but care for Mum and hang out talking to the tomatoes. I got really into cooking shows. Heston Blumenthal, Jamie Oliver, *Ramsay's Kitchen Nightmares. Boiling Point.*"

"Aha!" I say, recalling our first conversation at the bar. "Okay."

"And then I saw your dad's show."

"Nooooo," I say.

"*Nicolò's Mediterranean Adventures,*" he says in the same voice-over as the show.

"No. Way!" I reply, gasping.

"After Mum died, I went back to London and I looked up his restaurant. I went straight to Nicky's, knocked on the back door, and wouldn't leave until he gave me a job. He did. Washing dishes for almost two years. The bastard."

"It's where everyone starts," I say, laughing.

"It wasn't until much later I learned that the show was axed after one run," Leo says.

"It was a shame," I say.

"It was the hot-air-balloon gimmick," Leo says. "It never really took off."

I cackle. I'd heard my dad make this joke before.

"*Such* a silly idea," Leo says, shaking his head. "Your dad deserved better."

I nod, smoothing out the stiff industrial cotton of the bedsheets, as Leo fills both our glasses. "His glory days were when I was, like, eleven and twelve. The restaurant was packed all the time. We had a few minor celebrities come by."

"I've seen the photos," says Leo, laughing. "The one with the Wiggles is my personal favorite."

"By far the most exciting was when the footballers came in," I say.

"GUNNERS EAT FREE," says Leo, laughing. "Your dad had to take that sign down, you know. It was basically bankrupting him."

"Jesus," I say, making a show of rolling my eyes. Leo shakes his head slowly.

"He never had the head for it," he says grimly.

My mum did, I think.

"I guess I had moved on with Mum by then," I say. "I never saw you."

"And I never saw you," he says. "And I'd *definitely* remember."

I blush and he sees it, looking pleased with himself. He shuffles up a bit in bed, and the neck of his pajamas falls open, showing the smooth skin of his chest and the smallest hint of hair between his pecs. Gah. It's almost too much for me. I feel the enduring heat in my cheeks as I'm distracted by thoughts of touching him. Hell, even *seeing* his bare chest, and running my hands through his thick, dark hair.

Olive, I swear to god, rein yourself in.

"You know, Jamie Oliver annoyed the shit out of him," I say. "He was so young with his own TV show, making a lot of Italian food."

"Jamie came in once," Leo says, leaning forward a little.

I gasp. "He did *not*."

"He did. Like six years ago. And your dad fussed over him so much. It was hilarious." Leo stops to laugh at the memory, and I feel a pang of regret. But I also feel comforted by the fact that Leo and I are talking about Dad and I'm mostly okay with it. Enjoying it even. For the first time, I allow myself to be grateful that Dad had Leo.

"I bet he was starstruck," I say. "Did he get the gold-leaf grappa out? The little crystal glasses?"

"You know it," Leo says, cackling. "In fact, he was so nervous, he made *me* cook the meal while he stood over me pretending not to care but interfering with every step. 'Leo, please. You're grating the pecorino like a damn goat. Use the good oil.'"

Oh my god. I smile, tipping the wine back and enjoying the feeling of this moment. Of talking about my dad with someone who isn't Mum, and reflecting on all of him—the salty and the sweet. It is cathartic.

Leo's eyes go to my feet, and the little white polish at the ends of my toes. His gaze follows the length of my legs. He is not making much effort to hide his attraction now.

"More?" asks Leo.

He puts his glass down and folds his arms. Cocking his head to the side, he narrows his eyes.

"Can I just say, he definitely loved you," Leo says. "At least, he talked about you all the time. He—"

I jump in, cutting Leo off. "I hear you. It's just that he didn't act like it."

"I think if you'd come to the restaurant—" Leo tries, but I hold both my hands up.

"Look, it's hard to know what's true anymore. Put it this way: The inheritance was a total shock."

"It was?" Leo seems genuinely confused by this.

"I don't know what I thought he'd do," I admit. "I didn't really think about it."

"I loved your dad, but it sounds like he needed to listen more to your mum," he says. "All my talk of modernizing aside, the guy could *not* run the business side of things. He stayed with suppliers out of loyalty, even when they were clearly taking the piss. He believed there would be more TV shows and was *so* distracted by that. I remember one time he was getting new headshots done for his agent, fretting about his graying hair and whatnot. And I told him if he fixed the restaurant, people would come back. And he said, 'People come here for *me*. It's *me* I need to work on.'"

"Yikes," I say, laughing.

"I don't want to call it an ego," he says, grimacing.

"Oh, it's an ego. You can still love him and say that, I think."

Leo laughs.

"You know, the food critiquing was kind of a way to channel my anger, and I'm tired, Leo. I'm tired of critiquing everything. Of being the big bad guy when I walk into a restaurant. I hate my job, honestly," I say with a sigh.

"I knew it," he says, grinning.

Leo holds up the bottle, glancing at the remainder. Part of me wants to suggest I sneak up to the bar for another. "One more for the road?" he says.

"One for the water," I say, nodding out the window.

He leans forward and places a hand on my bare leg to steady himself as he reaches his other out to fill my glass. When he leans back he doesn't remove it. Instead, there is a gentle squeeze.

He yawns again and holds his glass aloft. "To Sicily?"

"To Dad?" I reply, looking back at him, glassy-eyed.

"To Nicky."

We sit in silence for a moment, finishing our wine. My nervous energy is off the charts.

I wriggle myself up, stretching out my neck. "I'm going to use the loo."

I head into the bathroom to pee and wash my face and then reapply my low-key makeup. I take a moment to quietly tell myself to be cool. To be calm. To try to just sleep.

I remind myself that nothing can happen. Nothing should happen. And that I need to keep a lid on my rocketing emotions. Nothing good will come of it. I take a deep breath and return to the cabin.

But Leo is already asleep.

17

THE NIGHT IS restless. I dream about Leo. I dream we're running through the narrow alleyways of Catania. Then I am alone with Leo at Nicky's. He is kissing me against the bar. As I slip my hand in between the buttons of his shirt and touch his warm skin, I feel the hard form of his muscles under my fingers. His shirt is softer than it should be. A soft, silky cotton. His chest flexes and I hear a breath in my ear as I reach my head forward and kiss the edge of his jaw once. Twice. Three times, before he pulls his head back.

I can feel his fingers trailing up my bare legs, leaving an electric fizzling in their wake. His hand, rough and large against my skin, reaches my thigh just at the edge of my shorts and stops . . . I hear myself moan. My hand moves down the lines of his chest, to his stomach, which hardens under my touch. I reach the waist of his pants now, and my hand skims under the bottom of his shirt until I make contact with his skin and pull at the waistband of his pants. I moan into his ear, moving closer to him, lifting my leg up and hooking it around him.

I am hungry for Leo. Starved. I want to reach down, farther

still, but just as I start to move, I feel a hand on my wrist and hear, "Olive," whispered gently in my ear. "You're dreaming."

And then I'm on a boat, and Leo is sailing the boat, but I want to get off. He can't hear me. I shout to him. "Leo.

"*Leo!*"

I wake with my heart racing, feeling a sense of urgency. Did I just shout his name? Did I wake myself shouting his name? I roll over and put my hand out, but Leo isn't there. It's still dark outside. Or just coming to sunrise. It must be around 4 a.m.

Confused, delirious, I fall back asleep.

The first sense that brings me back is the sound of water running in the bathroom. Then it's the smell of cheap, burned coffee.

Leo emerges a few minutes later, holding two paper cups.

"Hey, sleepy," he says, with an intimacy that makes my cheeks flame.

"Hey," I reply. Groggy. I clear my throat. "What time is it?"

"Six," he says.

"Did you sleep okay?" I ask, wishing he was still beside me. With the warmth of his body gone, all that remains is the dent in his pillow.

"Um . . . sure," he says, in a careful way that makes me uneasy.

"I was dreaming a lot," I say, aware, now, of the stickiness of my skin and the clamminess of the sheets.

"You *were*," he says quietly, putting the coffee on the dresser next to me.

"Shit," I mutter.

I look next to me; the blanket wall is now bunched at the foot of the bed, the duvet covers twisted almost into a spiral. Like a tornado has raced through. I raise my hands to my head and I start to cackle. Laughter and deflection are the only way to deal with my embarrassment.

"Oh no. Did I *actually* climb the wall and ravish you?" I point to the remains of the blanket wall.

Leo shakes his head slowly, a slight hint of a knowing smile on his face. "I'm afraid you didn't get that far, Olive."

Relief, followed by a lick of surprise. Then a rush of warmth to my cheeks. *I didn't get that far?* I pull the blankets up over my face and groan into them.

"Have your coffee," he says, and I can almost hear the smug smile on his face. "The sun is up and the mainland is in sight. We're docking soon."

AS IF THE universe wants to make up for the proximity of the previous night, when we board the train it's surprisingly empty. I tell Leo I'm going to sit alone and catch up on work emails. I read a message from my boss congratulating me on a takedown of a Michelin-starred eatery in Knightsbridge owned by some insurance billionaire. "It's gone viral, Olive."

I shudder. My last review. I want that to be my last review. I'll write about food trends and review kitchen products; I enjoy that stuff. But no more restaurant reviews. I'm done.

There is an email from one of the subeditors asking me if I'd be interested in covering the yuzu fruit trend or the rise of the butter board (artisanal butter) for next month's supplement. (*Butter*, I reply. Always butter.) Then I spot an email from that Realtor about listing Nicky's, with the subject: Some Good Prospects.

I sigh, gazing out the window as the train shuttles inland from the coast. The landscape is already so different from the burnished sandy tones of Catania. We're in lush, rolling green hills now, fresh from rainfall, with the sparkling sea well behind us.

I need to talk to my girls.

ME: Help.

KATE: Update?

ME: Um. I need to talk about Leo. We had to share a fucking bed last night

GINNY: 😮 OMG

KATE: We need a call

ME: Can't, he's sitting nearby

GINNY: I need more info

ME: Okay, hang on.

I get up and wander down to the far end of the train and move to the area between the two carriages, out of earshot.

"Hi, and yes, I have a glorious tan," I say quickly into the video call. "There was only one room booked on the overnight ferry, so we had to share it. Nothing happened. Although I did have a dream that something happened and I'm slightly nervous my dream may have crossed the threshold into reality for a moment."

I take a deep breath.

"I think I might have tried to, I don't know, *touch* him. *Super* inappropriately."

"Oh my god, Olive!" Ginny says, bursting into laughter.

"I think he was touching me too," I say, thinking of the hand trailing up my thigh and how real it felt. But perhaps I was dreaming.

Kate is more considered. "Oh dear."

Ginny jumps in, "Wait. Hang on, do you fancy him? Like, *properly*?"

"Yes. No. *Fuck!* Sorry," I say, as I slap my forehead. "It's complicated. It's a big fucking vat of boiling-hot complicated. First up, yes. I definitely fancy him. Like, *a lot*. I like our chats, I like the way he smiles, I like to talk with him about food. He's also kind, which I was not expecting."

"What were you expecting?"

"I drew a picture of him in my head where he was rude, obnoxious, arrogant—"

"We prefer kind," Kate says, cutting in.

"And hot," Ginny reminds us, putting her eye pencil down, listening intensely.

"If it was just the cookbook, and we got kind of entangled and had a summer fling while chopping tomatoes under the fucking Sicilian moonlight together, that would be fine, but the stuff with the restaurant. It's making my head hurt."

"What stuff with the restaurant?" Ginny asks.

"Oh, you didn't tell her?" I say to Kate, who shakes her head. "Gah. I've been having thoughts like maybe selling immediately is a little hasty. And those thoughts have only gotten stronger."

"Oh no," Kate says.

"Oh *yay*," Ginny says, clapping her hands.

"Ginny, it's messy as *fuck*," I say, biting the edge of my thumb.

"I agree," says Kate.

"Do you think he likes you?" Ginny asks, biting her lip in fizzy anticipation.

"Maybe," I say. I think about the way he looked at me at dinner. The almost kiss on the stairs. There have been moments. I'm sure of it. "This is a mess, isn't it? It snuck up on me. He's like objectively hot, but I thought he was a hot *asshole*, so that made it easier. But now I realize he's a hot nice guy. Thoughtful."

Ginny and Kate are both quiet for a moment, pulling frighteningly similar concerned faces, just as Leo starts to walk down the carriage, holding on to the backs of other chairs to steady himself.

"I have to go," I whisper suddenly.

"Oh, is the hot chef coming?" says Ginny loudly.

"Shh, Ginny," I whisper quickly, before looking up at an amused Leo with a single eyebrow raised. "Hi, Leo."

"Hey, Olive. You want anything from the restaurant car? I'm getting more astringent espresso and perhaps another one of those dry pastries."

I hear the girls both giggle. "That's Ginny and Kate," I explain.

"Hi, Ginny and Kate," says Leo, and I turn the screen around so they can wave at each other.

"I'm going to guess Olive called the espresso *astringent*," says Ginny.

"She did, but it was me who thought the pastry was a bit dry." And then Leo smiles his cutest smile into the screen at my best friends and I feel my knees start to buckle under me.

I turn the phone back round to face me.

"Good-bye, Leo," I say, waving him on.

"I think you mean Hot Chef," he replies, his eyes narrowing in wicked delight.

"*Fuck!* I'm hanging up now," I say to the girls, who are both bug-eyed at this exchange. I get back to the seat to a flurry of messages from them.

GINNY: OMG you're fucked

KATE: I agree

GINNY: He's adorable

KATE: I agree

ME: He's also not as awful as he was

KATE: Sort your feelings about the restaurant before anything else. You need to distance yourself from Leo romantically until you know. It's not fair on him, or you.

ME: I'm not sure it's romance. I think it's horniness.

KATE: Still . . .

GINNY: No. Don't refuse yourself happiness! Everything will figure itself out.

ME: I want to listen to Ginny.

KATE: No! You need to think about Leo as well.

ME: I know

GINNY: Don't be so cynical you guys.

KATE: Sort out Nicky's first. Promise me.

GINNY: Love destroyer

KATE: Realist

ME: I'll cool it. I have to. I need to find a bit of space.

KATE: Without being rude, just in case

GINNY: 😠

KATE: And call us any time. We're like your sponsors, okay?

ME: Emergency buzzkill hotline. Got it

GINNY: Sorry but I'd just encourage you to take one taste

KATE: Call me, not Ginny.

ME: xxx

I put my phone away feeling a sense of relief. Cool it, until I sort my head out about the restaurant. I can do that.

Leo shuffles back toward his seat, but when he gets to mine he stops.

"I spoke to my auntie. She's very excited. She wanted to know if you were keen to come to my third cousin's wedding with me," he says, with a sort of embarrassed half laugh.

"As your date?"

"Your dad was going to come with me," he says.

"As your date?" I say again.

"Well, I guess as my plus-one," he replies, laughing.

"I . . . um." I try not to think of the conversation I've just had with the girls. "Sure," I say, looking back down at my phone and closing our text thread. I can go to a wedding with Leo and still cool it. "I'll need to go shopping."

"Don't you have a Versace dress on you?" he says.

"Fine. I'll wear my nine-euro Versace knockoff," I shout down the aisle as he heads back to his seat, cackling, with his hand raised like he doesn't want to hear it. "Would you like that? Maybe I'll pick up a pair of matching Crocs? Is that Tuscan Wedding enough for you?"

18

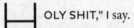

OLY SHIT," I say.

I am completely stunned by the beauty of it.

The villa, which will be our home for the next ten days, is nestled on the side of a hill, down a short gravel drive flanked by poplars, grapefruit trees, apricot trees, and a huge cherry tree, already showing plump black fruit. We stand for a moment taking it in, the sounds of a warm breeze rustling the leaves, the chirp of crickets, the cooing of a pair of turtledoves.

The front of the two-story stone villa is almost completely covered by crawling vines, with only the four square windows peeping through the foliage, their green shutters already closed to preserve the cool.

"Is *this* your auntie's house?"

"No," he says, looking across at my gawping face. "There was a change of plans."

"It's a good change."

"This is an Airbnb she manages, and there was a cancelation," he says.

"Is there . . . a pool?" I say, drooling.

"It has a pool," says Leo, dropping his suitcase at his feet, opening something up on his phone. "'Villa Sienna will help you avoid, as much as possible, contact with other people. A private cook, housekeeping, and gardener discreetly maintain the highest standard with utmost discretion during your stay. With both Sienna and Florence a short drive away, guests can enjoy all the excitement of Tuscany's most famous towns and retreat to the quiet of their luxury villa in the hills.'"

"Oh, I love it. I *love* the ivy," I say, sighing.

"The private cook? That's my aunt Chiara. So, not *that* private," he warns me.

"I look forward to meeting her," I say.

Leo looks like he wants to say something, but then he closes his mouth, smiling wryly.

"The view from the back must be incredible," I say, nodding toward the door. "Come on."

But just as we're about to enter, Leo's aunt—she must be seventy at least—skids by us on an electric bicycle, long skirt blowing behind her as she flies around us and comes to a stop by the door. She dismounts with some difficulty, unhitches her basket, and then smooths down her flowery dress and striped apron. Her hair is cropped short but maintains some serious height under the blue scarf she has fixed around her head.

"Hey, Zia Chiara," says Leo, looking like a bashful teenager.

"Il mio bambino," she says, kissing Leo on the forehead and pinching his cheek so hard I wince on his behalf. Then she turns to me. "Lui è il mio prezioso piccolo principe."

"Prince?" I whisper mockingly.

"And here is Olive Stone," she says, with a less enthusiastic smile. There's a slightly accusatory edge to the *here*.

"That's me," I say, holding a hand up to shake hers.

She stiffly takes it, looking me up and down. I mean, she literally looks at me from my feet to my face and then nods as if she's seen quite enough, thank you.

"Benvenuti," she says, accent thick, scowl prevalent.

"Thank you," I say, smarting a little from her not-very-welcoming welcome.

"Siete in anticipo, ma va bene. Non ci vorrà un momento," she says, awkwardly motioning for us to go ahead.

"We're early, but it won't take long," whispers Leo.

"I got that," I whisper back.

"E poi potrai riposare," Chiara says to Leo, pinching his cheeks again. "Oh, mamma mia, is good to see you, baby boy."

The entrance area is small but leads to an enormous lounge with big arched windows looking out across the Tuscan countryside, and just ahead, a huge pool with stone tiles and a single upright ladder leading into the water.

"La piscina," says Chiara unenthusiastically.

"I'll race you," I say to Leo, who laughs, but Chiara shakes her head.

"Sorry," I say, eyes straight to the ground.

"La cucina," she says, waving a hand toward a stone archway that leads into the most darling stone-tiled kitchen.

"Qui è dove ti siedi," she says, waving outside to a large wood-and-canvas umbrella with a darling table-and-chairs area underneath. We follow her back into the house and she continues. "Qui è dove ti siedi." The sofa.

"Qui è dove ti siedi." Two snuggly chairs by a bay window.

"Lots of places to sit," I say, smiling. She nods back with another tight smile.

We are then led up a wide staircase, the steps worn from hundreds of years of feet.

"Sonno," she says, waving at four doors, two beside us and two down the hall, which must face onto the front of the property. *No, thank you.* I want the view.

"You take your pick," says Leo, probably relieved we don't have to share a bed.

I push the iron handle of the wooden door on my left and light spills into the hallway. "This one!" I say, gasping at the view through the arched window. "I don't need to see anything else."

I throw my bag down on the bed and walk straight to the window, flinging it open and breathing in the sweet, luscious heat.

I consider a shower in the cute en suite bathroom but then spot the raised faucet outside. An outdoor shower, then a plunge in the pool? Yes, please.

THE WATER IS bracingly cold as it hits my skin, but the chill is welcome. I lean my head back under, wetting my hair, and then step out, wrapping a huge white bath towel over my head, and take a seat on the sun lounger.

I shield my face from the sun and look back up toward the house, where I spot Leo looking down at me from the open upstairs window in his bedroom. He quickly looks away to the sweeping view when my eyes catch his.

"Hurry up, this is *heaven*," I shout.

"I'll be down soon," he replies, moving back from the window and out of view.

Moments later, Chiara emerges from the house with a chilled cut-fruit plate and a tall glass of fresh orange juice.

"Grazie," I say, smiling, trying to make a connection. "Thank you so much."

"Prego," she says, with the most hilarious false smile, like she was elbowed in the ribs by the ghost of hospitality.

"Leo used to eat the pineapple so sweet," she says. "A delightful boy."

"Oh," I say, raising my eyebrows and smiling.

"We have video of his first tomato," she says. "I can show you?"

"No videos, Zia," Leo says as he comes outside and walks toward the shower.

"They're at my house," she says, "along with his Barbie. Before he fell in love with big red tractors, he only had eyes for his Olympic Skater Barbie."

"Olympic Skater Barbie?" I say slowly.

"Yes, she had the little sparkly dress and the bendy arms."

"The bendy arms, huh?" I say, stifling a laugh.

"He loves her," she says.

"There's a lot to unpack," I call out to Leo.

"That's enough, Zia," Leo calls out from under the water.

"I come later? Sì?" Chiara says as Leo steps out of the shower. She gives him a wet hug and then turns to me. "He's a very handsome boy, you think? Beautiful too, like his mamma."

I take in his tan, sculpted torso, the light sprinkling of chest hair that tapers into a line disappearing beneath his red swim trunks. "He's not *unpleasant* to look at," I say, and swallow as she sort of canters off into the house.

"I believe the term is *Hot Chef*," Leo says teasingly.

"Screw you," I say.

Leo just grins as he slides his sunglasses on and sits beside me on a sun lounger. I have to work hard not to stare at the glistening beads of water as they trail a path on his skin and quickly evaporate into the dry air. He leans over and takes a chilled half apricot off the plate. *Hot fucking Chef*, I mutter in my head.

"Hardly feels like work," he says. A reminder, I think, that at some point we'll need to do just that. "I have to say, for all the excitement and bustle of Catania, I'm going to love it here for a while."

"Same here," I say, stretching out, wiggling my travel-weary toes. "Now, *this* is paradise."

Leo says nothing for a moment, but I can feel his smile in my direction.

"What?" I ask, tipping my sunglasses to get a better look at his face.

"It's good to see your hard opinion won," comes the reply, with a wry smile. "Very *satisfying*."

I feel my skin tingle all over when he says the word *satisfying*.

"Leo. This is a real treat, and I'm glad to be here. Thank you. I can see why Dad loved it here. And your aunt is charming . . . in her way."

Leo laughs at this. "*In her way* is the quintessential caveat to an Olive compliment," he says when his laugh subsides.

We both lie there, faces to the sun, sunglasses on, for what feels like hours, interrupted only by the intermittent chorus of cicadas and the periodic clash of pans coming from the kitchen. Very occasionally, the sound of a car on gravel far in the distance.

"The almost silence," I say after a while, drowsy from falling in and out of sleep. "Your aunt, will she be visiting us a lot while we're here?"

"I don't know," he says, turning his face to me. "Probably. Why?"

"I feel like she has something to say to me."

"Oh, don't worry about it," he says, reaching for a jug of ice-cold water that appeared while we were dozing. "She has something to say to almost everyone."

"I almost don't want to think about it, but any food ideas for this route? Tuscany is tomatoes and bean stews and wild boar, isn't it?" I ask, raising myself onto my elbow, turning on my lounger to him, ready to enjoy a moment of uncomplicated food talk. "I'd love to keep up our pace from Catania and really get on top of it so we can also chill."

"Well, I've already got ideas . . . ," he says slowly. "Zia is going to show us her wild boar ragù tomorrow." He laughs, turning his head back to the sky. "Can you imagine? In this heat?"

I smile, lying back. "Hmm."

"She has an old heritage-tomato farm, and, *only if it works*, I'd love to include something from there."

"Sure," I say. "Absolutely."

"That's it? No fight?"

"Leo, it's got to be *tomatoes*. Dad hasn't done tomatoes yet, and it's a book on regional Italian cooking. I really believe he meant to do tomatoes in Tuscany, come on!"

"You're probably right," he says.

"I'm right," I say. "I just know it. And what kind of fool doesn't like tomatoes?"

"That was too easy," he says, laughing suspiciously.

"As long as you're not going to turn them into a tomato candy floss for the book, I'm all in," I say, laughing.

"Let's get it done. Then we can enjoy heaven with no deadline," he says.

"Yes, just the sun, this pool, cold fruit from the icebox, you, and me," I say mindlessly, my thoughts juddering to a halt as soon as the last part tumbles out. Leo makes no response. And, in the silence that follows, I feel a slight tingling down the back of my neck.

Leo removes his sunglasses and there's a question in his eyes, but I look to the sky.

"I'm going to make a coffee, and then I have to check my emails," he says wearily, sliding his sunglasses back on.

"Emails?" I say, with a comedy gasp.

"Yes, Olive, *emails*," he says. "I have a Zoom call tomorrow too."

"A Zoom call?" I say with another gasp. "The horror. Why do you have a Zoom call on holiday?"

Leo laughs, but stands and stretches. "First, this is a working holiday. And second, it's with a recruiter." I say nothing as he heads inside the house.

I stand too, but walk toward the pool, diving into the still blue water. When I come up, I shield my eyes so I can watch him through the glass doors, moving in the kitchen, fixing his coffee. I watch him slide into a chair at the old wooden farmhouse table, flip open his laptop, and then lift his arms, reaching around to the back of his head and curving his back in a long stretch. I think of Nicky's and allow myself to imagine a sledgehammer smashing through the wall at the back to open up the kitchen into the dining area. I allow myself to imagine Leo, covered in plaster, ducking out from behind the wreckage, his face covered in fine white powder. I reach up and clear the mess from his lips with my thumb.

Slowly, I sink into the bottom of the pool and try to cool the hot desire for Leo that is intensifying with every blistering moment.

19

THE NEXT MORNING, I emerge at the front of the house to find two bikes and Leo leaning against the stone wall checking his phone. He stands up straight as soon as he sees me, sliding his phone away.

"Are we . . . *cycling* to your aunt's house?" I ask, glancing up at the main road at the end of the drive. "Because I'm neither under twelve nor over forty."

"Yes," he says, mounting the larger bike and waiting for me to join. "It's only about a twenty-minute ride. Downhill most of the way."

"I hope we're getting a lift back in that case . . . ," I say, mounting the other and kicking back the stand.

Leo nods toward the drive, and I let him take the lead. The main road, which is a single-lane potholed nightmare, follows many tight corners, winding its way down into the valley. Several times I hastily pull over as a car comes flying around the corner toward us.

"There are electric bikes now," I shout to Leo, who is less steady on a bike than I am. "And by the way, isn't Italy the home of the fucking Vespa? Can you imagine my dad cycling back up this way?!"

"He usually hired a Vespa, to be fair," he shouts back, laughing.

At that exact moment, I hit a stone, and although I'm going as slowly downhill as balance will allow, I tumble inelegantly sideways and into a hedge.

"Shit!" I yelp as the bike clatters to the ground and I fall with a *thud*.

Leo looks back over his shoulder to see if I'm okay and also falls. In sympathy, I think.

"Shit!" he shouts.

"Fuck!" I shout.

A cacophony of profanity pierces the tranquility of the valley.

"I've hurt myself," I whimper.

"I'm coming," he says, propping his bike up against a railing and rushing back up the hill to tug me out of the hedge. I'm covered in tiny scratches, and wherever there is bare skin I feel a stinging.

I turn to the hedge, and lo and behold, it's a bush of nettles. *Nettles.*

Leo pulls a leaf from my hair, and then also clocks the nettles. "Ow, that's not good."

"Nettles," I moan, then I brace myself as the hot burning and itching start to present. "I'll need ten minutes of standing here silently screaming."

"Is there a dock leaf?" he says, glancing at but not touching the foliage by the roadside.

"Owwwww," I say, looking at the little dots that have appeared down my arms and legs.

"I don't have anything," he says. "I don't know how to help."

"Time and bravery," I say.

"What?"

"My mum always said time and bravery are all you need to get over beestings or nettle stings. She also said that about ex-husbands." I half laugh and grimace. Leo looks as though he wants to hold my hand or hug me, but I step back, quite sure it would make things worse.

"Your face is fine," Leo says, grimacing.

"Great. The modeling career can continue unabated." I moan, glancing down at the scrape on my knee, which is a little bloody.

"You'll need a Band-Aid," he says.

"Will I, Dr. Leo?" I say, licking my thumb and clearing the blood. "Bloody bikes."

"Sorry. I thought it would be fun cycling the Tuscan hills," he says.

"You know these hills, don't you? These very steep hills flanked by nettles!" I say.

"Sorry," he says again, trying not to laugh. "It was a good idea in my head."

I giggle and then wince. I use every ounce of will I have to avoid scratching the stings, and then slowly the pain subsides, and I feel like I can finally breathe out.

"I'm ready," I say. "I've survived. Not as bad as I remember, in fact."

"You're a grown woman now, Olive," he says, laughing.

I watch as he examines the scratch down his own leg and then nods for us to continue. "Let's go," he says.

"I'm going to walk the rest of the way down Death Hill, though, if you don't mind."

He waves his hands out at the view, not quite yet dusty with heat. It's clearer than yesterday and you can make out the different farming fields. A wheat field to one side, a vineyard farther in the distance. On one field, a tractor makes its way slowly, driving the tramlines in a golden sea of rapeseed flowers.

"Still do love a big red tractor," he says, before looking down at me with a twinkle in his eye.

"Are you manly enough to admit you owned a Barbie?"

"Yes. I have no choice with Chiara running her mouth off like she does," he says, gazing out to the rolling hills, a smirk across his face.

"I hope she's going to be a little nicer to me today," I say, nodding to Leo and raising my eyebrows as though I'm asking a question.

"She'll be fine," he says. "She's wonderful once you get to know her."

I tip my head and shake it slowly, smirking at him in disbelief.

We continue the walk down the hill, holding our bikes as we do, walking under the heavy branches of hazelnut, cypress, and occasionally a chestnut.

"There was a huge chestnut tree at the green near our home in London," I say, as we enter a dappled section of the path and disappear under the foliage. "I played in it as a kid. You know what it's like as an *only child*. The tree was basically my brother."

Leo looks across at me and frowns. "I know that feeling."

"I do want another chestnut tree one day," I say, running my hand along the branch of a young silver birch.

"I like that goal," he says, grinning.

I find myself wanting this walk to go on forever, as occasionally we catch each other's eye, the sweetest tingling of chemistry between us. It is becoming so I can feel his presence as he moves beside me, as though a million little threads are binding me to him and I'm allowing it.

"Leo, do you really think you could have turned Nicky's around?" I ask him, careful to put the past tense on everything.

"If your dad had let me, I could have given it a good shot, I think. I had this idea for a take-out window, serving focaccia sandwiches at lunchtime. You know, over the pandemic? Seven bucks. One meat, one vegan, every day. Classy. Wrapped in paper and brown string."

"Good idea," I say.

"Good *margins*," he says. "But your dad didn't want it. Said Nicky's was for sitting with your meal. Not feeding people who eat in offices."

I nod. "Hmm. Sounds like Dad."

"And yet, you know how in most cafés it's polite to buy an hourly coffee and whatever if you're going to, like, co-work at the table?"

"It's only fair," I say, as we come to a crossroad.

"Left," Leo says, and we turn and continue down the valley as it starts to flatten. "Well, when some fucking suit came in with his laptop to have minestrone, and sat there for like three hours, your dad would give them a coffee and cake on the house."

He turns to me, and in a perfect mimicry of my dad's voice and hand gesticulations, says, "He's lonely, Leo, fix the man a tir-amisu."

"Jesus," I say, a little squeeze on my heart, wondering if Dad was projecting his own loneliness.

"So," Leo says. "These were some examples of things your dad wouldn't do, and things he *shouldn't* have done. A combination of his traditional approach to dining and his overly generous nature."

"Overly generous is *generous*," I say. Though once more, Leo's explanation of the problems at Nicky's have given me pause. If there were basic things Dad wasn't getting right, the problem really wasn't so much Nicky's the restaurant but Nicky the *owner*.

A bird flies in our path, followed by a second, and a moment later a thunderous flock emerges, as if startled, from a huge linden tree, taking flight all at once into the sky, in a black cloud that rises, peaks, and then dives, shooting off onto the horizon.

"Swallow," Leo says, in awe.

"Only with the right guy," I reply, biting my lip.

Leo looks at me, his mouth open in shock, then bursts into laughter. "*Olive!*"

"I couldn't resist," I reply playfully. "Come on, let's ride."

I mount the bike again and shoot off down the narrow, windy lane.

"You don't know where you're going!" he calls out, climbing onto his bike and chasing me down the tree-lined road into the distance. "Wait!"

We arrive at Chiara's, sweaty, red-cheeked, and, dare I say it, slightly exhilarated from the ride, despite our tumbles.

"Was it so bad?" he says, kicking his bike stand down and parking next to me.

"It's like you *know* that nature and exercise are good for you, and yet, every single bone in your body says *nah*," I say, dismounting. "But then you do it, and you wonder why you waited, because you feel so fucking happy and charged with the good happy hormones."

I glance at him.

"Ready to cook?" he asks, a smirk on his face.

"No, Leo, that's your job," I say, rubbing my hands together. "I'm ready to taste."

"BUONGIORNO, ZIA," LEO calls out.

"Sì, sì. Come, come," Chiara says from somewhere out the back, her voice echoing through the stone house.

The house is not dissimilar to the villa in construction, though much smaller and without the spanking-new infinity pool. But the classic Tuscan garden that surrounds it is magical. I can see little naked stone statues holding forth bowls with running water standing guard next to winding, stony paths that disappear under vine-covered arches to a sloping terraced garden below. The smell is fragrant with lavender, herbs, and a heady back note of tomato, coming, I think, from the farm that must be down beyond my view.

Stepping into Chiara's kitchen is like stepping back in time. The walls with seemingly random exposed stone are finished in that classic rag-rolled dusty peach. We duck under a redbrick doorway and down a step into the cool stone room, which has only one small window, littered with potted herbs, overlooking greenery and a small patch of blue sky.

I glance down to the daintily painted floor tiling and across at the huge, square ceramic sink, and a very old Aga-type stove with three heavy doors and a hood for grilling. Above, a huge circular iron fitting with hooks for pots and pans, bunched drying herbs, and a variety of alien kitchen gadgets hang over us.

"Wow. This kitchen is *amazing*," I say.

"It's old," replies Chiara sharply. Then she nods to a row of brand-new SMEG small appliances on a stand-alone cabinet against the back wall, and her voice turns sweet. "But Leo helps me keep it modern." Chiara puts the little scissors she's been using to cut the top off a bunch of thyme into the pocket of her apron. She smiles at us both, holding her hands out in a welcome gesture that Leo takes as an invitation for a hug.

"She makes meals for the Airbnb here, and she didn't even have an electric kettle," says Leo, as he pulls back from her and she ruffles his hair.

Ah gods, why does he have to be so thoughtful?

"Come," she says to me, holding her hand out toward a flowery ceramic bowl filled with celery, carrot, and onion.

"Everyone cooks in Chiara's kitchen," Leo says as she thrusts a board of unbutchered boar into his hands.

"Dai, tritate! Sbrigatevi!" she says, waving at us both. "Per favore."

"Chop, chop," says Leo, laughing at us being bossed around by his grumpy aunt.

"I'm chopping. Trito, trito," I say, as I pull off a stem of celery and cut it in long lengths, then spin it to cut squares the same size as the onion.

Chiara orders us about, chopping, peeling, crushing, and in Leo's case, butchering the ingredients for the stew. Leo can do no wrong with his prep, whereas I am constantly being told to go più veloce, più lentamente . . . Meglio! Meglio! Meglio! It's clear she *really* has something to say to me.

When Chiara heads to the toilet, the two of us catch each other's eye.

"I prefer when it's just us in the kitchen," I say.

"I can be bossy too," he says, laughing.

"Can you, now?" I say with a wicked grin.

"Very bossy . . ." Leo claps a wooden spoon in his hand, slowly. *Playfully.* "I'm glad to hear you like working with me, though."

Leo straightens up, and I turn to see Chiara, fists on hips, blood down her apron, looking terrifying.

"You *like* to work with Leo?" she says.

"Yes," I say, smiling, unsure what's coming. I put down the knife and wipe my hands on a tea towel. "What is it, Chiara?"

"And yet you sell the restaurant," she continues, throwing her hands in the air.

"Oh. Okay. Now I get it," I murmur, feeling my heart sink into the pit of my stomach as I glance over at Leo, unsurprised he's told her.

Chiara frowns at me, rubs her hands down her front, and then stomps out of the kitchen again, leaving us alone in silence. I stop cutting and stare at Leo, exhausted.

"Sorry," he says, eyes to the ceiling. "I didn't think she'd react this way. I thought she was being short with you because . . ." His voice trails off, and he looks sheepish.

"How many reasons have you given her?" I ask.

"I didn't know you," he says.

"Can you talk to her?" I say to him, raising my shoulders questioningly.

"Of course," he says quietly. Then he joins Chiara in the hall and in very fast Italian they argue with each other. I hear snippets of *it should have been yours.* And then, *where has she been all these years?*, various versions of *mamma mia*, followed by *I can't believe she doesn't even want it*, from an indignant Chiara, and then from Leo: *she had a rough time with Nicky.*

"Chiara," I say, joining them in the hallway.

"And here she is," she says, raising her chin. Her eyes tell me she isn't angry, but upset for Leo.

"I understand why you're upset, you feel that Leo deserved the restaurant, but I didn't ask for it. It isn't my fault."

"Such a gift, and you don't even want it?" She turns to Leo. "And everything you did for him."

Chiara's face slackens into a look of such sadness, *such* heart-break for Leo.

"I can get another job, Zia. I probably should go out and spread my wings a little," he says, starting to look humiliated by this whole exchange. "It's her right to sell it if she doesn't want it."

"It's been hard. Of course I feel torn," I say, and Leo's brow descends in a split second of confusion.

"Then you're unsure?" Chiara jumps on it, her eyes rounding in hope.

"*No*. Not exactly . . ." I put my hands to my face and shake my head vigorously. It shouldn't have come out like this.

Chiara puts a hand on my shoulder, and I want to backpedal, explain myself. To dampen this beacon of hope that has arrived to complicate things further.

"*Shit*," I mutter into my hands.

"I leave you to talk," Chiara says, an annoyingly satisfied whisper of a smile on her face. "There is a salad, there is wine in the cellar. And then you go and see my tomatoes? Sì?"

Let her go, Leo mouths to me before I have a chance to protest, and I force a smile as she strides off.

I head back into the kitchen as Leo says good-bye. Then I resume my chopping, but Leo comes in and pushes me aside with his hip, moving in to dice my sofrito even further until the pieces are so small they are one knife swipe from a soup.

"I'm so embarrassed about all of that," he says quietly.

"Forget it," I say.

Leo looks at me like he wants to press me on my earlier admission, but he doesn't. Instead he turns into a machine, his body moving unconsciously through the steps of making the stew.

He sautés the sofrito, adds bay leaves and whole bruised garlic cloves. That mix is put to the side, while more olive oil is added and then the wild boar, dusted with salt, pepper, and a little flour, is fried. When the meat is brown and crusting on the edges, he tips in the sofrito, adds a glass of red wine, juniper berries, and a long sprig of rosemary, and then puts the lid on and motions toward the oven.

"Me?" I ask, standing back, both hands at my chest.

"Yep," he says, glancing at the oven again.

I open the oven door and see there is already an identical skillet in there. I grab a tea towel and lift it out, sliding it onto the stonework surface.

"One she made earlier?" I ask, turning back to the oven to put our freshly prepared stew in to cook.

"She was excited to help," he says, shaking his head, looking down at the stew. Then he pauses and apologizes again. "She worries too much about me. I'm a grown man, for god's sake."

I laugh lightly, as Leo lifts the lid, and after the steam drifts away, it is replaced by the deep umami of a long-and-slow-cooked ragù. He forks the boar apart so it's partially shredded, and I lean in to take a deep sniff.

"Looks amazing," I say, diving a fork in, much to Leo's amusement. "So good. Shall we cook some tagliatelle?"

"Yep, I'll prep it and bring it out, okay?"

He puts the lid back on and then both his palms flat on the

stone of the kitchen island. He stares down for a long while and then lifts his head up.

Here it comes.

"*Are* you feeling torn?" he says evenly. "Or was that just to get my auntie off your back?"

I take a breath.

"I'm uncertain about selling," I say, glancing nervously between Leo and the floor. "But I don't know what that means yet. It might mean nothing."

Leo studies my face.

"I see," he says, his eyes narrowing on me, a look, not of excitement at my admission, but of empathy.

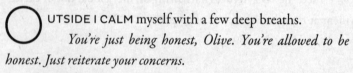

20

OUTSIDE I CALM myself with a few deep breaths.

You're just being honest, Olive. You're allowed to be honest. Just reiterate your concerns.

I head out onto the back porch, looking out at a view that is less expansive than the villa's, but from which I can just see the tops of tomato vines and a long white tunnel with a glass entrance, which must be the edge of the farm down the hill. I pull out my notebook and fold Chiara's handwritten recipe into it.

Leo comes out with the big salad and slides it into the middle of the table. He's also got a chilled bottle of San Pellegrino, which I open and pour into both our glasses.

"Do you want to talk about it?" he says.

"I don't know if you're the person I should voice my doubts to," I reply as I drag my hands down my face.

"I can listen without hope," he lies, and I shoot him a look. *No, you can't.*

"Okay, well. Allow a guy a little hope, Olive," he adds, with a laugh that makes me feel like my heart is in a goddamn vise.

"Can we talk tomatoes first?" I say. "We have a lot to do."

"Sure," he says breezily. *Too breezily.* The soft glow of hope radiates out of every pore on his body like a sunbeam. He glances at the ceramic bowl in front of him. "Here is a classic panzanella."

"Usually delivered with soggy bread and watery tomato," I say, trying to focus on the food. Trying not to think about the restaurant. Trying not to salivate over Leo's arms as he dishes us both out a portion with two wooden spoons.

It is not a panzanella like I've had before. This one is an absolute riot of summer color, with grilled yellow and red peppers; crunchy, garlicky croutons; enormous torn leaves of basil; and a vinaigrette so sharp it tingles my nose and makes my mouth water.

"She wants you to be impressed by the tomatoes," he says, stopping to groan as he takes a mouthful of the salad. "Her tomato farm can't compete with the mega-farms, and so that's why she looks after a handful of local Airbnbs. It's hard. She struggles. But at least I can help with some new equipment now and then."

I take a massive gulp of the water on the table, trying not to think about how kind Leo is. How much he loves and supports his only family. I try not to make the obvious comparisons with my dad, who made us basically homeless so he could keep the restaurant going.

"Well. Her tomatoes," I say, my mouth absolutely drooling with every forkful. "Bloody hell, they're incredible."

I scribble a few notes in my book, as Leo tries to guess the ratio of vinegar to oil, capers to anchovies, lemon zest to basil leaf. We discuss a sourdough alternative for the croutons and whether we could opt out of the finely sliced red onion.

"No. But they need to be soaked," he says. "Auntie hasn't soaked these and they're too sharp."

"Agreed," I say, jotting down the note.

"We need to see the farm before we go," he says, nodding toward the back of the garden.

"Also agreed," I say again, offering a little smile to Leo, feeling the weight of a pending conversation bearing down on me. *Just be honest*, I tell myself for the hundredth time.

"Look at us, agreeing on things," he says, smiling.

"Well, it's only a salad," I say. "What the hell could you do to ruin a salad?"

"Oh, you'd be surprised," he says, chuckling as he offers a hand to help me stand.

Leo and I walk down toward the back of the garden through a hedge lane, under a leafy archway made from bent hazelnut branches, and down toward the rows of trellised vines. The smell is strong and sweet. We snake down through the vines toward a greenhouse, where rows of baby tomato plants are meticulously organized, labeled, and sprayed from above with a light mist of water.

Leo reaches up to hang on to a metal frame above his head. I notice the bulge of muscle in the undersides of his arms. That hint of his tattoo in remembrance of his mamma. My heart does a funny flutter and I sort of snort-cough, turning away from him.

I hear him come up behind me to look at the tomato I'm pretending to examine so I don't have to look at his bulging biceps.

"Can you imagine Italian food before tomatoes? They only came here in—"

"Yes, the fifteenth or sixteenth century, I know," I say, rolling my eyes at him. "They came from South America. Everyone knows that."

"Can you actually imagine European food without South America? No cocoa, no potatoes."

"No corn, no vanilla."

"No tobacco," he adds, "not that I'd miss that, I suppose."

"You never smoked?"

"Two years," he says, laughing. "Your dad knocked that out of me."

I watch him touching the edge of the little seedling with his finger. Something about his finger gently touching that delicate green leaf makes me fizz inside, and I quickly take a few steps away to get out of his space.

I glance down at my watch.

"Shall we head back to the villa?" I ask.

"Sure," he says.

"I need a shower," I say. "I'm covered in nettles, thyme, and boar juice and oil and tomato seeds. I smell like onions."

"Hot," he says, smelling the backs of his own hands. "And I'm not actually kidding."

I feel the tension melt slightly as I laugh.

"Come on," he says, as he nods toward the back of the house. We make our way back up the long field to the bicycles. As we near them, Leo stops and turns to me, shielding his face from the sun with his hand.

"Look. I know this is presumptuous and I don't want to pressure you, but I worked on some ideas for Nicky's," he says. "A new direction for it. A new menu. I tried to show your dad, but . . ."

"He wasn't interested?"

Leo shakes his head. "Would you like to see it?"

I nod, feeling the prickle of the sun on my skin, as I consider my answer carefully. All I can do is be honest, and I want to see his ideas. I want to open myself up to keeping Nicky's.

"Yes," I say. "I'd like that."

THE RIDE BACK is grueling, although I'm pleased to see that I'm fitter than Leo and beat him by some minutes. I am already gulping down water in the kitchen when he arrives.

I watch as he uses the bottom of his T-shirt to wipe the sweat off his brow. I sigh, averting my eyes from his body.

"I've got a Zoom call," he says, glancing at his watch.

"I'm going to go call my mum," I say.

But when she doesn't answer, I decide to make use of the bath in my en suite.

I stand up and pull my dress off and wander, yawning, into the bathroom. Then I hear a yelp.

I spin around, *naked*, and there is Leo, in *my* bathroom. Standing on the bath mat dripping wet, just out of the shower.

Also completely naked.

There is a moment where our eyes meet, then his flicker down my body and mine down his, tracing the lines of his chest and the curving muscles on his stomach, beads of water trailing down to pool on the floor. I feel an instant reaction inside, a coiling of a spring that pulls tight from my chest to my thighs.

I stare at him and the whole universe narrows to *this* moment. His stomach flexes, and his hands clench, his eyes on the curve where my neck meets my shoulder, and then they drop to my breasts and I feel all my blood rush to where his gaze rests, my breath shallowing to tiny gasps for air.

I am drawn toward him. I lift my hand just a fraction, my

fingers reaching forward, and he spots the signal, his eyes once again locking with mine. But now they are dark, his pupils dilated, his face tense with desire.

I don't move a muscle.

Don't do it, Olive. The warning that sits somewhere in the back of my mind right now is so slight, but it catches me. I feel it pierce the bubble around us.

I drop my eyes.

"You were on a Zoom," I say.

"I wanted to shower first," he explains.

"Shit."

Then everything moves quickly. I grab a fluffy white towel to cover myself. But Leo hasn't anything within reach and so he pulls on the shower curtain, so hard that it comes off its metal pole, one ring popping off at a time. *Pop! Pop! Pop!*

My eyes dart back across his body to the huge erection that the flimsy plastic sheet cannot hide.

"Fuck," he says, trying to cover up. The pole that held up the shower curtain falls, hitting him on the back of his head before landing in the bath with an almighty clatter. "Shit."

"Sorry, I thought this was *my* bathroom," I yelp, now spotting Leo's soap bag next to the sink. "Oh my god. *Sorry.*"

"Olive," he replies, his eyes softening. It is the hint of tenderness on his face that snaps me out of the moment.

I rush out the door and jump onto my bed, red-faced.

"I'm so fucking sorry!" I shout.

"It's a shared bathroom," he calls out, clearly trying to fake laugh, but it comes out like a high-pitched machine gun. "I didn't realize. Sorry!"

"I didn't know either," I call back again, fake laughing

hysterically in return, the picture of Leo's naked body and huge boner flashing in my mind.

I then hear the banging of what I think is the pole being hastily reerected, followed by some mild stomping, and then, after some time, a knock on the door to the bathroom.

"Come in, Leo," I say, trying not to laugh.

"The bathroom is all yours," he says through the door.

"You *can* come in," I say, but there is no response. "I'm covered up."

I stand and I walk to the door and open it. Leo is leaning against the frame in boxer shorts and a clean white T-shirt, his hand up on the edge of the doorway. My heart jolts at the distilled sex appeal of this man. I know that sex appeal is subjective. I know that if I put Leo in a room with a hundred women, maybe only a handful would be this attracted to him. But he was made with me in mind, I swear it.

"Can we laugh about this?" he says, grimacing, and then he drops his hand and steps back.

"Sure," I say, as lightly as I can. And then I add, jauntily, despite my cheeks burning, "Who here hasn't had a wank in the shower?" I chuckle like a murderous clown, dying a little bit inside.

"I wasn't . . . *Olive!*" He looks absolutely mortified.

"Sorry, I thought . . ." I look toward his crotch and then bite both my lips together to stop myself from talking.

"You were *naked* right in front of me," he says, eyes narrowing on me again. "I'm only human."

A compliment of sorts, and I burn with a heady mix of pleasure and mortification.

"Let's stop talking about this," I say, catching my breath. "Forget it ever happened. We're both adults."

"Yes. Let's bonfire the last seven minutes," he replies, with a relieved chuckle.

"Fucking burn it and toss the ashes into the wind," I reply, looking guiltily over toward Dad's urn, which I can see poking out from behind the curtains. "Bad metaphor, but you get the picture."

His face cracks into a relieved smile. "I have to do this call."

And then he turns and heads into his bedroom. I watch him go, my heart thundering in my chest. I lie back on my bed and wonder how the hell I'll sleep tonight.

21

THE NEXT AFTERNOON Leo is outside with a red Vespa and the face of a man who has plans.

"Can I play tour guide?" he says as he tosses me a helmet. It's a little cooler today, and he's wearing khaki pants with a tight white T-shirt and an open short-sleeved button-down.

This morning I came downstairs to hear him on a call with a recruiter. I stood in the stairwell listening to him talk; it was clear the job was a pastry chef as part of a chain of hotel restaurants. I hated listening to him selling himself, talking about how he was looking forward to improving his skills with desserts. That no, unfortunately he didn't have a reference. That yes, he could potentially start soon.

"Where are we going?" I ask, glancing down at my knee-length skirt and contemplating changing.

"Don't change," he says with a grin, "you look great."

I roll my eyes at him, unable to absorb the compliment. And then I move toward him.

"I want to drive," I say, and he nods, sliding to the back of the seat and motioning for me to get on. I've driven a Vespa before; we had one in London and Dad let me drive it illegally a few times. When I was twenty-five, I bought a secondhand one for zipping around London, but it cost a fortune to keep it running.

I jump on and pull on my helmet. Leo reaches back and holds the handles on the seat behind him, but his hard chest brushes against my back, his thighs fitted snuggly behind mine, and I'm too aware of the delicious heat of him.

"Head up the hill and follow the signs for Florence," he says.

"We're going to Florence?"

"No. I'll nudge you when we're turning off."

The scooter kicks forward and we're away, whizzing up the country roads.

After about fifteen minutes, Leo points to a turnoff and we drive down a smaller road up a hill and to a walled mountain frazione, a small medieval village with a market in the center.

Leo guides me to an area behind a fountain to park, and we dismount, pink-cheeked and windswept.

"So good to be here again," says Leo, shoving our helmets into the little boot at the back.

"Again?"

"Yes, I used to come here in the summer when my mum was sick. Do you remember I said that I got really into cooking shows?" he says, grinning. "I also got into something else."

"What?" I say, following him into a bakery. A gorgeous, tiny store with a round stone doorway and just a few dozen loaves of bread on shelves behind the counter. He pays for a small ciabatta loaf and a couple of pesche di prato.

"What did you get into?" I say. "Shopping?"

"Come," he says.

I follow him down a small, paved alleyway, taking in the

pretty village with its terra-cotta-colored roofs, yellow and orange weathered plaster, each balcony spilling with potted flowers and herbs. A couple of women hang washing from a line above us, while groceries are off-loaded from a three-wheeled van into a tiny eatery ahead.

"Come with me," he says, nodding toward a little alley off the edge of the town's piazza. We wander down the narrow lane and come to a tiny yellow building with *Forelli* in black script scrawled across the top.

Leo pushes open the door and guides me in.

"One of the last artisanal pasta factories in Tuscany. All handmade. Some dried, some, like these tortellini, packaged fresh."

The factory is more like a large industrial kitchen, with huge stainless-steel work surfaces, enormous dough mixers, and all sorts of contraptions for creating different shapes.

Near the front a woman looks up from a bench dusted in flour as she hand rolls out a large flat layer of fresh pasta. It's brighter yellow than I've seen before.

"Semolina, durum wheat, and egg yolk," Leo explains.

I watch as she spoons tiny rounds of spinach and ricotta in a line along the square, and then expertly lays a second sheet of pasta on top. After squeezing out the air with her thumb and forefinger, she runs a cutter down the length of it.

"She makes it look so easy."

"I like to see kitchen prep, but I'm just a chef," he says, laughing.

"I like it too, actually," I say. "But I don't get it. Are we eating here?"

"No," he says.

Leo grins and nods to the lady behind the counter as she

comes over to serve him, and I loiter near the front, marveling at the shelves, fully stocked with nests of fettuccini, pappardelle, testaroli, and pici. I love the traditional design of the packages, a yellow paper bag rolled shut at the top and fixed with staples. The logo is simple: the year 1925, and the ingredients list.

I turn back to Leo, who is taking something warm in a bag and has borrowed a long roll of foil to wrap it up.

"What's in the bag?"

"So many questions, Olive," he says, laughing as he holds open the door for me.

We head back to the bike, and he gently slides the food into the boot, first removing the helmets. Then he jumps on the front of the bike, checking his watch.

"If you're wondering if it's time to eat, it is!" I say, laughing.

"One more stop," he says.

I lean back and hold on to the rail just behind me. I'm tempted to lean forward and put my arms around his waist and my cheek against his back, but I don't.

The next stop is a village down in the valley, where Leo parks outside a rustic cottage attached to a large, modern farmhouse. I wait by a wood fence, watching cows lazily chew their cud in the field. It doesn't appear to be a shop, but Leo emerges a few minutes later with a small block of cheese wrapped in paper.

He nods at the bike. "Come on," he says.

I climb back on, Leo still driving, and we start to climb up.

"Where are we going?" I say. "It's getting late! The sun is going to start setting soon and I don't fancy this ride back in the dark."

"Trust me," he shouts back, as we head through the woods and emerge at the top of a valley, lit in an almost golden shine from the evening sun. Leo pulls over to a clearing.

"A picnic?" I say at last, gazing out across the view.

Leo removes his helmet and starts to unpack everything from the bike. Two beers wrapped in a cold tea towel. The bread. The Sicilian olive oil. Knives. Forks. A couple of ceramic bowls. He drops a wide blanket onto the long grass and motions for me to sit.

"Not just a picnic," he says, looking at his watch. "Come on, sit."

I salute his command and take a place on the blanket as Leo lays the food out.

"This is the best bread in the area," he says. "The very best pecorino. The most delicious ravioli with a simple tomato sauce. My favorite Italian sweet pastry for dessert. And two beers, because that's what I liked to drink at eighteen."

"You found all these places?"

"I made a sport of finding the best food I could, and every time I come back, I go to the same places to make sure they've not dropped their standards."

I laugh, patting the blanket for him to join me. "I like this Leo. This Leo is a very good Leo."

Ahead, I can see two villages on the other side of the valley, but my eye catches on what looks like an amphitheater in the distance.

And then the music starts.

I gasp, turning to Leo, who is watching me with delight. Then he laughs.

"Look at you," he says, flicking the top off the beer. "You can't come to Tuscany and not find a way to listen to opera for free."

"You've done this before?"

"Auntie Chiara showed me," he says, laughing. "There are

people all along this hill hidden between the trees, sitting having picnics."

A lone woman's soprano voice ascends the valley and soars through the air on the wind. The song is so desperately sad and beautiful, wavering with sorrow and despair.

"'O mio babbino caro,'" he says quietly as the voice lifts above the strings.

"I know it," I say. "I've heard it. What's it called?"

He nods. "It's from *Gianni Schicchi* by Puccini. It means 'My Dear Daddy.'"

I feel my eyes prickle as he says it, the voice rising up the valley so haunting, so special.

"Everything will be Puccini," he says. "He's the local composer. In Sicily it's all about Bellini, but in Tuscany, we love Puccini."

"It's not a football team, Leo," I say. "Quiet, please."

The song continues and I'm utterly spellbound. "I'm not going to cry at the opera," I say, sniffing, but the moment that Leo has put together: the sun starting to set, the music filling the valley, the picnic . . . it is all just so special.

"What's the song about?" I ask him.

"Um." Leo frowns again and then stares out into the distance, grimacing further. "It's about an inheritance."

"It's about an inheritance," I say, laughing as a tear rolls down my cheek.

"I didn't think about it," he says, shaking his head.

And just like that, the next song begins, a man—a tenor— singing something a little more upbeat and jaunty.

We eat, and we lie on the blanket as Puccini fills the air, the sound beginning to fade as the wind picks up. Leo tells me about his childhood spent roaming farmers' markets in Central London with his mother, hating her interest in food when all he wanted was a burger. He talks about trips to Tuscany for summers, and I feel a strong connection to him as he describes pebbled beaches and burned skin and large gatherings in piazzas where the children climbed in the fountains and the parents sipped on Campari and soda and ate too much food. "Conversations were so boring," Leo says, laughing.

"Especially as they got more drunk," I agree.

I talk about my favorite places to eat in London. We laugh. On the ride home, Leo drives, and this time, I put my arms around his waist.

"It's safer," I suggest.

"It's also warmer," he says, as I relish the feeling of his body against mine, my head resting against his back.

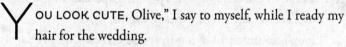

22

YOU LOOK CUTE, Olive," I say to myself, while I ready my hair for the wedding.

My new dress is cornflower blue and falls in an empire line to the floor, with small, puffed sleeves that can be pushed up or pulled down off the shoulder.

I picked it up at the market yesterday, while Leo went shopping for groceries. We took lunch at a small trattoria. So far, we've settled on panzanella and the simple tomato sauce, but we still need another dish that really sings with tomato. We shared slow-roasted porchetta with porcini and burned leek, and Leo had a redfish soup with sea snails, which turned my stomach, much to his amusement.

"Why do macho chefs always order the weirdest thing on the menu?" I'd said, eyebrow raised. "Dad did it all the time. Tripe and intestine stew? Yes, please. Duck poo ragù? Rack that nasty shit up."

"You know, for a food writer, you're pretty unadventurous," he'd said, waving a fleshy lump of snail toward me.

"You enjoy your slimy mollusk, my friend," I'd said, teasing as he struggled to swallow it, desperately trying to pretend it was delicious. "Go on, Leo, chew that baby down."

We both had a couple of days of decidedly *not* drinking and, instead, sitting by the pool as Leo worked on dishes in Chiara's kitchen and I flicked through my dad's manuscript. I can describe my time in Catania. I can paint the sky with words, but those *stories* are not coming.

The truth is I feel awkward being sentimental. Every time I write something *from the heart* (as Leo is fond of advising me to do), it feels soppy and embarrassing, like I'm standing naked in front of the school and everyone's pointing and laughing at me.

I will keep at it, though. I'm *determined*.

I look into the bathroom mirror and feel elegant. My hair is pinned up, my fringe swept to the side and fixed with a small pearl clasp.

"Bathroom's all yours," I call out as I close the door and make my way downstairs.

Leo comes down moments later, fiddling with the cuffs of his crisp white shirt. He looks utterly perfect in a straw-colored suit and matching hat with brown trim.

"I'm excited to go to a proper Italian wedding," I say, coming to join him by the front door. "How will we get there? Shall I call a car?"

"Oh. We're not driving," he says, turning, finally, to look at me. "Wow."

"Thanks," I say, curtsying. "Just a little something I found at the market."

"Um. Before we go, though, can I give you this?" Leo hands me a bound stack of printed paper with *Nicky's* written across the front.

"The proposal?" I say.

"I wanted to update it a little," he says, looking down at me with those big brown eyes. "Now that I know what you like."

"I'm going to leave it here so I don't lose it," I say, dropping it on the side table by the door.

Leo nods. "You make a far more attractive plus-one than your dad would have," he says, as we head out onto the driveway and he stuffs his phone into the pocket inside his jacket. I admire the way his shirt clings to his body, the belt hugging his hips.

And then I hear the *clip, clip, clippity clip* of horses' hooves coming down the road, just out of view. I look back at Leo, confused, as the breeze blows the soft layers of my skirt. It's slightly cooler today.

"Is that what I think it is?"

"I'm afraid so," he says, nodding as four chestnut horses pulling an old wooden wagon appear around the bend. It's gorgeous—the canvas cover is decorated with ivy and little white flowers, and it's filled with women in pretty, colorful dresses and men in their best summer suits.

The driver yanks back on the reins and calls out to us.

"Benvenuti a bordo! Potete sedervi dietro!"

Leo grabs my hand and pulls me toward the wagon, where we climb aboard and join the dozen other guests, making our way to the only available seats at the very back facing the road behind us.

Holy shit, I mouth to Leo. *This is so cool*.

I take a seat, holding on to an iron post for balance, as Leo shyly chats to a couple of the guests before joining me.

"Sorry I didn't introduce you," he says, sitting. "I don't know their names. I need Chiara." And then we're off. Swaying down the gravel road.

The seating is tight, and Leo and I sit thigh to thigh, rocking into each other as we move.

"*This* might be good inspiration for your Tuscan story," he says, as we turn down a lane and make our way through a woody area, the canopy of trees thick with the pungent smell of earth.

"How about no cookbook talk today?" I say, gazing out across the hazy fields to two horses lazily chewing on grass. Both lift their heads to look our way before resuming their meal. "We're so on top of it. What about a day off?"

I turn to Leo, and he nods, lifting his hat and running his hand through his hair.

"And no Nicky's," he says, grinning. "Got it."

The church is a humble eleventh-century stone structure flanked by a small cemetery on one side and a row of poplars on the other. It's tiny, really, compared to the great cathedrals of Florence or Sienna. It has only two windows high up on the left side, above a line of medieval paintings, which are deep brown with bloodred accents; images of men either sacrificing stuff or receiving their tax bills, I presume, by the anguish on their faces.

The wood bench seating is old, full of grooves from worms, and on each place is a folded order of service fixed with a ribbon down the spine.

We are the last group to arrive, and we take a seat in the back row, with a few guests opting to stand.

"Gianna and Alessandro," I whisper. "How do you know them?"

"Alessandro is a third cousin," he whispers back.

"I don't think I even know a single third cousin."

"On average, apparently, everyone has a hundred and ninety third cousins," Leo says, laughing.

"How do you know that?" I ask, nudging him.

"I looked it up when I lived here with my mum," he replies.

"Now, why on earth did an eighteen-year-old Leo need to look *that* up?" I ask playfully.

"Country-life hazard," he says, laughing. "You *can* date your third cousin, though."

"Right," I say, giggling enough to elicit a shush from a buttoned-up lady in a pink fascinator, who stares at the pulled-down puffed sleeves of my dress with such outrage that I quickly pull them up onto my shoulders, much to Leo's amusement.

"Church sleeves," I explain.

Leo only glances sideways at me, raising an eyebrow.

The service takes about an hour, and by the time they are kissing, I'm crying. The bride looks unbelievable in layers and layers of white silk fitted to an intricate lace bodice with little cap sleeves. Her eight bridesmaids are wearing pale gray dresses in different designs. The men wear black suits with suspenders and bow ties.

Leo hands me a handkerchief, and I blow my nose loudly.

"Didn't take you for such a sentimental type, Olive," he says.

"I am a total sucker for a wedding," I reply. "I love that people are so blindly and naïvely caught up in the moment. It's so pure. Because, you know, most of these marriages end, don't they."

"Jesus, *that's* why you were crying?"

"No," I snap, and then smooth the skirt of my dress across my thighs. "Maybe a little."

Leo looks sympathetic, if a little concerned by my admission. "They don't *all* end."

"Nope, but every couple thinks *they'll* be the lucky ones," I say with a whisper. "It's a huge leap of faith."

"Come on," he says, standing as the bride and groom pass,

beaming at their guests, and we start to file back out. "Let's go eat and dance."

We walk about ten minutes down a blue stone path toward a huge villa with a perfect lawn overlooking a vineyard below. There are two long tables, each seating about forty guests, running almost the length of the grass, with curved iron poles wrapped in green vines holding elaborate chandeliers and crisscrossed fairy lights above the tables.

"Wow," I say. "This is going to be magical as the sun goes down."

"Gorgeous, isn't it?"

"How did you get an invite to your third cousin's wedding, anyway?" I ask, as we collect glasses of champagne from a table stacked with welcome drinks and nibbles. I am noticing that Leo doesn't seem to know a lot of people here, and those he does know, he's a little awkward around.

"Chiara," he says with a laugh. "When Mum was dying, I think she worried about me being all alone with no family back in London. I didn't really grow up with this lot." He waves his glass toward the guests milling around on the grass, kissing cheeks and raising toasts while the bride and groom stand on the stairs doing photos.

"She's been on a mission to integrate me with the family here. If I'm in town, no one is allowed to throw even a dinner party without inviting *poor Leo*," he says.

"What about your dad?"

"Oh, he's no one," he says. "Left when I was a baby. Bit of a dickhead, by all accounts."

We are interrupted by Chiara, bowling through the crowd toward us with her arms outstretched as she pulls Leo into an embrace. And then she turns to me and does the same.

"Forgive me these last days," she says, patting me on the back. "I'm just an old lady who loves her nephew a little too much."

"It's fine, Chiara," I say. "I'm glad someone likes him."

Leo narrows his eyes at me, and I tip my glass toward him.

"Come, come," she says to me. "Did you see the house?"

This is clearly code for *I want to talk to you*.

I'm almost dragged away from Leo, who stands alone in the middle of the lawn, but he's quickly joined by a couple of other men, his eyes lighting up when they approach. Chiara motions for me to head up the stone stairs and onto the little balcony to look at the view. I slow my pace as she struggles to keep up with me.

I gaze out across the hills, the sun bearing down as the afternoon heat peaks and a humid breeze threatens rain. Chiara joins me and waves a hand out.

"Sì," she says, simply. "It's beautiful."

But I know we are not here to look at the view.

"Olive," she says.

"Yes, Chiara."

"I'm sorry I wasn't very kind to you, Olive," she says. "I got a surprise. I talked to Leo after Nicky died and asked him what happens with the restaurant, and he was waiting to learn."

"I see," I say, biting my bottom lip as I fold my arms protectively.

"Every year Leo comes here, sometimes with your father as well, and Leo used to say, 'Nicky, please let me make some changes.' And he would say, 'Maybe one day, Leonardo. One day. One day. One day.'"

She briefly chuckles at the memory. "Old men like your papà don't like being told what to do, Olive."

I smile at her, unfolding my arms, waiting for her to continue as we stand side by side looking out at the view.

"And when we learned you will inherit the restaurant and he . . . Well, Leo makes the best of things, and he was very happy to work with you," she says. "Very happy."

"He was?" I say, surprised.

"And I didn't know the latest news that you will sell," she says, holding a hand to her heart. "And so I felt so bad for him. Sorry, Olive. Is not your fault."

"He will be *fine*, Chiara. Whatever happens."

"Sì," she says, nodding once. A strong, determined nod. I turn to her.

"He *will* be," I say.

"Olive, I have to ask why you do not want your family business," she says, genuinely confused, eyes rounded and moist.

"It ruined my family," I say. "That *family* business. My dad didn't listen to Mum. Lost a lot of money. And eventually, Mum couldn't take it anymore."

Chiara is quiet and contemplative. "Men," she says. "And people wonder why I never married."

I laugh at this, glancing toward Chiara, leaning forward on the redbrick banister, which is hot to the touch.

"But Leo is not your father," she says.

I seek him out and spot him collecting a drink and chatting easily to a pair of groomsmen. At that moment they turn to face us, and Leo points up. Unsure whether he's talking about me or Chiara, I look away, feeling myself blush.

"Leo doesn't have Nicky's big ego," she continues.

"It was part of Dad's charm," I say, feeling the need to defend my father. His big ego was part of what made him so charismatic.

"Leo puts other people's feelings first. Always has done. It's even maybe a problem," she says woefully.

I don't know that she means it as an accusation, yet I feel accused. "You don't need to tell me what a good man Leo is. I've seen," I say shortly, wanting this conversation to end.

I think about a young parentless Leo and what he went through. And then, how grateful I am my dad took him in. I stare hard into the distance, at a row of angry-looking dark clouds far away on the horizon, and then down at Leo, who has his hand on his hat to keep it from blowing away. Is there a change coming?

"Leo says your father would have done anything for the restaurant," Chiara says.

"I know," I say, sighing. "And that was the whole problem."

Chiara lifts her hand to stop me from speaking. "Your father would have done anything for the restaurant," she says again. "Leo, he would do anything for the people he cares for." Chiara is talking about *us*. About me and Leo as a partnership beyond business. What has she seen? What does she think is going on?

"Anything, huh? Including walking away from Nicky's?" I ask, my eyebrow raised.

"Including that," she says.

LATER, I FIND Leo wandering down the aisle between the two tables, scouting for our seats. I am glad to be back with him, and I thread my arm through his.

"I count four Matteos and three Mias," he says, glancing at my arm as it slides through his. "But no Leo."

We continue walking, the sound of chatting increasing in volume as the guests continue to drink. The warm wind whips up the scent of lavender from the bushes that grow along the stone fence at the foot of the garden. Waiters start to place long wooden platters filled with antipasti on the gaps in the runner and to open bottles of wine.

"Leo," he says triumphantly, before pointing to the seat next to him and grimacing. "Sorry, someone didn't get the memo."

I know before I look that I'll be sitting at a table with the card name *Nicolò*.

"It's fine," I say. "And, Leo, you know how we're not talking about the restaurant or the book today?"

"Dad too?" he says, picking up the name card and shoving it in his pocket.

"Yes, please," I say. "I want to get wedding drunk and wedding dance, happy in the knowledge that I can embarrass myself and never have to see these people again."

Leo laughs, just as a quartet of violins begins a beautiful song, Vivaldi perhaps, designed to usher the guests to their seats.

"I don't want to know what Chiara said to you, do I?" he says, as he pulls out the chair for me.

Leo and I find ourselves placed between couples around our age, and I play *guess the cousin* quietly to myself as we make our introductions. Everyone speaks excellent English except for the Polish partner of the girl to my right, and the pretty Tyrolian who has only just moved to Rome. The conversation is lively and switches between Italian and English with ease.

We eat plates of milky cheese with peppery oils and salty olive tapenades. The wine is a light Pinot Grigio with our antipasto; an odd choice, I think, in a region known for its Sangiovese grapes and its squat-bottled Chianti in straw baskets.

"This is a fresh pairing," says Andrea diplomatically, and I raise my eyebrows in agreement. She introduces herself as a wine merchant from Sienna, and her partner, Luna, owns a small stud farm in the valley.

I notice with a degree of amusement that the couple directly opposite Leo and me are also *freshly paired*, unable to keep their hands off each other. Stopping to kiss in that unashamed way new lovers do, cheeks flushed, bare skin stroked. Leo watches me watching them, and I look away, thinking thoughts of Leo that I'd kept at bay for most of the day.

"Third-cousin love," whispers Leo to me, and I shove him, laughing.

The Chianti comes out with the next course, a mushroom tagliatelle with truffle oil, and then some kind of slow-cooked beef cheek in red wine. I'm surprised there are no speeches, but Leo tells me that will probably happen during the cutting of the three-tiered wedding cake.

By the time the meal is finished, I'm feeling tipsy and pleasantly full, and many people are already milling over onto the stone patio area for dancing. Children hold hands in circles, and a drunk grandfather lifts his little girl up high into the sky while she squeals with delight.

The wind has picked up considerably, meaning the music from the band becomes muted, and then explosively loud as the sound carries with the gusts. Hats fly, and the tablecloth billows.

"What a day to have a storm roll in," I say, trying to tuck my hair behind my ears as Leo slides his grappa onto the table and motions to the dance floor.

"How about it?"

"You want to *dance*?" I say, clocking the slight sway in his stance. He's a little drunk.

"Can you resist this jaunty accordion version of an Ed Sheeran song?" he says.

"Nobody can," I say, nodding to the guests filing onto the floor.

"Come on!"

Leo grabs my hands and pulls me toward the dance floor, passing a far-too-pleased-looking Chiara as we go. The wind blows the lights overhead, which swing dramatically, giving the effect of disco lights flashing, and I pick up the skirt of my dress and dance awkwardly opposite Leo, pumping my fist unenthusiastically in the air as he shuffles from side to side with alarmingly bad rhythm.

"You don't like dancing?" he calls out across the noise.

"I'm shit at dancing," I say, which isn't exactly true, but I feel awkward in this moment. "You know there's going to suddenly be a slow song and we're going to need an escape plan."

"What if I don't want one?" he says, thrusting his hips to the left and right before it slowly dawns on me that he's trying to embarrass me.

"I'm not slow dancing with you. You're a mess," I say, pointing to his outstretched palms, making a weird horse-riding motion in the famous Gangnam Style.

He laughs, snapping himself back into a more dignified groove, his eyes on me as lightning cracks in the distance and thunder follows with a roll so loud, a few people around us flinch.

I move increasingly awkwardly as the man next to me starts to do the Macarena, and I shout, "Wrong song!"

"Let the guy Macarena," Leo says, laughing. "Let him live, for fuck's sake."

I can't help but laugh at myself. I realize I'm being ridiculously uptight.

I hold my finger up to him, make my way quickly to the drinks table, down a grappa, and return to the dance floor, just as the lights dim and a dreamy Italian ballad begins.

"See, I told you this would happen. I swear they plan it that way," I say, hands on my hips. "Shall we back out awkwardly, Macarena back to our seats like it was our plan all along? Two-person conga?"

Leo reaches out and grabs my hand, pulling me in tight with one expert tug.

My body hits his and we are suddenly hip to hip, chest to chest, my heart thumping hard against my rib cage. He lifts my left hand up and tightens the grip on his other around my waist, pulling me even closer, before he whispers into my ear.

"Or we could just keep dancing," he says, with a tipsy grin, his eyes hooded.

"I wouldn't call what you are doing dancing," I say teasingly, as I feel his hips rocking, his moves suddenly feeling expert against my body. My heart kicks harder and I allow myself to fall further into his arms.

Leo's breath hits my ear as he spins me around, and I feel the first drops of rain on my arms. Leo spots them too.

"Not now, storm," he says sharply. "How rude."

"It's not too late to run for cover," I say meekly, my voice strangled and weak.

"Let's have this one dance," he says as he spins me again. "As us." He pulls me in a little closer still, so that all my concerns float away and my body melts into his.

"As Olive and Leo," I say, dreamily imagining he's just a guy I met at a wedding. And not . . . whatever entanglement we do have.

I give in and rest my head against his chest, listening to his heart, as another lightning strike cracks overhead and the heavens start to open. The band, who are sheltering under cover, continue to play as the dance floor heaves with drunken guests, not caring as the rain falls.

"This is completely cheesy," I say, closing my eyes as my dress slowly soaks through, clinging to me. "Dancing in our best clothes in the rain."

"So cheesy," he replies. "And yet . . ."

I look up at him and suddenly our eyes are locked, staring into each other. Leo's shirt clings to his body, the outline of his muscles hard under the soaked cotton. I have never wanted anyone as much as I do him in this moment.

His eyes drop to my lips and I will him to do it. *Kiss me, Leo*, I think, tipping my head back slightly.

"You're too much," he says, his body stiffening against mine, the tension unbearable.

"I'm wet," I reply.

And then he groans a little and pushes his mouth to my ear, dragging his lips across my cheek and then back again. "Tell me more about that," he says.

"Stop it," I say, laughing, putting my hands up on his chest, feeling it tighten under my fingers. There is just this slight, wet fabric between my hands and his smooth skin, I think with longing. I drop my head forward and I bury my face in his neck, breathing in the smell of summer rain and cinnamon and the hint of sweet sweat. It is intoxicating.

"Stop it now," I say more firmly, into his neck.

"It would be messy," he agrees, his nose in my hair, his hot breath doing more than enough to feed the desire that is threatening to overwhelm me.

And then his lips move slowly toward mine. Leo and I are lost in this moment as his lips meet mine in the softest, most gentle kiss. Not even a kiss really, just his lips touching mine, the wet of the rain making everything slick.

He pulls back to look at me, and I'm burning with a desire that I'm willing myself to fight.

"Leonardo!" says a voice from above us on the terrace.

I snap my head up to see Chiara, looking down at us and waving frantically.

"Dai! Come inside!" she calls out. "We move inside. They're cutting the cake!"

"Coming, Zia!" Leo calls, and then he looks down at me again and pulls himself away, tugging on the leg of his pants as he does. I fold my arms around my dress—soaking wet, clinging to every inch of me.

"I'm not done with you," he says. "Whatever happens." He looks up at the house and then nods for me to follow him.

"Leo," I say, panicked. Afraid to leave it like this. "We *can't* do that again. Not before we've gone through the proposal. Before we've closed the door on Nicky's. It's too confusing. *Please*." I wring my hands as his eyes trace the line of my body underneath my soaking dress.

His eyes fix on me, and I watch his face fill with a sudden clarity. He nods.

"Do what?" he says with a wry smile. "We were just dancing. I don't remember a thing."

23

THE NEXT MORNING, I throw open the curtains, make my-self a cup of tea, and settle in to read Leo's proposal.

It was an awkward return home from the wedding, with Leo and me sheepishly heading straight for bed.

"Is a drunken wedding kiss even really a kiss?" he'd said, look-ing at my anxious face as we stood on the landing outside our rooms.

"After that much Limoncello?" I added gratefully.

"On a dance floor," he'd added.

"In the rain," I replied, feeling my heart aching.

"We didn't stand a chance," he said, a timid smile on his face.

I lie back on the bed, thinking about that kiss. How soft his lips were, how alive with desire *I* was. I sigh. And then I flick open the proposal.

The essence of his pitch is a laid-back but chic pasta bar. The kitchen at the rear, opened out with a large surface for rolling out fresh pasta in front of the guests. The bar is shortened, the beer taps removed, the old-fashioned overhang pulled down. The old oak bar top is replaced by cool black-and-white marble, giving it a vintage touch. Outside the tables are small, with chairs facing outward in that classic European sidewalk style.

It's slick. Modern Italian, but with a great old-school feel.

But it isn't just the ideas for renovation that are both surprising and impressive; it's the menu, which is not only simple and delicious. It's quietly designed to make real money.

Pasta. One hundred percent fresh. With several different fillings and sauces to choose from. That is the entire menu, along with sourdough ciabatta and some hand-selected antipasti meats and three desserts. The key to the menu is that pasta is cheap to make, and constantly changing the menu means that although there are only six dishes to choose from, they are always seasonal, and therefore always cost-effective. The meat is slow-cooked, cheaper cuts. No super-pricey aged sirloin. It's smart.

I imagine my dad balking at it. *Where's the bistecca? Where's the osso bucco?*

But Leo is right. Dining in London is changing, and people don't want these heavy, homely, traditional meaty meals like they used to. Pasta can be vegan. Pasta can be light. Pasta is *always* delicious. The new furnishings will create more atmospheric sound, introducing a vibrant, lively feel so that going out for a meal feels like going fucking out.

This is a restaurant you can go to for a good time and an inexpensive meal that is so delicious, you'd be happy to queue for a table.

Which brings me to his final idea: no bookings. A risky business that shows an almost arrogant self-belief while remaining accessible for all.

I groan. It's good. It's not perfect. I'm not sure about the blandness of the interiors. I think we need something else warm on the menu: a daily special of Tuscan bean stew or even a soup. Not everyone likes pasta. The fools.

I put down the proposal and gaze at Leo from the window as he manages a few laps with great vigor and then runs quickly out of steam. This is good, I think. Hang on to these imperfections, Olive. You can make them bigger, make them an issue. You're an Olympic champion in finding the *ick*. This is your moment. But as I watch him lift himself up and sit on the edge of the pool, the water cascading off his bare torso, I have to retreat back to bed to recover from the flawlessness of him.

I'm feeling more confused than ever when my phone buzzes. It's Ginny.

"Dude, I'm really in trouble," I open.

"Sexy trouble?" says Ginny, sounding unhelpfully excited.

"Leo gave me a proposal for what he'd do to the restaurant. And it is really, really good, Ginny. And smart."

"That's a good thing, isn't it?"

"I was kind of hoping it would be terrible," I say. "It would make everything easier. You know, I could sell up and then when he forgave me, maybe we could even date?" My voice is pitiful.

"You want your cake," she says. "Fair enough. Cake is *good*."

"I can't have the cake," I say. "No matter how I slice it, I can't have the damn cake. I can't keep the restaurant and start a business with Leo *and* start a relationship too. It can't be done."

Ginny laughs, lowering her voice. "Olive, you really like him, right?"

"I really do."

"And you're sure he feels the same?" Ginny asks.

I think about the wedding. Then, I think about his erection in the bathroom.

"I'm pretty sure," I say, clearing my throat. "And I'm pretty sure he's as concerned as I am about acting on it."

I groan into my hands. "I want someone to tell me what to do. I can't talk to my mum about any of this. *You're* far too reckless..."

"Hey!"

"You're like the romantic equivalent of a bungee jump," I say. "And Kate is too sensible. She has checklists."

"What's stopping you from making big decisions in your life?" Ginny asks, her voice soft and gentle.

"Fear of getting it wrong."

"And if you got it wrong..."

"Catastrophe. Loneliness. Mess. Horror. Cataclysmic-end-of-the-world-type feelings."

"Well, that's just ridiculous," she says. "The worst-case scenario is that you ... um, I dunno ..."

"Fuck Leo and keep the restaurant. The restaurant fails, I lose loads of money, and Leo takes me to an employment tribunal because I shagged an employee."

"Or," Ginny says brightly, "you end up with an amazing business, with a partner you love, who is also your business partner."

"The first feels more likely," I say.

"Why don't you want to speak to your mum?"

"She has a negative opinion of hospitality, and a negative opinion of Nicky's," I say, sighing, gazing down again at Leo, who is unhelpfully applying suntan oil across his muscular golden arms in broad, slick strokes.

"She might surprise you," she says.

"Maybe," I say, walking into the shared bathroom, checking to make sure Leo's door is secure.

"Take the leap," Ginny says. "If you want to be with Leo, you should be with Leo. If you want to keep the restaurant, you should keep the restaurant."

"When did I become such a wimp?" I say, looking hard at myself in the mirror.

"When there were real stakes," she says.

AFTER PACING MY room for a while, I can no longer resist the urge to call my mother. She has been my counsel my whole life, and I need her.

She is folding towels when I call, a practice that felt like a dark art when I was growing up. *"No, that's a bath towel, Olive. Nope. That's downstairs toilet. Face, not the hands. Those are the guest towels. No one should be using those."*

I would learn later that guest towels had a hierarchy too. There were guests worthy of the guest towels, but not *all* guests. I reflect on my mum's incredible organizational skills and wonder how the hell she ever put up with Dad.

"Olive," she says brightly. "Is everything okay?"

"Yes, yes." I take in a big breath.

"Yes," she says, before covering the phone with her hand to speak to George, even though we're on a video call. *"You need to wash those bike shorts, George, you can't just keep wearing them. No. They're full of bacteria in the crotch area. Do they help with the chafing or not? Put some of that cream on."*

"I can call back?" I say, recoiling from my phone.

"No, darling," she says to me, and then, off the receiver again, she says, *"Earl Grey. But just a dash of nonfat milk this time. Stop trying to push the oat milk on me!"* I hear the throaty chortle of a man off-screen and then the sound of a door pushing shut.

It is weirdly reassuring to hear Mum asserting herself in her relationship with George. I'd worried, at times, that Dad was too big for her, and she'd shrunk too much.

"Oat milk!" she says to me, aghast, clutching a gray hand towel to her heart.

"It's really good. And better for the environment," I say, my mind wandering to Leo's menu and wondering how we could incorporate a greener footprint into the proposal.

"George has an electric bike." This is my mother's comeback to any hint that she could change her boomer ways.

"Speaking of bikes, I fell into a nettle bush the other day," I say.

"Well. That's never fun."

"I was thinking about what you used to say. Time and bravery," I say.

"Oh!" she says, raising her hand to her chest. "I loved your little brave face, Olive. Your lips all screwed up and a big line between your brows." She tuts and then sighs at the sweet memory. "It's a terrible thing to say, but the upside to any of your daily bonks and beestings was always that I got to see that little determined face. Determined to be brave."

"Sadist," I tease, and Mum chuckles, smoothing a facecloth before rolling it and placing it in a little basket.

"I've been thinking about Nicky's, Mum."

There is a small, barely perceptible gasp.

"Yes?" she says, stiffly.

"The chef, Leo, he's given me a proposal for what he would have done with the place, and . . . it's kind of upended me a little." I stand up and pace back and forth in the room.

"I see," she says, sighing.

"What do you think?" I ask, chewing on the side of my

thumbnail, sending prayers to the heavens that I'm not upsetting her.

"What. Do. I. Think," she says, repeating the words slowly to herself.

"Yes," I say.

There is another long pause.

"Are you seriously considering it?" she says.

"Not *seriously*," I lie.

The silence on Mum's end of the phone tells me she's thinking about her next words very carefully. I watch her as she nods slowly to herself.

"It's not completely crazy," she says. "You'd be good at it. *My* problems with Nicky's largely came from your father. You know the story, Olive. It was his way or the highway."

"But if it was differently set up . . . ," I begin.

"If you remove the small matter of the chef being such a blinkered creative tour de force? Or Pol Pots and Pans, as I used to call him." She pauses to consider her next words. "Then running a restaurant is rewarding. *Very* hard work, mind," she adds with serious warning.

I hear the shower turn on in the bathroom, and I lower my voice.

"I know, I know," I whisper quickly.

"This is a big decision, Olive. You need to talk to creditors, to the bank, to the estate attorney. You need good suppliers. Preferably not friends like your father had. Someone who understands how to set up a menu," she says.

"Like I said. I'm not seriously considering it."

Another pregnant pause. Mum can usually tell when I'm lying, but I hope like hell she can't right now.

"Anyway, it's too big of a project for me," I say, trying to laugh.

"I hope *that* isn't what's stopping you."

"It's not," I say, shaking my head a little too vigorously. "Forget about it, Mum. I just got the proposal and it made me pause, that's all."

"Because, Olive, it's not *that* big. You break it down into small steps. Plan everything. You just need to take your time, do the research, and then . . . leap of faith."

Time and bravery, I think to myself.

AFTER AN HOUR of attempting to write about our bike ride, and then fussing over the draft of my Catania story, I head downstairs to find Leo flicking through the channels on the TV with a bottle of wine. When he sees me, he turns it off.

"You can watch something," I say, picking up the open bottle and making my way toward the kitchen to get a glass. "Don't mind me. I'm just looking for wine."

Leo springs up to help.

"Stay put," I say. "You look relaxed."

"That I am," he says, sitting back down, before shooting me a look. "*Mostly.*"

The proposal. My heart squeezes. I am going to have to give him something.

"I've read it," I say quickly.

"And?"

"It's good. You *know* it's good," I say, smiling wryly. "You could probably get investment to start it yourself somewhere."

"That's my plan B," he shoots back, plucking a kalamata olive from a small ceramic bowl before placing his drink back down on the coffee table.

Must not give him too much hope.

"I don't want to drag this out," I say. "But I do need time to think it through, talk to some people, and I have a *lot* of questions."

"Why don't we go over it together?" he says. "I could cook for you. Some of the dishes? I know we're going to Liguria in a few days, and we should make time to do it before we get to Roger's."

My dad's best friend, Roger. Another emotional tidal wave to get through.

"Yeah. Let's do that," I say, nodding. "You cook for me, I'll get my questions together, and at the very least I can give you real, thorough feedback."

I reach for my glass and smile to myself.

"You're considering it!" he exclaims. Then he narrows his eyes on me. "Aren't you? This isn't a no. I think if it was a no you'd tell me right away."

"It's not a yes," I say, folding my arms, feeling myself tense.

"Sorry," he says, raising both his hands. "I want you to know, it won't change what I think of you, Olive, if you decide to sell."

I look over at him and smile gratefully. Although I'm not sure it's true. How can it be?

"I wonder what Dad had in mind," I say wistfully, staring out the huge windows into the darkening sky outside. "Was it as simple as, if he gives me the restaurant, I drop everything and take it over?"

Leo leans forward.

"You asked me once if your dad ever talked about you," he says. "And I want you to know that he did. Olive, he had a folder of all your press clippings in the office. He framed that one you wrote about Le Grappa. He used to read lines out from it all the time. One line I will never forget: 'Le Grappa is cosplaying as an Italian eatery wearing cheap Prada knockoffs.'"

I wince, and then my breath catches in my throat as the information starts to sink in.

"And he . . ." Leo stops for a moment, seeming to consider whether he should continue talking.

"Go on," I say.

"He had a picture of you next to the red kitchen clock."

"He did?"

"Yeah," Leo says, laughing. "You were so cute. You had these long plaits. I think you were like ten or something. He used to say that you would come back." Leo stares at me, catching the look of grief that threatens to overwhelm me.

"Why didn't he tell *me*?" I say, my voice cracking slightly, but I wrestle my emotions and steady myself.

"I don't know," he says, shrugging.

"He called, I mean, we spoke and whatever. I did see him sometimes. I know he asked me to the restaurant, and I never went, but it felt like a betrayal to my mother to step foot in there. Why didn't he do more to, like, I don't know, spend time with me? Connect with me as an adult away from the fucking restaurant?"

"Maybe he didn't call enough. But you were always there," he says. "Right next to the clock."

"Christ, that's so infuriating," I say.

"I felt like he was waiting for you," he says, squeezing his lips together. "I'll probably wake up tomorrow and regret saying it. But you should know how much he loved you, in case . . ."

"In case I want to walk away because I think he didn't care."

"Yes," he says. "He did care. So much so that I thought it was *you* who broke *his* heart."

He leans forward, reaching out his hand as he places it over mine, and I sit for a moment, letting him comfort me while I process. I push the wine away, unable to stomach any more.

"Thanks," I say, finally.

I remove my hand from under his, but he leaves his there for a moment, fingers outstretched. The smallest physical hint that he doesn't want me to go.

24

W HAT IS THIS one?" I ask, holding up an enormous pear-shaped tomato.

"For saucing," the stall owner says. "Pera d'Abruzzo."

Leo took a quick trip to the market to gather ingredients for his proposal dinner tonight, and I've been ordered back to pick up the forgotten tomatoes. Of all the things to forget.

But this afternoon I was happy to disappear and let the ideas in his proposal percolate before I speak to him. So on the bicycle I climbed, and to the little food market in the square I have come. But "Can you pick up some tomatoes?" has turned into quite a chore.

"The classic Tuscan tomato," the stall owner says, handing me two other specimens.

"I'm going to need to call the chef," I reply, holding up my phone. "Grazie, grazie. Un momento. Mio amico."

The stall owner nods as I hit Leo's number.

"Leo," I say sharply into the phone, "there are about four million types of bloody tomatoes and I really need more information. This isn't your classic cherry or vine or beefsteak tomato scenario."

"Datterini and some cuore di bue," he says, laughing. "I can talk to the stall owner."

"I can handle it," I say defiantly, hanging up. Leo is going to properly cook for me tonight, and it's probably the final piece of this puzzle. I know he can cook, but can he set my soul on fire?

I return with a basket filled with tomatoes to Leo cooking. I watch him as I haul the basket up onto the dining table.

"Is it safe to come in and make a coffee?" I call out.

"Not really," he says, laughing. "I *can* put one on for you, though."

He slides his knife onto the countertop, stirring something on the stove. I see the pasta roller is out and clipped to the benchtop. I pull out the seat and watch him work for a bit.

"I got every kind of tomato possible," I call out, as he fills the stove-top espresso machine and places it carefully on the gas stove. "Cupido, Piccadilly, pomodoro, the list goes on."

"Bene, bene," he says, looking up at me and laughing. It's hard to concentrate on tomatoes when I look at him. It's hard to concentrate on anything, especially when he's dressed like that. All in black but for a frilly floral apron that he's clearly found tucked away in some drawer. I need to go and write.

"I'm gonna head upstairs and hit the keyboard with my head. What time will we start?"

"Six?" he says, emerging from the kitchen holding a coffee and side-eyeing the enormous pile of tomatoes with a grin.

"I also got cherries. See you in a few hours?" I say, and he nods confidently.

"I'll be ready."

"WE WOULD ONLY have a couple of in-season starters," Leo says, laying a plate of fried courgette flower and goat's cheese in front of me. "The tempura is more like the Japanese style, superlight. The honey would be field honey, to keep with the spring and summer theme."

He taps the edge of the plate. The presentation is simple and elegant, and it looks delicious.

"I love it," I say. "Although I have to admit, I was expecting something a bit more ostentatious."

"You're missing the micro herbs and reduced honey foam after all, Olive?" he says, sitting opposite me, folding his arms, tea towel tossed over his shoulder. "As you know, I *can* be restrained when I need to be."

I raise a suggestive eyebrow, and he laughs at me. It's too easy to fall into this flirtatious banter with him, but I can't. I mustn't.

"So, you say in the proposal you would do this alongside an ever-changing antipasti platter. One vegan, one meat. And then just the six pasta mains?"

"Yes. And I think we should pull a few from original dishes from Nicky's. The famous mushroom tortellini, for example," he says, pointing at me.

"It's not still on the menu, is it?" I say, thinking back to me and Dad rolling our little parcels all those years ago.

"It sure is. Still called Olive's tortellini too," he says.

"Oh man." I shake my head, laughing, while I dive my fork into the courgette and my mouth explodes with the sweet honey and the salty cheese.

Leo serves wine from the cellar, an incredibly savory Monteraponi with notes of saffron and capers. Then he brings out a rustic bowl of tomato soup.

"You know, I think this dish works well for the cookbook, as well as a potential dish for Nicky's," he says, sliding it in front of me. "It ticks all your boxes, I think."

"What are my boxes?" I ask, tipping my head to the side.

"Authentic, inexpensive, and unfussy," he says.

I nod. It's true. Those *are* my boxes. "Tomatoes, leftover bread, good olive oil, garlic," I say. *Delicious.*

"What do you think?" says Leo as he tips a little more wine into my glass.

"I can't find much to critique," I say, smirking, as I spoon mouthfuls of the soup.

"That was actually my mamma's recipe," he says. "Using Chiara's heritage tomatoes. But we can do a really low price point on that."

"Well then. Good for Nicky's and straight into the cookbook," I say. "Like I said the other day, I do miss something fresh on the menu. A salad or some simple beans. Just a couple of options."

"I agree," he says, emerging from the kitchen with a very basic tomato salad. Not a panzanella, just fresh-cut tomatoes—and all the shapes and colors from green through to yellow and red. Torn basil and a simple dressing of oil and balsamic. A few sprinkled crushed, roasted hazelnuts and pine nuts finish off the dish.

He's thinking, adapting, listening to me.

"You didn't do any kind of budget for the renovations," I say, as I fish the last slice of tomato from the dish.

"I have to hold my hands up and say I don't know enough about that," he says. "Those ideas are just ideas."

"Right." I think, wondering about Ginny's capacity to take a look for me. If ever there was a time to have an interior architect as a friend, it's now.

"Cacio e pepe," Leo explains, as he brings out one of the pasta dishes. "Another low price point, and a dish we can expand with fresh truffles when the season allows. The dish is spun into a perfect round, finished with large wide flakes of shaved Parmesan."

"I like this presentation," I say, taking a mouthful of the pasta. "God, this is incredible. How did you get such a deep peppery flavor into the pasta?"

"I infused it," he says, taking his own forkful.

My jaw drops in mock amusement. "Fuck off," I say, reaching for more.

"I did, I added some white pepper to the pasta itself, and then a little bag of peppercorns to the cooking water," he explains, with a smug look on his pretty face. "I *infused* the flavor."

"It does not anger me," I say, rolling my eyes.

"Good," he says, laughing.

"I can see the vision," I say, smiling. "Let's talk about the interior."

I open the printed proposal and turn to the page with the renovation sketches.

"Honestly, you should leave the bar the size it is now," I say, pointing to the row of three tables on the sketch where the bar currently is.

"Why? It takes up so much room where we could put tables. More tables, more covers."

"But a bar adds *so much* to the atmosphere," I say. "People waiting for tables, enjoying a drink. Booze markup is always good. Makes the place feel buzzy and busy."

"Except that it never happens," says Leo.

"It will if the food is this good," I say, waving my fork around the table.

Leo grins. "I see." But before he has a chance to say any more, I hold up my finger to stop him.

"I *can* see it, Leo," I say, closing the proposal and putting my hand on top of it. "I can see it. And I *do* like it." I sigh, tipping my head to the side, wondering what to say next.

"So, what now?" he says.

"I don't know. I need to talk to people. Talk to the bank, a solicitor," I say. "My mum properly. Take a big breather and sit around in my flat in London and think about it away from here, from you and all of this. I need to look at this from every angle."

"More time," he says, nodding in understanding.

"It's not a no, Leo," I say, seriously. "But it's not a yes either. You get that, right?"

"It's progress," he says, putting his fork down, grinning. "But seriously. I get it. I'm happy that you were open enough to listen to my ideas. That first night at Nicky's when I bumped into you in the darkness, I thought—"

"*Who even is this bitch?*" I say, laughing.

"No," he says, folding his arms on the table, leaning toward me. "I thought, holy shit, that's Nicky's girl. I've heard so much about her, and now here she is. You were almost like a ghost to me. Everywhere I looked: Olive."

"I didn't think he cared," I say, shaking my head.

Leo shrugs and then frowns. "You do what you need to do, Olive. I mean it."

I stare at him, searching his eyes for bullshit, but it isn't there.

"Dessert?" I say, breaking the moment, looking hungrily toward the kitchen.

"I'm afraid I couldn't quite manage that. But shall we take it outside and watch the sun go down?" he suggests, and I nod, scooping up our wineglasses in one hand and the bottle in the other.

IT IS SPECTACULAR, the golden glow lighting up the patio in a shimmer. Leo has managed to find a sheet of paper that explains how to connect our phones to the outside speakers and tasked me with finding some music while he fills our glasses.

"I know we're not celebrating," he assures me. "But I feel good. Do you feel good?"

"I feel good," I say, smiling. "Shall I put on an album, or hit shuffle?"

"Shuffle is always dangerous," he says.

"I'm not afraid to live dangerously," I reply, hitting shuffle, waiting anxiously until an old Prince track comes on. I smirk across at him.

"Lucky break," he says. "I wouldn't want to be you every four minutes for the next hour."

"You're revealing more about your own shuffle," I say, too stubborn to put an album on now.

Leo laughs and then sits back in his chair, letting out a big sigh. "I'm pretty wiped out. It's some bloody pressure cooking for Olive fucking Stone."

"It was good, my friend," I say, tipping my glass in his direction. "Five forks out of five."

"I've never wanted to be forked so much in my life," he says as we stare out across the valley at the last flame of red on the horizon.

"Fork off," I say, stealing a glance his way and grinning. "Ooh, can I bring out the chilled cherries in the icebox?"

"Yes, please," he says, waving a hand as he kicks his sandals off.

While I'm inside, I take a moment, checking my hair in the mirror in the hall. I talk to myself. Remind myself that this is *Leo. Don't get carried away. Things are still complicated.* I take a breath. "Be cool, bitch," I say into the mirror.

"Cherry?" I say, returning with the brown paper bag.

"Please," he says, grabbing the bag from me and taking a handful.

I toy with a cherry against my lips for a moment, and Leo watches me as I bite it in half. It's sweet, tart, and fat, with juicy bloodred flesh. I look down at my stained fingers. Try in vain to remove the red color by sucking the tip of each finger.

Leo clears his throat, then reaches forward to take a cherry, lifting two, holding them above his mouth, before dropping the first one in whole. Then the second. I watch as he chews them, red juice running down the side of his mouth, which he clears with the edge of his tongue. The whole thing is extremely erotic, and I feel the return of want. Whenever there is silence between Leo and me, the vastness of my desire begins to call out.

"Leo," I say, shaking my head. "I've had *almost* enough wine to find you eating cherries kinda hot."

Leo turns his head slowly, his eyes rising to meet mine. "Almost enough?" he says teasingly. He reaches for the bottle and tops me up, pouring slowly. Deliberately.

I almost shoot back something daring. Witty. Heavily flirtatious. But I stop myself, turning from Leo's gaze and staring out into the darkening night.

"I had this memory in Sicily of eating oranges in the sea. It was so the juice could run down your face, straight into the water," I say. "No sticky fingers."

I stand up and take my glass to the pool area, the soft lighting underneath the water giving the whole pool an otherworldly blue glow. The stone is still warm against my bare feet. I bring the bag of cherries with me. "Come on, Leo," I say.

He stands, removing his shirt and joining me with our wine. He sets the glasses on the side of the pool next to the cherries and then dives straight in.

"That was well needed," he says, emerging from the water, brushing his hair backward.

I point to the darkness beyond the edge of the pool and motion for him to turn around.

I lift my sundress up and toss it back toward the table, left in my black knickers and bra, and lower myself in. Then I turn to the brown paper bag full of cherries and hold two out to Leo. He swims over, and we stand, leaning against the stone, letting the bloodred juice run down our chins and into the water.

The fairy lights bathe our faces in a warm yellow glow.

"See," I say, tonguing a cherry and dropping it into my mouth.

"It's a life hack," he says, finishing his wine. Leo rests his arms on the side of the pool and frowns like he wants to say something. But instead, he picks up another cherry, spinning the stem between his fingers.

One move here, and it's all over.

Mazzy Star's "Fade into You" comes on over the speakers; her tender voice and gentle acoustic guitar throw a deep, beautiful banket across us. It's achingly romantic, the candlelight, the starry sky. Leo.

"Shuffle," he says, as her voice guides us closer together, just inches from each other.

"It's always a risky game," I say as her voice sails above us. "It can really ruin a party."

Leo's eyes are all over my shoulders, my neck. Everywhere. And then after a moment they settle on mine, our faces lit by the silvery blue of the pool, then drop to my mouth. I feel my lips start to tingle under his gaze, and I move my tongue forward to wet them. Leo's eyes trail from my mouth back to my eyes.

I want this.

I close my eyes, and I feel his lips touch mine. They are warm, and his kiss is gentle, light as a feather, but my entire body reacts immediately, like an electric shock has jolted through me. The smallest of moans escapes my lips, and Leo reaches up to my cheek, his hand moving behind my head, fingers tangling through my hair as the pressure of his kiss increases. His tongue gently teases my mouth open and I respond by reaching my hands around his neck and pressing my body into his.

I can feel his breath quicken as he kisses me, more hungrily now. He moves his hands down to my hips, pulling me closer into him, grinding into me.

"Olive," he says into my neck, a hand now reaching up again, tugging on my wet hair.

His voice and my name bring me back into the moment, and I pull back, ready to stop, but then . . . I look at him. I take a deep breath and really look. I reach up and run my finger around the curl of hair that has fallen forward across his brows. A small line of concern has formed between them, his eyes darting between mine, waiting hungrily, nervously, for my green light. Beads of water on his shoulders catch the light like glitter, and it feels impossible to do anything but give in completely.

"Upstairs. *Now*," I say.

His face sags with relief as he looks skyward and then back down to me, grinning, pulling me tightly against him into another deep kiss.

We break apart and are out of the pool quickly, Leo following me as I open the sliding door into the house, leaving damp footprints on the stone tiles as we race toward the stairs. We arrive on the cool upstairs landing and he pulls me in hungrily again.

"Your place or mine," I say into his mouth, but he's already dragging me toward his bedroom. This is what I want. What *I* want.

Leo kicks the door shut behind us and then leans into me against the wall, stares into my eyes, searching my face. "You're beautiful," he says.

"Stop it," I say, laughing lightly as he puts his hand on my throat and drags it down my body, leaving a trail of sparkling heat in its wake.

"You want me to stop?" he says, grinning as he moves his hand toward my breast, pulling my damp bra gently aside, the cool air stiffening its peak immediately. I feel my eyes roll backward at the pleasure, and my knees weaken in anticipation. He lifts my chin up with his hand as he looks into my eyes. "I can't believe you want me as much as I want you," he says hoarsely.

"What are you waiting for?" I ask, my hands on his chest, my fingers sliding easily against his damp skin and around his neck to pull him down to me for a kiss.

Then he lifts me up and I wrap my legs around his waist. "I told you I wasn't done with you yet," he says with a small laugh as he kisses my neck, his arms holding my thighs in place as he pushes me back into the wall.

I grasp for purchase, angling myself higher against his hips as he frees a hand to pull down on my bra, pinching my nipple so I cry out and arch my back in delight. Leo laughs, deep and husky, into my ear as I do.

He palms my breast and studies me again for a moment, stroking his hand upward to my neck, kissing me tenderly, biting my top lip gently. I can feel his smile against my mouth.

Then we're moving again, and he carries me over to the bed. Leo lies beside me, head propped on his hand as his eyes hungrily peruse my body. I watch his pupils dilate, my breath quickening in tandem with his. When he finally touches me I gasp, his fingers cool against the heat of my belly. He trails them down my stomach, down between my legs, and strokes me with his thumb through the lacy fabric of my underwear, while kissing my collarbone in fluttery, gentle kisses.

I close my eyes and moan, pressing both palms against the headboard so I can move myself closer to his hand. He teases me through my underwear until I groan in frustration, pulling a throaty chuckle from him. Finally, he pushes the fabric of my knickers aside, and when he slides a finger inside me, I feel like a dam about to burst.

I want to scream out and very nearly do, turning my head to bite at his shoulder.

"Please," I say, breathless, unable to get the words out.

"Let go," he says, pausing to kiss the spot on my neck just below my ear.

I feel his hard cock press into my thigh while he works me with expert strokes until I am on the very edge.

"I want more," I say, pulling on his arms, anything I can grab. He climbs on top of me, taking the tip of my nipple into his mouth so my back bows, and he slides his free hand underneath me to the curve in my lower back.

Leo tugs my knickers down fast, and then his own boxer shorts until he is gloriously naked on top of me, still damp and glistening from the pool. His skin is as soft and warm as I could have imagined. I feel him pushing against me, the sensation electric. With both hands I pull his face to mine, kissing him deeply, willing him to hurry the hell up.

And he does, moaning once, deeply, against my shoulder as he slides in. A feeling that reverberates through my body, a sizzling, sparking sensation at each point that our skin touches. And when he begins to move I groan, my hand scratching up his back and plunging into his hair, tugging his lips toward mine.

He reaches down and hooks his arm under one of my legs, kissing my knee as he enters me slowly.

"Oh, that's good," I say breathlessly. It's relief and desire all at once as my mind scatters in all directions like billiards after the cracking of a cue ball.

"Are you okay?" he says, his voice ragged.

"I want more," I say.

He moves faster then, pulling my hips up off the bed so he can move deeper inside me, and it's all I can do to stop myself from screaming.

"More," I say as he moves faster, taking me to the very edge before I open my eyes, and the look on his face is so wicked, so delirious, so hot, I am finally, breathlessly, hopelessly undone.

Leo rolls off me and we both lie naked, sweaty, our hair still damp, our hearts racing, as the breeze drifts in through the window, cooling our skin. He reaches out, putting a hand on my stomach, his fingers fanning out and holding me in place.

"How long have I got?" he says.

"Until what?" I reply, putting my hand on his, threading our fingers, feeling the rise and fall of my breath start to slow.

"Until you worry," he says, squeezing my hand.

I laugh, rolling onto my side and running my fingers down his chest, resting my hand on his rib cage.

"At least until sunrise," I say.

25

I T ISN'T QUITE sunrise when I begin to worry.

His arm is across my stomach, and I try to lift it slowly without waking him. But he stirs.

"Bathroom," I whisper.

"Come back to me," he moans softly and rolls over.

My heart squeezes as I pull myself slowly up.

I find my bra on the floor and my bunched-up knickers near the window.

"Olive," he says, sounding more awake. "Come here."

"I need the—"

"You're clearly sneaking off," he says, laughing as he rolls over and holds his arm out toward me. I glance out his window and down to the pool area.

It looks a little like a crime scene where two people vanished. Piles of clothes sit outside where we cast them off. Two wineglasses, one toppled over. A wine bottle. The bag of half-eaten cherries has been mauled by something, leaving a bloodred stain on the stone.

I wanted this.

"Olive," he says again, and I don't resist, walking back over and climbing in next to him.

"Was this a terrible idea?"

"No. It was an excellent idea," he says, kissing my shoulder, his featherlight touch disintegrating my thoughts.

"Why do I feel like it was?" I say quietly. In the stillness of the early morning I hear the first birds beginning to chirp and the threat of a new day, filled with time to panic.

Leo props himself up onto his elbow and pulls the light blanket over me, tucking me in. "So you can't get away," he says with a grin. Then he strokes the side of my cheek and says, "Talk to me."

"Can you see how this complicates everything?"

"Yes," he says, nodding.

"It must be the dumbest, most stupid idea in the world to get into business with someone with whom you are romantically entangled."

"You're thinking about the business seriously?" he says.

I nod. "I am. I have been. I've been so worried about getting your hopes up, though. There are a lot of hurdles. I've never run a restaurant. I couldn't expect to walk in and be an open-heart surgeon just 'cause my dad was."

"You'll be fine," he says. "I mean, you could do some courses while we plan. I do know quite a lot about how to run Nicky's. I ran every area at some point. I just didn't have the authority to change anything."

"But now we've slept together. What if . . . ," I trail off.

Leo nods. "People do it all the time. Fall in love and work with their partners."

Fall in love?

I swallow. "What if it turns sour?"

"Can you try to imagine a reality where it only gets better?"

"It's a fantasy."

"It's not," he says, his brows descending as he places his hand gently on my belly. "Look at Rocco and Isabella, for one. Small family businesses have kept the world turning since forever."

I need to speak to Kate, I think.

"I don't do well in relationships, Leo. I am a faultfinder. I get the ick easily."

"Well now, that's a challenge," he says, grinning. And then he puts his hand on my face and turns me toward him. "Olive. Tell me this isn't special. Tell me you haven't been wanting to do this since the first night in Catania."

"Definitely not on the first night," I say, laughing. "Or the second. Perhaps things started to change when you bought me a macchiato. You know the way to a girl's heart."

Leo puts his hands under the blanket and turns my whole body toward him so we are lying face-to-face, inches apart. He kisses my nose. My cheek. My chin.

"It took you a while too, right?" I say.

Leo laughs, pulling back to look at me.

"The first thing I thought when I saw you was that you were hot and, thankfully, you looked nothing like your dad. The second thing I thought was, truthfully, that you were vacuum sealed."

"Vacuum sealed?"

"Yes, that you were holding everything so tightly inside, you might burst. You wouldn't accept my help. So fucking stubborn."

I laugh, blushing at the memory. "I was so nervous."

"I get that now," he says.

I smile at him and kiss him on the mouth.

"I should have reached out more. You think your parents are going to live forever," I say.

"He didn't fight hard enough for you," he says more firmly. "I wish I understood why."

He reaches around me and pulls me closer, our naked bodies flush against each other.

"Leo, do you really think we could do it?" I ask again. "Explore rebuilding Nicky's? Would you be able to take it if I said it was too hard? Too expensive? If I pulled out at the eleventh hour?"

"Yes," he says, nodding decisively. "Will you tell me when I'm getting carried away? Because I've never run my own kitchen." He grimaces. "But I'm ready. I'm so ready."

"If I knew you'd listen," I say.

"I promise," he says. "Come on. Let's enjoy our time together here. London is so far away. Nicky's is so far away. I want to enjoy you, in Italy, without any distractions."

"Erm . . . you know we have a book to finish," I say, grumbling at him.

But Leo disappears under the bedsheets and kisses his way gently down my body. "I can't hear you," he says as he pulls my thigh around his head and buries his face into me.

Later, utterly spent, my body like jelly, I do manage to sneak out of bed and head downstairs for an outside shower. I want to speak to Kate.

ME: SOS. Can we speak before you go to work?

Kate calls back just as Leo emerges into the lounge downstairs looking sleepy and delicious in nothing but a pair of gray boxers.

"Hi, give me a minute while I go upstairs," I whisper to Kate.

As I pass Leo, he reaches out a hand to pull me in, but I dance around it, smiling at him.

"I just have to take this," I say.

Leo frowns. "Don't freak out," he pleads.

I stop, turn, and kiss him, hard. "I won't," I say.

I rush upstairs, closing the door behind me, and make sure the door to the bathroom is secure before I fall onto my bed, lying on my stomach with my head in one hand.

"Don't freak out?" Kate says, having heard the exchange.

"We did it," I say breathlessly.

"What are you, *sixteen*? You *did it*?" Kate says, shutting the door to her office. I am suddenly wishing I called Ginny, but I know I need the hard talk right now. And the hard talk only comes from Kate.

"I gave in to temptation."

"I'm not a priest, honey," Kate says, laughing. "Sounds like the ship of good intentions has sailed."

"It sailed multiple wonderful times."

"Well, *that's* impressive," she says. "Sounds like quite the sailor."

"He certainly knows his way around the stern," I say, the hairs on my arms standing up as I hazily recall him kissing his way up the backs of my thighs.

"You've lost me. What end is the stern?" Kate says, laughing.

"Kate. I love his ideas for the restaurant," I say, my voice serious.

"I see," she replies.

"And I just had the best shag of my life," I say, holding a hand to my heart. "And I like him, Kate. I'm not just attracted to him.

I like *him*. I like Leo. He's sexy and funny and kind and playful. He works really fucking hard. He's loyal as hell. He loves his family."

"Oh shit," she says.

"I'm freaking out, Kate. Freaking out," I say. "I have started imagining the two of us working together and it feels exciting, like spring-out-of-bed-at-five-a.m. exciting . . ."

"The bed you'd likely share with him," Kate reminds me.

"Exactly. It *terrifies* me."

"Okay, that's a *little* dramatic," Kate says. "If you did end up together and try to work on a business together, you wouldn't be the first couple in the world to do that."

"Leo said that," I point out.

"Tight contracts, clear objectives. You can legal paperwork the hell out of it in case it all turns to shit."

"I keep thinking . . . am I gonna end up like my mum?"

"What do you mean?"

"She started out all in love and excited about working with this man, her *husband*," I say. "And then she ended up miserable. And forgotten. And sidelined. Would that be my future?"

"You can't tar Leo with your dad's pastry brush," says Kate. "Besides, you'd own the restaurant, Olive. If anything, Leo is the one in danger of being sidelined."

"And what about the cost? The fucking investment I'd need to make in the renovations? The place needs so much work, Kate. And what if I don't have what it takes? What if Leo doesn't?"

"Sounds like a list of things to figure out, not necessarily roadblocks," she says, a little wearily. "Are you sure about this, Olive?"

"No, that's why I'm calling you. To tell me I'm being stupid," I say, exasperated.

But Kate is quiet on the other end, so I keep speaking, the fears falling out of me, hard and fast, like a summer rain shower.

"I've not seen him run a kitchen. I don't know what kind of boss he is to the staff. I don't know if I'd actually like to have my own business. There is so much I don't know. It's all too big. And then there's the fucking cookbook I'm supposed to be doing."

"How's that going?"

"It's okay but it needs my attention. I need to write three achingly beautiful stories like the ones my dad wrote. Heartfelt stories about the regions and all my feels about the food, and at the moment all I can think about is how good it feels to be underneath Leo fucking Ricci."

"Okay," says Kate, breathing out slowly and then laughing gently. Kindly. "Let's breathe, Olive. One thing at a time."

"I feel like I'm already toying with him. I can't give him an answer to the restaurant question, not *properly*."

Kate tuts. "Olive, listen. You need to go downstairs and tell Leo how you feel. Tell him you have feelings for him and then tell him that you need some serious space to finish the book and then look at the restaurant. You need to take one step at a time. If he is any kind of good man, he will wait."

I make a kind of whimpering noise.

"No, you can't hide your feelings away from this one, Olive. You need to say it straight," she says. "Leo is active in all of this too."

"Fine," I say, looking over at my father's urn. "Damn, some-times I wonder if my dad knew all this would happen."

Kate laughs. "That you'd end up in bed with his sous chef?"

"No. *Ewww*," I say. "I mean that if I spent time with Leo that I might consider coming back to Nicky's."

"Go talk to Leo," she says. "Cookbook first, then you'll need to do a lot of research and talking to the right people before you can begin to think about the restaurant."

"Okay," I say, nodding.

"And for god's sake tell him how you feel about him."

I skulk down the stairs pulling on a dressing gown and look around for Leo. The sun is out, and Leo is lying on a sun lounger with a coffee next to him, reading an old magazine. I wander out, slowly, nervously, and take a seat next to him.

He sits up, shading his eyes from the sun, swinging his legs off the lounger to face me. "Freaking out?" he asks, his face squished in concern as he tries to catch my eye. But I can't make contact. I have to get this out.

"A little," I say, rubbing my hands together.

"Please don't," he says, reaching his hand out. I take it and climb onto him, falling into his arms.

"We have to finish this book, Leo," I say, my head on his shoulder, my legs entwined with his on the single sunbed. "And then I need time to decide about Nicky's."

"Of course. I'm not asking for an answer on that. We don't need to think about what's next right now. Can't we just dance in the rain for a while?"

I smile, running my fingers across his chest.

"I think we can do that," I say, rolling my eyes at his sentimentality, which from Leo is a treasure. The sunbed creaks under our combined weight, and I take it as a cue to stand.

"I need to write these chapters for the book. I've struggled with the stories. I need to write about tomatoes and opera music and prepare for Liguria and seeing my dad's best friend. I need to throw those ashes somewhere."

There is a long beat of silence where I hear nothing but the chugging of the pool cleaner and the sound of a bird high in one of the trees. The heat starts to bear down on my skin as I pull the gap in my dressing gown closed.

"It's a lot," he says gently.

Leo reaches out and takes my hand, and he kisses my knuckles. We hold hands for a moment, and he circles his thumb on mine gently as emotions threaten to overwhelm me.

"Let's get this book done," I say, and Leo nods once, in absolute agreement.

"Anything to do other than pack before we head to Portofino?"

"I can think of a few things," he says, eyes glinting mischievously.

26

Liguria

JUST THINK IT'S *obvious* the next key ingredient should be basil," I say to Leo as our taxi pulls into a car park at a basil farm just outside Genoa.

He doesn't want to be here. Not one bit.

I've insisted we stop at an obscure biodynamic basil farm on the way to our hotel in Genoa, since I doubt either of us will want to visit a farm once we're based in Portofino, exploring the stunning coastline of the Italian Riviera. We are leaving the classical rural beauty of Tuscany for the old Italian glamour of that coast. No more tractors; now it's strictly boat shoes, parading on promenades, window-shopping for Gucci, Formula One driver spotting, and diving off rocks into azure waters after half a bottle of fizz.

But we're not feeling fancy right now. We got ninety percent of the way here by bus. A beast of a thing with a broken air-conditioning unit. The trip was five long hours inland from Florence, through Pisa for a quick stop, and then onto the motorway that follows the curve of the coast north. When we get to Genoa, we'll have a night, just the two of us, in a hotel, and then we're being picked up by Roger's boat.

I felt sad to say good-bye to Chiara, who begged me to come back again someday, *with Leo*. I took two bottles of her homemade passata, a small bag of mixed tomato seeds, and a handwritten recipe for her tomato and bread soup, which we are going to have photographed for our section on Tuscany. She wrote it down in 1973 and it's as gloriously oil-stained and brown as you would hope. I did promise to return. And I meant it.

"All *I'm* saying is that I wouldn't call basil a *key* ingredient," says Leo, shutting the door to the taxi before bobbing down to apologize to the driver. "Scusi, un momento."

"He doesn't know when he's wrong," I tell the driver.

"Who's paying?" the driver asks, emphasizing his frustration with pinched fingers.

"She is!" "He is!" Leo and I say in unison, pointing at each other.

"So, I get paid twice? Bene, bene. My lucky day," the driver says.

"*No*," we both say.

"Then just forty-seven euros," he says.

"*Just*," mutters Leo, fishing around in his wallet.

"There was no other way to get here," I say, glaring at Leo.

The driver takes off down the road, stuffing his million euros in his front pocket, leaving us in a cloud of dust outside what I think might be a closed basil farm with our luggage and no way to get to Genoa. It will be fine, and I definitely cannot give Leo the luxury of hearing me admit I may have made a *little* mistake here.

"Liguria is pesto, potatoes, purple asparagus, beans and legumes, and, I don't know, basil was the most appealing."

"You, Olive, have clearly never had a good bean," says Leo, wandering up to the entrance to the farm shop and peering in the window.

"Basil is not an ingredient," I mutter, mimicking Leo's deep voice, checking my phone for coverage, and finding one single bar. I quietly google the farm, but it takes ages to load, costing a fucking fortune too, probably. "How can you say it's not an ingredient? You're basically saying all herbs are not ingredients."

"I'm saying *key* ingredient," he says, tossing his arms in the air in frustration. "If we're going to hook the entire Ligurian chapter on a key ingredient—which is what we're supposed to do—why in god's name would you choose basil when *beans* are right there?"

"Oh, Leo," I say. "Are you even Italian?"

I narrow my eyes at him, and then finally the basil farm opening hours load, and I grimace. Closed on Mondays. Fucking closed. "How can a farm close? Like, don't you need to water things and whatnot?"

Leo sighs. "Olive, let's just go to the coast. Check into our hotel. Sit in the balcony spa pool and fuck."

"I can't understand how you'd rather do that than visit a basil farm," I say cheekily.

Leo laughs at me, picking up his roller suitcase and standing, waiting for me to do something. "All right. I'm letting you lead."

"Success!" I say, stopping him in his tracks. "I've found a basil farm two kilometers from here, which is both open and also has a café."

Leo grimaces, then chuckles, grabbing my hand and pulling me in for a kiss. "Are we walking?"

"We're walking!" I say triumphantly, pulling back from his embrace and heading off down the main road as Leo reluctantly follows, dragging his suitcase behind him.

"We're walking this way!" I say, looking at the blue dot on my phone, doing a U-turn, and correcting course.

"We could be naked in a hotel," he says, "right now."

Thirty-seven minutes later, and we're both hot, sweaty, and angry, and I'm feeling sheepish. The second basil farm does, thankfully, have a café, and I drop my bag on the ground, carefully placing the urn in its tote bag on one of the available chairs next to me.

"I'm sorry, okay? I fucked up. We should have just gone to the hotel and relaxed."

"It's fine," he says grumpily.

"I made good progress on the writing for Sicily this morning," I say, hoping to appease Leo as he drops the handle of his suitcase and sits down. "And I just wanted to start the final leg off by looking into the key ingredient *first*. I know when we get to Roger's it's going to be a bit of whirlwind."

I grimace inwardly. Roger, I remember, is a big character, like my father. He likes to eat, he likes to drink, and my mother used to find his presence around my father stressful. If my mother was always a little highly strung, when Roger came to town her anxiety surged. As Dad and Roger drank, tales of their history would emerge: working on boats in the summer, jazz festivals in the south, Roger's trips to London when I was just a baby. The stories were lively and hilarious, full of swear words and adult innuendo and talk about boozing and the stupid things young men did. Mum *hated* it. I could barely follow it, but I loved to watch them laughing. It was always exciting when Roger came to stay.

"He needs to watch what he says in front of Olive," she'd warned my father more than once.

"Yes, I've only met Roger once, but I suspect we're not going to get much work done. He's a man of pleasure," says Leo, grabbing my hand to pull me down next to him.

"A coffee?" I propose. "And then we can go."

"Coffee is good," he says, grabbing the laminated menu from between the salt and pepper shakers. "Ice coffee, even. You?"

"Oh, the same," I say, "a milky one, please."

Leo stands up and heads to the counter, and while he's gone I take a minute to pull up all the dishes I've found that are both native to the region and stuffed full of basil. Or at least feature it as a *key* ingredient.

Leo returns with a tray and two drinks, plus a huge two-liter bottle of water, of which we each guzzle half. "Right. I've spoken to the lady," says Leo. "We can go through and look at the nursery and the large fields out the back. There isn't much beyond that and a massive shop selling pesto, which is made elsewhere."

"Well, great," I say. "Sounds like we can make this error of mine very quick."

My phone buzzes in my hand.

"One sec," I say, standing up and walking slightly away from Leo so he cannot overhear our conversation.

"Hey, Olive," Ginny says. "I heard you climbed the leaning tower of Pizza."

"Pisa," I correct.

"But was it a tower or . . ." She has to stop talking since she's giggling uncontrollably.

"Jesus, Ginny," I say, giggling too as I glance across at Leo. "He's here, so I can't really talk."

"Fine," she says. "Are you okay, though? Are you freaking out?"

"Yes. But he's keeping my feet on the ground," I say. "We're just going to try to enjoy the trip and get the book done. We can face the question of Nicky's when we get back to London."

"But you want Leo *and* the restaurant?" she asks, almost breathless.

"I think so," I say, feeling my cheeks burn at the admission. "I think so."

As I return to the table, Leo points at my ice coffee, which no longer has any ice in it, and then raises his eyebrows toward the empty chair. I sit obediently.

"Who was that?"

"Ginny," I reply, sucking back on my straw. "She just wanted an update on . . ."

"*Things*," he says, smirking. "Well, I've booked a car. I've also called Roger and told him we will be at the dock at eleven forty-five a.m. tomorrow, so we will arrive in time for lunch."

"Thank you," I say, impulsively leaning across to kiss his cheek.

He pulls me close and then whispers into my ear, "I've found four dishes we can look into that have basil but are not all pesto."

"Hot," I say, turning back to him and kissing him on the mouth.

Leo laughs, gently pushing me away. "You in those little shorts. It's too much."

"We're going to have to sneak around like teenagers at Roger's house."

"Which is why we should be at that hotel. *Now*."

Leo closes his laptop and leans forward, folding his hands together. "Also, Olive, can you stop fucking around and send me your story on Catania?" he says. "The new introduction to Sicily you said you did such great work on this morning?"

My heart rate picks up slightly, and I grimace. "Oh, do I have to?"

"You're going to have to," he says. "I mean, you're going to have to show *some* people, Olive." He laughs.

I'm panicking about sharing it. My original introduction focused on Rocco, his relationship to my father, their training together, and a story about the day my dad made Sicilian blood-orange sorbet for a wedding and forgot the sugar. While it was a sweet story, it should be *my own story*. And so I rewrote it. *Again.*

I pull it up on my laptop, and after Leo has put his own phone away, I hit send.

"Can we do this basil thing, then go to the hotel?" Leo says, standing.

"Fine," I say, standing to join him. He looks at me, scowling, and then pulls me in for a kiss. I make a show of sighing, pulling back, and wagging a finger at him. "But it would be nice to see a little more commitment to the project from you."

"I'm very good at multitasking," he says, smiling wickedly before he lowers his mouth to mine.

27

🍴

"O H, HELL YES," I say, putting my toes onto the wooden deck of Roger's boat, which he's kindly sent to pick us up. "This was worth getting out of that cheap hotel bed for."

Leo, who is holding on to a rope as he jumps down from the side of the boat, swings around so he can roll his eyes at me.

Every time I look at him I get full flashing images of the night before, like just the sight of him sparks a fully immersive Technicolor experience in every cell of my body. His skin. My skin. His hands on every part of me. Leo can see it, and he pulls me down onto the deck and throws his arms around my neck.

"Beautiful," he says into my ear, breath tickling. "Just beautiful."

"Get it out of your system," I say as he kisses my neck. "I don't want us to be hanging off each other in front of Roger."

The boat is small but perfectly kept: a bright white with blue and red stripes and dark wood interiors. Plush cushioned seating below deck. It's called *Sofia*, after Roger's wife. They met during a summer jaunt around the Riviera. She was the daughter of a wealthy Bulgarian businessman, and he was the working-class kid from Hackney cooking for them on their luxury yacht. They made an odd pair that no one gave much of a chance. My mother, for example, would often ask Roger as part of her welcoming small talk if "Sofia has had enough of you yet." It struck me as a bit unkind, even as a child. But it was always delivered in such jest that Roger belly laughed.

Roger has worked hard and built up a catering business supplying boats in the area.

"He never minded a bit of competition," my dad used to say.

Leo sits on the small table behind the helm, while the captain fusses around us with ropes and sails. A young boy who couldn't be more than fifteen offers us both a glass of champagne, which I decline but Leo accepts.

"Can't believe we have to take this boat all the way to Roger's house," I whisper to Leo. "Such a drag."

"A reminder that it's a *yacht*," says Leo, who has already relaxed into his seat, holding a small espresso in one hand and a flute of champagne in the other. He looks up to grin at me.

"It's a hard life," he adds, shrugging. "Sit with me, Olive."

I take a seat opposite him and momentarily am swept away by the sheer thrill of it. As we watch Genoa fall away into the distance, the captain explains we'll be hugging the coast down south toward Portofino, through the *Italian* Riviera.

"For *Italians*," he adds, grinning.

He means that this stretch is not quite as populated by tourists. It's a small strip of the Mediterranean where Italians come with their families to stretch out on beaches under the blue skies and swim in the still cobalt seas. From the water, we pass bay after bay, where colorful buildings climb into the dramatic cliff faces, and busy restaurants buzzing with hungry sun-fatigued guests line the promenades.

"The other Cinque Terre," the captain says proudly. "With better food."

"It's called Golfo Paradiso," Leo says to me as he reaches out and threads his fingers through mine.

"Sure looks like paradise," I say, resting my head on his shoulder.

This is the Italy of sixties cinema. Winding cliff-top roads, naked torsos weaving through traffic on Vespas, pretty girls drinking Campari al fresco, children with sticky gelato fingers tearing past, towels streaming behind them, toward the sea.

At each bay, fishing boats tussle like suckling pigs for moorings in small harbors. Huge shiny white mega-yachts float far from the squawking of children and gulls, their crisply uniformed crews tending to the sunbathing "beautiful people." I glance back to Leo, feeling giddy with the thrill of it.

"Anchovies," says the captain as we pass a village called Sori.

Then, later, as we pass another unassuming little village, he points again. "Pansotti. And focaccia di Recco."

I glance down at my phone and search it up. It's a thinner kind of focaccia, flatbread almost, filled with gooey cheese, the recipe for which dates to the twelfth century.

"Every town has their food," says the captain, grinning. "But Recco? That is the food capital of Italy."

"We gotta go there," I say to Leo.

Leo pulls back, reaching for his laptop. "I'm sorry I didn't get to this last night," he says.

"You were a little distracted, Leo," I reply, grinning. "Oh, don't read it now!"

"I have to. Before we get to Roger's," he says.

I nod, sitting back, my thumb to my mouth, chewing on the nail nervously.

"My first encounter with the bittersweet taste of the Moro, a Sicilian blood orange, was sitting outside under a gnarled olive tree, during the height of a June heat wave. Small puffs of cloud the only blemish in the otherwise perfect blue sky, the bloodred flesh yielding a juice so refreshing it felt as close to perfect as I've ever come. The second encounter came at a fish market in Catania, where a group of men in flat caps spooned red-orange mounds of Moro granita into their mouths between games of cards. I was back in my dad's world, and the memories of oranges were everywhere.

"'It's the color of sunset on the outside, and a bleeding heart inside,' said the sous chef at legendary Catania eatery Rocco's—"

"Okay, stop now," I say, mortified.

"'The tangy hint reminds one of the tart sweetness of raspberry or cranberry . . .'" He peers over his laptop. "You know, you should be a food writer."

"Fuck off," I say, staring across the sea, the Ligurian water bright and reflective in the midday sun.

"It's really good," he says quickly.

Leo continues reading in silence, and I try not to think about what he might be making of the rewrite. Over the past week we've spoken at length about the approach: Should we try to mimic Dad's voice? Ghostwrite the section, so to speak? Or should it be my voice? Should the last three chapters, after his death, be written by his daughter while she travels to his favorite places?

There was no argument. This part of the book *has* to be my journey to get to know my father, and the food and the places that helped shape him.

"It's beautiful, Olive," says Leo after some time.

I ignore him.

"I'm ignoring you," I say, to drive home the point.

"You're going to have to learn to take compliments," he says.

I blush and redirect.

"Shall we send it to the publisher?" I ask. "I mean, I've nearly finished the Tuscany section, and if she hates it we should know sooner rather than later."

"She isn't going to hate it," says Leo. "Are you worried, Olive, about getting a bad review?"

I narrow my eyes at him, grinning playfully. "You know, I'd take a four out of five. There is nothing wrong with four out of five. One or two out of five? If you know you're good at what you do, then you don't have to take those reviews to heart. You can dismiss them. But a three-star? That's mediocrity. That's the review to break your heart."

Leo laughs. "There is nothing mediocre about this," he says, nodding toward the screen. I look back at the view, nervous anticipation about seeing Roger starting to build.

"See, this is why I love the North," says Leo as we finally chug toward Portofino's tiny harbor, the colorful buildings clinging to the cliffs above the small rocky bay.

"It's just, wow," I say. "Lucky old Roger, eh? Imagine meeting someone with a home here. Nothing bonds the heart like a house on the cliffs and a big-ass fucking boat."

"Yacht." Leo shakes his head at me. "I hope you don't think I'm into you because of your big-ass fucking inheritance."

"No," I say quickly, confused for a moment by the idea of it. "It hadn't crossed my mind." I step in to take one last hug before we see Roger. "But now that you mention it . . . ," I add with a grin.

Leo kisses me on the mouth and then fixes his eyes on me, determined. "Last destination. Let's get this job done, all right? Then I want to get you back to London."

As we near the jetty, the yacht starts to slow.

"We take a small boat in," Leo explains.

"Can't we dock all the way?" I ask Leo, frowning.

"Only if you have about three grand to spend," he says.

"Three grand?"

"Well, at least you get the whole day for that," he says, grinning.

"Is why he keeps the boat in Santa Margherita," explains the captain.

We board a small runabout that comes out to meet us and then we chug slowly toward the jetty. I start to feel nervous as we approach. This is my dad's best friend. And in a way part of my family until I was fifteen. I try to pull all the memories of Roger together, his jolly, playful nature, bellowing voice, and loud, machine-gun laugh. His scaring my mum by appearing at the side window in a Darth Vader mask. He and Dad drinking outside, listening to old Italian music, dancing sometimes. "Reliving their halcyon days," Mum used to say, eyes rolling.

"There he is," says Leo, pointing at a very tanned tall man in cream slacks, a blue striped shirt, and a white hat with a black band. On his arm, a slender woman with blond hair and an enormous straw sun hat; a tailored, sleeveless jumpsuit in lemon; and heeled espadrilles. *Effortless summer.*

I feel my heart quicken a little. "I feel nervous as hell suddenly," I say to Leo.

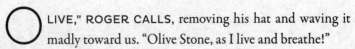

28

O LIVE," ROGER CALLS, removing his hat and waving it madly toward us. "Olive Stone, as I live and breathe!"

I glance over at Leo for reassurance, take a deep breath, and wave back.

"Hi, Roger," I shout as the boat pulls closer and our driver tosses a rope over a metal bollard and tugs us in.

Roger is beaming. Close-up he's heavily lined everywhere but the forehead, with a thick head of silvery hair. His wife, Sofia, is a picture of style and grace, and also, I think, a little Botox.

Roger sticks his hand out to help me up onto the jetty, and I feel so glamorous standing on this gorgeous pier lined with restaurants, in the middle of a bay surrounded by cliffs, the blue sky shining above. Everywhere perfect hair and tailored slacks, everywhere Gucci glasses, Prada shirts, Valentino summer frocks, Balenciaga bags with small dogs at pretty sandaled feet.

"Gosh, it's so fancy here," comes tumbling out of my mouth, as I shake Sofia's perfectly manicured hand.

"Wait till the tour boats come in!" says Roger, looking at his watch. "The great unwashed arrive to buy an ice cream and piss in the bay."

"Roger," says Sofia, hitting him with the back of her hand playfully.

"So, Olive, last time I saw you was in Cinque Terre, I think. Sofia and I were trying to remember," he says. "What did we decide, love?"

"It *was* in Cinque Terre!" she says warmly. "You came for two days on the boat, do you remember?"

"Oh yeah," I say, pulling out the memory. One of our very last visits, I think.

"Sofia, honey, can we take them straight to lunch? Neither of them really has any luggage. How do you travel so light? Sofia needs her own camel. Or tugboat," he says jokingly.

Sofia gives him a look, sighing good-naturedly as she guides us down the promenade, each restaurant filled with diners plunging bread into oil and sipping on their bright orange Camparis and Aperols. The smells of barbecued seafood waft through the air, and I think about the crazy difference between here, with its blue sea and salty air; luscious, green Tuscany; and sun-burnished Sicily.

"Roger is so happy you came, Olive," she says. "He was very sad about your father's death and couldn't face the funeral at such short notice."

"Oh," I say, feeling my cheeks redden. "I probably would have missed him anyway. It was all a bit of a blur. I was a mess that day."

"Of course you were. He was your father. Such a shock," she says quickly, her eyes flickering back to Roger in a way that unsettles me.

We turn down an alley at the end of the pier, and instead of having lunch in one of these fancy waterside places, we climb a set of stairs until Sofia ushers me into a barely signposted eatery with a wave of her hand.

The restaurant is low-key, dark, with a pretty little roof terrace that peers out over the peaks of rooftops and then onto the main square, which runs straight into the sea ahead. Truly a spectacular view of Portofino, the opposite of all the photos that look from the water into the colorful bay. From this angle, we're looking out toward the sea. Our vantage is that of a resident, *not* a visitor.

The host leads us up some spiral stairs and we are surrounded by Italian voices, not a single English word spoken, except by Roger.

"Here, here," he says. "Your father's favorite place, my favorite place, Sofia's favorite place, and now *yours*." He beams at me.

"Wow," I say, glancing down at the bay teeming with little boats bobbing like corks in the gentle swell. "This is . . . special."

"We practically live here," says Roger, dropping his hat on the back of the chair and pulling out his seat. "Sit, sit," he says excitedly.

"A place so good you don't need the foot traffic," I say, grinning at the bustling promenade that wraps around the cliffs and out of view.

I glance over at Leo as we move into place at the table, and he subtly tips his head toward the seat next to him. I move decisively and slide into the chair. It's a surprisingly rickety old chair in a place with a million-dollar view. You get the feeling that these kinds of eateries are on the endangered list, if not extinct, in the best spots on the planet.

"Allow me please to do the ordering, as if you were eating with us at home," Roger says. "You will *not* be disappointed, I promise."

"I can't imagine," I say, as the smells of garlic and prawns and chili waft around us.

"Sweetheart, I have thought about you every day since the news," Roger says, leaning toward me.

I don't know what to say that I haven't said a hundred times already on this trip, but Leo takes the reins right away.

"It all happened very fast," he says. "But he was happy."

"You've been such a rock for him these last years, Leo," Roger says, before catching himself and quickly turning to me to explain. "Nicky saw Leo rather like a son, I think. I mean, he would, wouldn't he? Spending all those hours together in the kitchen."

I shift in my seat uncomfortably, and Roger, realizing what he's said, adds, "But nothing could be as precious as you were. Little Olive. The apple of his eye."

Not teenage Olive, I think. *Not adult Olive. Only the little Olive who still loved him.* I feel glum suddenly, realizing that Roger is going to be by far the toughest test for me.

"And you're both here to finish his wonderful book!" says Sofia, moving the conversation along as she spots my slumping mood.

"You know, without wishing to get all macabre about it, this was supposed to be him, sitting here at this table," Roger says, hands up in the air as the waiter arrives and he politely waves away the offer of a menu. "He sent me this email when he booked the trip. Let me find it."

I get a shiver of impending doom as Roger slides his phone out and starts searching through it. "You know it was always his dream, Olive, to do a cookbook. Here it is!

"'Rog. Coming though in July to finish the book. Want to do something with beans. Nobody thinks about beans enough, don't you agree? *Nicolò.*'"

Leo coughs into this hand, and I glare in his direction.

"That was the last message from Dad," I say, mouth dropping open. Leo can no longer contain his laughter. "Nobody thinks about beans enough?" I repeat. It makes me giggle too. I can imagine him in the flesh saying it. Gesticulating, almost glassy-eyed over it. It would have come across as so profound, so *true*. You would leave the conversation musing over it for days, feeling vaguely depressed even, that beans have been all but forgotten. But read out by Roger, stripped of the passion of my dad's voice, it sounds absurd.

"Beans it is," I say, looking to Leo, laughing. "I concede defeat."

"I don't want to say I was right," he replies. "But I was definitely right."

"You were going to come here and not do beans?" Roger says, frowning. "My god, just as well I have the evidence."

"Doubly good, because we're having Liguria's famous beans and pesto for lunch," says Sofia. "And Roger has some other bean dishes he wants to share with you this week. And the place on the hill—Roger, we have to take them there for that green minestrone. The one with the cannellini that we ate."

"We're going to do it all!" he says, beaming with delight. It is impossible not to be caught up in his enthusiasm and love for *living*. Like Rocco's, his personality is big. Like Dad's too. But Roger has a warmth and softness to him also. And it's obvious he dotes on Sofia, who clearly adores him too.

"Oh, wonderful," I say, as Sofia, who must have slipped away, arrives with a waiter clutching a bottle of pale pink vintage champagne.

"I know it's French," she says, "but it's a celebration, sì?"

"Sì," we all say in unison as she takes the bottle, pops the cork, and fills our tall, stemmed crystal glasses and we all cheer happily as the liquid pours out.

"So how's the trip been so far?" Roger asks.

"It's been amazing. It's been a bit of a bonding experience for me . . . you know, with Dad. Belated bonding."

Leo pushes his knee gently into mine.

"Oh yes," says Sofia. "It must be so strangely wonderful to come on this trip he would have taken. I'm so glad you've had each other to share it with."

It's hard not to laugh considering what has gone on between Leo and me, and I feel myself blushing as Leo looks over at me with a sweet smile. I shake my head at him. *Stop it.*

But I'm so grateful he's here. He's opened my eyes to a side of my dad I'd let slip away. He's reminded me of all the things I used to love about him, and that even if for the last decade I felt such resentment and maybe even anger toward my dad, I also missed him. Maybe I'll never understand what happened; humans are complicated beings after all. And sometimes we close ourselves off to the big love, to avoid feeling any pain. Is that what I did when we packed our bags and left all those years ago?

Is that what Dad did?

I feel Leo's hand on my thigh now, and I put mine over his, squeezing to thank him for the support. Our hands stay there. I leave mine on top, and our fingers interlink. They're just out of view of Sofia and Roger, but it will be obvious if we stay like this too long. I lift my hand and place it on the glass on the table, and a moment later, I feel the warmth of Leo's hand leave my thigh.

"You had a tough time together in the last decade or so," says Roger, making a decade sound like a few lost hours rather than the eternity it feels to me now.

I shrug. "It was difficult after my parents separated."

"And how is your mother? Jean. How is *she*?" he says, pouring a little more champagne for me. I feel a strange penetration in his stare.

"Um, yeah, she's, you know, good. She's remarried now. Very happy. They live in Yorkshire, near her sister," I say, unsure how much detail Roger really wants. "She's struggled a bit with it all too."

"She has?" he says.

"Of course she has," says Sofia.

I find myself in defense of my mother under Roger's gaze. Not that he's accusing her of anything, but there is an underlying tone of judgment. The way best friends feel, I suppose. The way Ginny or Kate would feel for me.

"Yes, of course." I splutter a little to find the words. "I mean, he's her ex-husband. He's my father."

"Yes," he says, drawing the word out.

"It was hard on her too," I say.

"It was all very hard on them both, pet," Roger says, patting my hand with his. He glances across at Sofia again, and then back at me.

"Yes. Of course," I say quickly.

Two waiters appear clutching bowls of pasta, and we are served simultaneously, like a choreographed dance move. The bowls have wide, flat, exaggerated rims. The pesto pasta—linguine—is spun into a perfect mound, with green beans and pan-fried potatoes decoratively placed on top.

"It's not how you'll find it in Genoa or Rapallo," says Roger, nodding toward his dish, "but it's a very good version indeed. The pesto is leafier than most, which is why you have this green oil pooling at the edges."

Leo lifts his dish slightly to watch the incandescent green roll in thick stripes toward the edge of the bowl.

"Nice," he says. "That's a hell of a green."

"Basil is a very special plant," I say. "A key ingredient, wouldn't you say, Roger?"

"A what?" he replies, leaning forward, holding a hand around his ear.

"Never mind," I say, knocking Leo's knee with mine.

"Let's eat," says Sofia.

I'm still thinking about Dad, wondering if there could be some healing ahead, as I twist my fork through the pasta and scoop it up to my mouth.

"Oh, wow, this is amazing," I say, over and over.

Leo looks across at me, concerned. "Are you okay?" he whispers. But Roger catches it.

"Is there something wrong?"

"No," I say. "No." I glance at Leo. "Why?"

"Oh, just you said the dish was *amazing* four times. And so I was just making sure you were okay," Leo says with a wicked grin, and I slap him on the arm. Leo is back. Or at least, he is putting on a show for me, to help me get through this first lunch.

"If we've rendered our guest speechless with a little linguine, I can't wait to show you what I can do with my Limoncello," Roger says, laughing.

Later, as our lunch dishes are removed, Roger is about to start another story about Dad when Sofia interrupts. "Roger, I'm sure Olive doesn't want to go over and over stories about him all day," she says. "Save a few. We've got a week together."

"It's okay, I'm kind of used to it now," I say, smiling at her gratefully.

"But still," Leo says quickly.

Roger looks momentarily deflated and I feel for him. He's lost his best friend, and he's sitting with the man's daughter and sous chef and he wants to sink into memories, just like he used to at home with Dad all those years ago.

Sofia seems to sense this too, and kisses him on the forehead. "Come on, darling, let's get them a shower and a rest. I want to get you settled in," she says to Leo and me, "and then we can open the grappa and Roger can whip you up a tiramisu."

"Ohhhhh . . . you're going to like that," he says, completely distracted and perky again. He grins at me. "I make a killer tiramisu. Better than Nicky ever did."

"Come on, you've had quite enough. You'll fall asleep on the pier again," she says, and then glances at us, quickly adding, "I'm kidding. He's actually rather teetotal when we're alone. It's like he saves all his most outrageous behavior for guests."

She chuckles, and I stand to join her as we make our way back down the spiral staircase and Sofia leads us through one of the small alleys that shoots from the bay and up to the cliffs above. Roger waves his hat to almost every business owner on the way, it feels like, receiving enthusiastic waves in return. Leo and I share a few amused looks as we wander behind the two, weighed down by our bags.

Sofia points ahead to her house, indicating that it isn't far to walk. I'm surprised by how small the house is, but I suspect small in Portofino is still out-of-this-world expensive. Besides, Roger tells us, this is the second house. The first is on Lake Como. They are mostly only here in the summer months.

"Sea, lake, and mountain," he says, "the holy trinity."

29

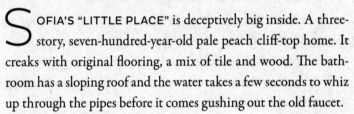

S OFIA'S "LITTLE PLACE" is deceptively big inside. A three-story, seven-hundred-year-old pale peach cliff-top home. It creaks with original flooring, a mix of tile and wood. The bathroom has a sloping roof and the water takes a few seconds to whiz up through the pipes before it comes gushing out the old faucet.

"It's a bit of a fixer-upper," she says, waving at some scaffolding holding up the top-floor balcony.

"It's incredible," I say, looking across at Leo as she shows us to my room, which is beautifully decorated, mostly in whites and dusty green with little orange shutters that open out onto the bay.

"What Sofia means is that it constantly needs fixing up," says Roger. "And you can't change anything, bloody regulations everywhere."

"It's perfect," I say, gushing at the charm of it, while knowing I'm incurring none of the expense of having to fix the place up or pay to stay here.

"And, Leo, you're in here," says Sofia, opening the door next to mine. "Unless . . ."

"No, that's fine," Leo says, and Sofia nods, glancing between the two of us. She is wondering. Women never miss these things. Perhaps she's spotted the sham: an awkward, almost playacted distance between us, with the moments of true tenderness piercing through the facade. A classic case of two lovers trying and failing to keep their feelings under wraps.

"The bathroom is down the hall," says Sofia. "It's shared, I'm afraid, and there is no lock, so just be aware."

Leo and I catch each other's eye and I suppress a smile, remembering our shared bathroom back in Tuscany.

"Noted," says Leo. "Did you note that, Olive?"

"I noted it, Leo," I say, shaking my head at him.

Sofia watches our interaction with amusement, and I know she can tell that there is something going on between us.

"Roger and I will get coffee and dessert and grappa and probably cigars ready for you," she says, giving me a cheeky *knowing* look as she sails down the stairs.

"What was that look about?" says Leo as soon as she's out of earshot.

"I think she thinks that we . . . you know . . . are . . . something."

"Well. She's right," he says, with a laugh. "We definitely are something."

Leo looks at me with his piercing dark eyes and he shakes his head.

"We sure are," I say, grinning.

"I'm going to quickly freshen up," he says and then kisses my forehead. "See you downstairs in five, Olive."

I do too. I pull out a long skirt and a little tank top, both of which I haven't worn since I picked them up in Tuscany. I have a quick shower, taking my time to reapply my makeup. I even wash my hair, slicking it back, wet, into a low bun.

By the time I get downstairs I see that Leo is already sitting out on the terrace with Sofia, grappa in hand, while Roger stands, one hand resting on the mantel above an old outdoor fireplace, talking loudly about the quality of the local markets. On a wood coffee table, a communal tiramisu in a ceramic bowl has been poked at, a few spoons standing out of it. I have a violent feeling of déjà vu as I take in this image. Dad often did this when he was too tipsy at a dinner party and had had enough with formalities.

"My friend Salvatore, he sends me a video every morning," Roger says, pulling out a phone and holding up a video of a fish market. "Plaice, calamari, gambas the size of your fist."

"The size of a fist?" I say, moving toward them. Leo turns to me and smiles, tipping his head slightly, as his eyes run down my body, taking in my outfit, and I feel a thousand little sparklers fly off me in his gaze's wake. I relish the feeling without letting the pleasure of it show on my face.

Sofia hands me a grappa immediately.

"Please help yourself to the dessert. Roger insists on eating it this way," she says, nodding at the bowl.

"Dad did too, sometimes," I reply, and Roger laughs.

"I like it," I say, leaning forward and taking a fresh spoon. I scoop up a mouthful, and it is as messy and delicious as it looks, the eggy mascarpone landing across my chin.

"Nice one, Olive," I say, reaching for a napkin. "*Classy.*"

I can feel Leo's eyes on me, and I take my time to clear my mouth, dragging the napkin across my lips. I am distracted by thoughts of him. His hard body. His rough kisses.

"It's a beautiful view out there," I say, dropping the napkin and turning to Sofia.

"So, Olive, how are you in life? Your dad said you're a food critic now," Roger says, sitting back in his seat. "Yes. Nicky said you were out there tearing shreds off the inauthentic. What did he say, Sofia?"

"I can't remember, Roger," Sofia says, waving away the conversation. She turns to me, explaining, "The two of them would go on and on. You end up switching off your brain."

"I remember what he said," Roger continues, "He said, 'At least I gave her good taste.'" He grins, proud of himself.

"Oh god," I say, feeling simultaneously proud that my dad thought that and embarrassed. "I'm not sure I will go back to it, truthfully."

"Why so, Olive?" Roger asks.

"I think I've had enough of finding fault in everything all the time," I say, giving a sidelong glance in Leo's direction.

"Critics have their place," says Roger. "They're a necessary part of the machine. There are a hundred and eighty restaurants in this small town. How are you going to know where to eat without reading a review or two?"

"Yeah, sure. But I reviewed for clicks," I say. It's the first time I've said it out loud. "Every review was a rebellion."

"Your father said that too," Roger says, laughing so hard, it's difficult not to join in. "He used to say, she's not reviewing the White Swan, she's reviewing her childhood."

I cringe inwardly.

"I can't do this toxic grappa. I'm going to get some more champagne, what do you think?" Sofia says, her eyes darting between Leo and me.

"Great idea. We need a toast! A toast to Nicky," Roger says.

While Sofia is gone, Roger slides a large leather photo album across the table toward me. "The summer Nicky and I finished a stint cooking on a yacht, an absolute dream job. And some photos from your parents' first trip here. And this one is from the summer of 1996, when you were four or five."

"Oh, how cool," I say, sliding down onto the floor so I'm closer to the coffee table. I touch the first album, the one from my own visit. "Can I?"

"Go ahead, just shout if you have any questions!"

I flick through several pages of a thirty-something Roger, who looks like a young Jude Law, and Sofia with a pixie cut, looking as chic as she does today. There are snaps next to cars, outside heritage buildings. A photo of Roger with a Vespa.

"He crashed it into a tree," says Sofia, returning with the champagne.

"Have the pin in my leg to prove it," says Roger, wincing. Another popped cork. Another sweet smile between Sofia and Roger.

Then there are some photos of Dad and Roger on the huge yacht, arms around each other in swimming trunks. A Polaroid of Dad in a kitchen somewhere.

"Couple of singles, taking on Italy," Roger says, laughing. I look across at him, savoring the thought of the two of them up to no good, cooking for millionaires, along the Italian coast.

And then I see Dad and Mum.

"There's Nicky and Jean," says Sofia, pointing at the photo of the two of them sitting inside Nicky's. Wineglasses, empty plates, a lit cigarette trailing smoke from a ceramic ashtray. Mum in a wide-brimmed straw hat, Dad with his arm around her, smiling like the cat that got the cream.

"You look so much like your mum there," Leo says, leaning in almost as close as me. I can feel his warm breath on my neck and touch the spot with my fingers.

"I wish," I say, turning the page. A photo of Mum in a bikini on the back of a boat, smiling at the camera. A photo of Dad behind a barbecue, two fish smoking away on the grill.

"Well, it's great you never got to look like that old bastard," he says, pointing to a particularly unflattering photo of my sunburned dad, reclined on a seat at a dinner table that has recently been savaged, sticking his stomach out and pointing at it.

Sofia pours the wine, and Roger raises a glass in the air.

"To Nicky," says Sofia. "May he be eating all the best kinds of pasta."

"To Nicky," Roger says. "A great friend."

"To Nicky," Leo says, "A great boss and mentor. *Mostly*."

Everyone laughs and then their eyes turn to me and I clam up immediately. Holding my glass in the air, I shake my head furiously.

"I can do yours, Olive," says Leo quickly, but before he has a chance, Roger clinks his glass with mine.

"For taking you on as his very own," he says.

I frown. "Pardon?" I say, leaning into Roger. "What did you say?"

"For adopting you," he says, looking over at Leo and then Sofia as his face slowly starts to fall and his eyes widen.

"Oh my god, Olive," he says, his voice tight and panicked. "I assumed you knew. Oh my god. Sofia?"

"Darling," Sofia says, gliding across the room, putting her hands on my shoulders.

"What are you saying?" I mumble, my voice cracking, as the

glass slides out of my hand and Leo manages to scoop it up just before it hits the floor.

I shrug Sofia's hands off my shoulders and look back to Roger. "He's not my father?"

My entire world shrinks to this thought, this feeling, this truth.

I cannot see, suddenly, and I'm swimming through the room.

"I need a moment . . . ," I say, walking backward a couple of paces, looking at Leo for help. *Help me. Make this stop.*

And then I turn and run.

30

TAKE THE STAIRS up to my room, two at a time, hearing Leo's footsteps following more deliberately behind me. I throw open the shutters onto the balconette and perch myself on the end of my bed. A moment or two later, I hear a gentle knock on my door.

"Olive?" Leo says.

"Yes, Leo," I reply.

"Let me in."

I walk to the door and open it. Leo clocks my face with immediate concern. "You're really pale. You need to sit."

"Did you hear that?" I say, my breath ragged. "You heard it, right?"

"Can it be true?" Leo asks, his face etched with worry.

A hundred little things sharpen in my mind. The crystal clarity of my life playing back with new color and new understanding. My mother's face comes into view and I feel it so hard, it knocks the breath out of me.

"Oh my god," I say again.

Leo closes his eyes, and for a moment I feel a stab of anger toward him. Did he know?

"He's not my father."

Everything around me starts to swim, and I move in slow motion.

"Mum already had me," I say, muttering. "Dad met Mum when she already had me."

"Roger might not know the full story," Leo says, sitting me down, putting his hands on my shoulders, running them up and down. Calming. Soothing me. "You can't be sure. You should ask him."

"No," I say. "He told me I was *his Olive*. That I was a gift from God."

"Oh no," Leo says, his voice tight now too. "You need to speak to your mum."

"I have to go," I say. I stand up and fish around for my clothing, eyes starting to prickle with tears.

"They lied to me, and when they broke up, they didn't tell me . . . because why? Because Dad didn't want me to know? Because Mum didn't? I don't even look like him. I've *never* looked like him."

"Olive, slow down," he says. But he isn't correcting me. He isn't telling me I'm wrong.

I lean into the sobering feeling of anger, turning to Leo. "Did you know?"

"Of course not," Leo says. I feel like someone took a sledgehammer to my heart and it shattered like glass all over the floor. "I knew there was something complicated going on between you. I knew there was something amiss with how much he loved you, and how little he . . ."

"Fought for me," I say, slumping against the wall. "It wasn't just *me* staying away."

"Olive, you need to take a breath, you look really pale," he says, trying to maneuver me back to the bed. "Sit down. You really, really need to call your mum."

I nod furiously, searching now for my mobile. I pull it out of my purse and immediately drop it on the floor, along with the contents of my bag.

"He wasn't my father," I say again.

"Does it matter?" Leo says.

"It matters," I say, feeling my eyes start to glass over as I let Leo pull me in for a long embrace, but I hold myself as firmly as I can, refusing to let the tears come. "It matters," I say again.

"Try to take a deep breath," he says into my ear, stroking my hair. "Let me get you a glass of water, or tea? Would you like a cup of tea?"

I nod, although I don't want one. I just want Leo out for a moment so I can think.

When he leaves the room, I find my mum's number and I hit call.

It rings off. And I immediately send her a text message.

ME: CALL ME

And then I ring again, because waiting is not an option. I need confirmation right away. This time she picks up within moments.

"Olive?" she says, slightly breathless herself. "Is everything all right?"

"Hi," I say, my mind going blank suddenly. How do I ask? What do I say? "Mum. I just wondered if you could answer a question for me."

"Of course," she says, "are you okay? You sound funny, Olive. Have you been drinking?"

"I am funny," I say. "I have been drinking."

She sighs. "Where are you? Are you at Roger's?"

"Yes. And he told me, Mum. He just came out and said it. That Dad was a great man taking me on as his own," I say, and then, as I feel tears threatening again: "I have to know. Is Dad, you know, my dad?"

A pause. A pause long enough to confirm it. But then she lies.

"Of course he was, darling," she says, a small nervous chuckle escaping her lips. "What a question."

"My biological dad. Is he my *real* dad?"

"Oh, Olive," she says, but I hear the fragility in her voice. "He loved you so much."

Leo comes in with the tea and I look up at him. I drop the hand holding my phone to my side.

I can hear the tinny sound of my mum's voice coming through the earpiece. "Olive! Olive?"

"Speak to her," says Leo, as he pulls me back down to sit on the edge of the bed. I lift the phone back up to my ear. "I have to go," I say, hanging up on her.

A moment later, before I've had a chance to collect my thoughts, the phone starts vibrating in my hand. Mum. I let it ring out, staring at the screen for what feels like an eternity. Then I switch off my phone.

"Olive," says Leo. He puts his arms around me and pulls me in, tight. "You need to speak to her."

"I need to get out of here." I feel utterly trapped suddenly, in this little inlet with its towering cliffs and its tiny roads. "How do I get out of here?"

"Where are you going to go?" he says gently. "Why don't we talk this through? Let's ask Roger and Sofia. Olive, there could be a million reasons why they never told you. The most likely version was to protect you."

"To protect themselves," I say bitterly.

"Olive," he says, reaching out to try to hold me again, and I let him, falling limply into him.

"I need to go home," I say quietly. "I need to speak to her."

"Well, we can't get you out of here right now," he says. "We'd need to arrange a boat, or a bus or something."

"Boat," I say, frowning. "I need to get a flight. I want to go. I want to go *now*."

"I'll come with you," says Leo.

I nod, not looking at him, and he slips out the bedroom door. I suddenly feel very, very alone and unsure of myself.

I sit on the edge of the bed and my eyes fall on the urn, and I begin to cry.

31

'M ALREADY AT the end of the street before Sofia and Roger have noticed I've left, but Leo is on the case right away, telling me to stay there as he scurries back toward them to explain. I don't know what he's saying. I don't know what he could say. I keep walking and don't look back.

My bag is bulging from a hasty packing, and my eyes are red from the last hour of crying while Leo sat beside me, swearing and muttering to himself. I did not want him to speak. I do not want to know what he knows anymore. I already feel too betrayed to take any more betrayal.

I watch as the water taxi Leo ordered me chugs to the pier, and the driver waves me toward him. Leo is coming with me, although I don't want him to.

"Olive, wait," I hear him say as I toss my bag onto the back of the taxi.

"You should stay and finish the book," I say, unable to look him in the eye. "You were right about the beans anyway. It should have been just you doing the book. It should have been all you, Leo. All of it."

"Stop that," he says.

"Please don't come," I say. "This is between my mother and me. It will be fine. I just need some answers."

"I want to make sure you're okay," he says, telling the driver in Italian to take us to Santa Margherita and to *hurry*. Leo is carrying the ashes. I refuse to touch them.

I don't have the energy to argue. My mind is swimming. The questions too numerous to know where to begin.

When did they meet?

Why wasn't I told?

Who even is my real father?

"You don't know anything for sure," was all Leo kept saying. "Wait and talk to your mother."

I keep staring at the bag with the ashes. I want to toss them overboard and have them sink to the bottom of the ocean, inside the urn.

"Leo," I say. "Can you pass them to me? The ashes? I want to throw them into the sea."

"You want to do it now, from the back of a taxi boat?"

"I don't want to lug them all the way home. I'm never coming back here. I hate it. I want to go home," I say.

"You don't like Italy?" the driver asks, shouting over his shoulder. Leo whispers something in his ear, and he nods, glancing back at me with a look of concern.

"Don't you see? I'm not even Italian," I say, shaking my head. "Give them to me."

"No," he says sharply.

"Yes," I reply, reaching out my hand. I watch as his mouth tightens into a line, and he appears to want to protest, but then his body slumps and he swings the bag off his shoulder.

"Fucking monkey on my back for weeks," I say, snatching it off him and pulling the urn out. "Why did he want *me* to do it, anyway?"

My heart tugs at the feeling that as soon as Mum and Dad split, he just let me go. *He didn't need to deal with me anymore.* And then it swings to the other idea. The one I feel is the real truth: that he loved me with everything in his heart, and when my parents split, he felt he didn't have the right to demand more from me. That he was too scared to tell me the truth in case he lost me forever. I feel my stomach turn at the thought of it. The awful, upsetting, heartbreaking thought.

I can't open the fucking urn. I try to twist the round lid, then I try flicking it open, breaking a nail in the process.

"Fuck," I say, sucking on my thumb.

Then I put a little more pressure on the lid and hear something give, a dull snapping sound, and then it comes off easily in my hand. Inside there is a plastic bag sealed with a white tag.

I cannot handle this being all that is left of my dad. A thick plastic bag, stuffed inside an urn. The tears come again, and my head slumps forward.

"I hate this," I say, crying.

"It's okay, Olive," says Leo, taking the urn back from me as the boat approaches the pier. "Why don't I keep it until you know what you're doing."

And then my body kind of shuts down and I let Leo guide me from the boat to a taxi service that takes me to Genoa. On the trip I think about moments in my life, Dad at the kitchen counter telling stories, Mum slipping around quietly. The contrast between them was always deep, but now I see it through a new lens.

When we get to the airport, I feel a horrible numbness wash

over me. Staring at the check-in counter, I pick up my bag, ignoring the urn.

"You take it," I say, averting my eyes from Leo. "And please don't come. Go back. Finish the book."

Leo dismisses me out of hand, grabbing his own bag and paying the driver, a move that irritates me.

"I said don't come," I say, my eyes lifting to his. Numb. Numb. "I don't want you to come."

"Olive," he says, firmly now. "I don't think you should be alone."

"I want to be alone," I say. "I haven't been properly alone in weeks and I want to be alone now. I'm going to go through security and I'm going to call my best friends. And then I'm going to call my mother to tell her I'm coming to Yorkshire. And I don't want you to come through there with me. *Please.*"

Leo looks momentarily furious but accepts what I'm saying.

"Stubborn," he says.

"You are," I reply, sniffing, wiping my face with the back of my hand.

"I'm sorry, Olive," he begins, but I hold my hand up to stop him from talking.

"Later," I say.

He glances back at the taxi stand, and the huge queue that is forming. He pulls his phone out of his bag and then finally looks as though he's going to give up. I am relieved. I need him gone so I can clear my head.

"Fine," he says. "I don't like leaving you alone, but I'm not going to keep fighting you. Call Ginny and Kate as soon as you get through to the other side. If you can't talk to me, talk to them."

"I will," I say.

"Olive," he says. "This shouldn't change anything. Don't let it . . ."

I cut him off. "I know. I do know that."

He grabs my arm and tries to tug me in, but I shrug him off. And then he nods as the seriousness of my feelings sinks in.

"I'll find out what Roger knows," he says. "Let me at least do that for you."

I nod quickly, grateful. "I'll call you," I say, wanting to lean into him, but instead turning and heading for security. I look back only once and see that Leo is on his phone, his face etched with concern. I wonder what all this means. What it means for the restaurant. For Leo. For us.

32

Home

MUM IS NOT surprised to see me. She jumps out of the porch chair and rushes toward me as though I'm a small child. In a way, it's how I feel. Her house in the country has never felt like my old home, but coming to see her feels as close as it could get.

The gray-stone cottage looks small from the front with its ancient thatched roof and small wood-framed windows, but in fact, it leads to a large open-plan kitchen and lounge, which spill out onto a quintessentially British lawn, with three beehives, and at the far end, a hedgerow breaking Mum's yard from the farm behind.

"Olive," she says. Her hair is grayer than it was the last time I saw her, but the immaculate bob remains with the short fringe she's always had. Mum has always been so stylish and so graceful.

She puts her arms around me, and when she pulls me in, I allow myself to feel comforted by it, despite my anger.

"I finally got through to Leo and he said you might be heading here."

I feel numb, empty. I just want to get to the truth of why I came.

"Come inside," she says, motioning for me to sit. "I'm so sorry. I am so very sorry, Olive. You must feel . . ."

I look up at her, my eyes moist, red from crying. "Lied to?"

I want to say more, but I have Kate in my head, telling me to lead with compassion.

I called them both when I got through security. Ginny was devastated for me in the way I needed, affirming my right to be furious and validating my feelings of betrayal. But it was Kate who knew exactly what I should do next.

"DNA is just DNA. Being a father is something else entirely," Kate said. "You need to get to the heart of why they didn't tell you. The rest, the *is he really my father* stuff, is all up to you. It's really just an adjustment of fact. Nothing else changes."

Mum rushes into the kitchen to retrieve iced lemon water and some scones with jam and cream and brings them out on a silver tray. I have not eaten in twenty-four hours and the sight of the clotted cream in the little silver bowl makes me want to retch.

"Do you want a tea or a coffee?" she asks, glancing at her watch.

"I can't take the caffeine," I say glumly.

"You must be exhausted. Leo said you got in late. You will stay tonight?" she asks.

"Yes. *Maybe*," I say, shrugging.

Mum hovers for a bit and then heads inside. "I'll make a pot," she says, her voice all tight with nerves. *How long must we string this out?* I wonder. Better to rip the Band-Aid off.

I try to breathe; I focus on being compassionate.

Mum sits, finally, and there is a moment of quiet. I don't want to ask again and so I wait. I can feel Mum looking at me, fidgeting. But I don't offer any comfort. I need the information.

"We never meant to keep it from you," she says finally, pouring a coffee for herself. I look at her and nod slowly, before turning and staring out at a lavender bush by the edge of the patio. Watching a bumblebee fly drunkenly between flowers. "Not for as long as we did."

I glance at her, nodding. "Tell me everything, Mum. From the beginning."

She nods.

"Well, as you know, I met Nicky when I worked in that little dress shop near Angel, and he used to walk past on his way to his job on Upper Street. He came into the dress shop every day for a week, pretending to be looking for things. Men's socks one day. A pair of gym shoes the next. I mean, it was a women's dress shop," she says with half a chuckle, her voice unbearably strained, like an old rubber band about to snap. "Anyway, I was pregnant at the time but not showing. Obviously, I said no."

"You were already pregnant? With me?" I say, as I pick at the scones in front of me.

Mum sighs, resting her chin on her hand, eyes joining mine briefly, before she sits back and smooths out her white blouse.

"He'd left me," she says, frowning. "The man who . . ."

Her voice trails off. My *real* father left her while she was pregnant. I'm not sure I'm ready to hear it. "Tell me about you and Dad," I say quickly.

"Yes," she says, nodding. "It was very early days. I didn't tell Nicky I was pregnant; there didn't seem any point. He was kind and flirty, but I just told him no and that I was dating someone and thank you but no thank you. But we liked each other. I liked him very much indeed. Anyway, he went back that year to work some more in Italy . . ."

"Back to Rocco," I say. I'd known Dad had gone back and forth a few times over those early years. It had never occurred to me to really look at those timelines.

"That's right," she says. "And when he came back from his trip, he came into the shop to say hello, and there you were."

"Okay," I say, imagining his face when he saw Mum with a new baby.

"It didn't take long for him to figure out there was no father in the picture. And bless him, he just kept pursuing me. And he was *so* smitten with you."

I bite my lower lip to keep it from wobbling.

"We dated for a few months, then he asked me to marry him. And part of that deal was that he would adopt you."

"A condition?" I say, frowning.

"No. Not like that. For Nicky it was very clear. We would be a family, properly. You would be his. And I said yes to all of it. I loved him. I loved you."

"Were you ever going to tell me?" I ask.

"We'd agreed to do it when you were older. Maybe around your sixteenth or eighteenth birthday, we thought," she says, frowning. "But then the separation happened, and he begged me not to."

I bring my hands up to my face.

"You were already so angry with him, Olive. He was worried he would lose you if you knew," she said. "I was so upset myself; I probably didn't do enough to reassure him."

I look up at her, and I see her eyes are glassy now too.

"But he lost me anyway," I reply, feeling it like a sucker punch to the gut.

"Olive," she says. "I should have told you. We should have told you. I've thought about it a thousand times since he died."

"I feel like you said a lot of things about him that affected my view of him, Mum. You called him selfish. You said he only thought about Nicky's. Is all of that really true?"

"He can have been a good father, a good partner, but also have got some things wrong. Or maybe we both did," she says wearily.

My mind wanders to Leo. I get a striking memory of us sitting in Rocco's, and he tells me, *"He wasn't perfect, I'll give you that."*

"And it was right to be angry with him. He sold our house. He was a great chef, a fabulous host, a wonderful father and partner, but he was so convinced he knew best when it came to the restaurant . . ." Her voice trails off, and, again, I think of Leo's stories of trying to get Dad to modernize.

I look at Mum and I reach over and put my hand on hers. "I was angry with him," she says. "I just was. And I shared too much of that with you."

I don't say it, but she's right. She did.

"I love you, Mum," I say instead.

"Oh, Olive. I never wanted to run a restaurant. It's not in my bones like it was his. Or it is *yours*. I left him because I was tired of the package. Nicky came with Nicky's."

I squeeze her hand.

"I'd already put all the money my parents gave me when we got married into the restaurant and I had nothing really of my own. I didn't go to university. I worked in a dress shop, Olive."

I reach forward for water to quench my sudden thirst.

"I know," I say quietly. "Mum, I can't believe you didn't make him sell the restaurant when you divorced. Leo says he slowly ran it into the ground without your help."

"He might have done that either way," she says, shaking her head, a regretful smile on her face. She looks over at me, her eyes round and glassy. "I couldn't have done it to him."

I nod. I get that part.

"And anyway, in the end, the money comes back to you," she says, and I look quickly away from her gaze.

"I wanted to sell the restaurant and pay you out." I can hear the past tense in my sentence, and maybe Mum can hear it too. She smiles.

"I don't need you to do that," she says, holding her hands out to indicate her pretty house. "I want you to do what *you* want with it."

"Mmm," I say. "Who *is* my dad?" I ask, my voice tight with nerves.

"He's from Glasgow. And I tried to contact him, many times very early on, but he didn't respond. I assume he's still there. I will happily give you everything I know about him. But, Olive, he was not a good man."

I nod slowly, and a part of me seems to peel away. I feel a single tear on my cheek, but I do not dare move.

"Nicky loved you, Olive. He was as good as a father can be. He was so doting. So in love . . . He fell in love with you like I'd never seen. And I was happy. We were happy."

I let out a small, miserable laugh at that. Not meaning to be cruel, but saddened by it all.

"My name," I say.

"He thought it was fate," she says, her eyes glassy. "*Olive Stone.*"

At that moment, George comes out of the kitchen area,

wearing a sweatband around his head, and very short gym shorts. He makes an abrupt about-turn when he sees us both.

I turn back to my mother.

"We made a lot of dumb mistakes. But many of them were out of love for you."

I don't say anything. It's Mum's big plea for understanding, and while I do understand, I still feel so incredibly sad. What if I'd known? What if I'd actually known? How would I have felt at fifteen?

"He was your father, Olive," she says, rubbing her temples as though she has a migraine coming on. "He raised you. He loved you. We both made a mistake keeping the truth from you, and I've regretted it for years and years."

I reach down into my bag and pull out my wallet. Unzipping the compartment at the back, I pull out the Polaroid of me and Dad. The one where I'm holding an ice cream and my dad is looking at me, *beaming* at me. I hand the photo to my mum.

"He loved me," I say. "I do know that. I just feel like I didn't have the full story. Like maybe I would have acted differently when you two split up."

"That's my fault," she says, her voice wavering now. "I was so frustrated with him."

"I know," I say. "I've just always felt like, over those ten years, that it was me keeping distance, you know? But I do think now that a part of him was scared to push me."

Mum nods. She knew it too.

"He begged me not to tell you. I felt so guilty about everything, I agreed," she says, confirming my suspicions.

After a minute, she says, "How do you feel, Olive?"

"Heartbroken," I say.

I feel the tears falling down my cheeks. My heart breaks for my dad, who fell in love with me as a baby and took me on as his own. I take the photo off my mum, and through tears, I see the love in his eyes, the look of pride on his face, and I start to cry, heavily. The depth of the ache is physical. It hits me like a punch to the stomach and I cry out in agony at the pain of it. The pain is so hollow I find myself desperate for breath. There is nothing there. No way to tell him I love him. No way to thank him. He's gone. My love has nowhere to go, and my regret can never be atoned for.

"I'm so sorry, Olive," my mum says, as I slump on the table and cry.

33

G INNY AND KATE are waiting for me outside my house when I get back. As soon as I see them the tears start again. But this time, they are tears of relief to be back somewhere safe. With my friends. In their arms.

"Let's get you inside," Ginny says, opening the door to my house as she leads me into the lounge room. They've tidied up. Like, it's immaculate. There are flowers on the kitchen table.

I read the little card attached to the flowers.

Dearest O. We love you. You are loved. Kate & Ginny xx

"How long did it take you to agree on the message?" I say, holding the card out to both of them, sniffing as my tears subside.

"Kate's wording," says Ginny, shrugging. "On this I had to let her win."

Kate shrugs. "I just want you to see clearly that the most important truth in all of this is that you are loved, Olive. By us and your mum and dad. Loved so much."

I nod slowly.

"Yep," I say. "But every time I look at it from a new angle, I get confused."

"I'm going to make us a cocktail," says Ginny unhelpfully.

"Can we just have tea?" Kate says, frowning at Ginny.

"I know a good cocktail with peppermint tea. It's with gin. Do you have gin?"

"Ginny!" I say, laughing now.

"I'm sorry, it's just such a historical event, it feels like we need to drink," she says, frowning.

I flick the kettle on and tap a chair, indicating Ginny should sit, and Kate goes to the cupboard to grab a few mismatched mugs and the tea.

It takes about an hour to get them up to speed on everything. My mother; my terrible biological father, whom I don't want to talk about. And then my dad and what it all means.

"How do you feel about it now?" Ginny asks with a wide, uncomfortable grimace on her face.

I shrug. "I don't know."

I watch Kate and Ginny catch each other's eye.

"How did you leave it?" Kate asks.

"We hugged," I say, shrugging. "I was mostly in shock, I think. I felt angry for a while after I left. But I also get it. I get how the lie happened and how there was never a good time to reveal the truth."

"A mistake, but one you can forgive?" Kate asks, and I nod.

"I think so," I say with a shrug. "I try to work out his thinking. It's like he begged my mum, *Please don't take my daughter*, and then kind of let me go anyway?"

"It was almost certainly both of you pulling back for different reasons," Kate says quickly. "You pushed your dad away, and he felt some conflict in chasing you too much. Of course he did, Olive. How could he force a father-daughter relationship on you with such a burden of a lie? He probably felt he couldn't make demands on you. He didn't have the right to grab you by the ear and make you come back to the kitchen and go to culinary school or whatever."

I nod. Kate is always right. Even if she is serving it a little hot today.

"I'm sure he was carrying plenty of his own guilt, Olive," says Kate.

"I want to speak to him," I say, my voice a little shaky again. "Like one last time. I hate that I will never have all the answers."

"Did you try—"

"The empty chair? Yes. And no, I'm not trying that again," I say, chuckling now, as I wipe away the snot trickling down my face. "I must look like shit, my god."

"Actually, I think all the crying has given you a nice glow," says Ginny, leaning forward to touch my arm. "You'd pay a lot at Charlotte Tilbury for that dewy pink."

"What about the restaurant?" Kate says. "What will you do about Nicky's?"

"Well. As you know I originally wanted to sell it, to give Mum back some money, but then I'm there at her house in the country and her happy, settled life with George," I say dreamily. "She's happy now. Really happy. George is lovely with his bees and she says she doesn't need it."

"I bet she could use it," Ginny says.

"She doesn't want Olive to give it to her," Kate says, frowning at Ginny.

"It feels like it isn't this big thing I need to make right

anymore," I say. "Two things I do know. One: I can't change the past. I need to find peace with her mistakes. And two: I want to keep Nicky's."

"Aghhhhh," says Ginny, pretending to faint dramatically. "Thank god."

Kate raises an eyebrow, her reaction more subdued.

"Because of Leo?"

"No," I say. "Because I'll always regret not trying."

"Do you want to run a restaurant?"

I think of Rocco and Isabella. I think about the early days of Nicky's—me and my father and our mismatched tortellini. I think of my mother, who never wanted to do it but gave it everything she had until she had no more.

She and I are different. Because I want this. I've always wanted this.

And Leo and Dad are different because, well, they're different.

"I want to try," I say, nodding. "I want to give it a go with all that I know and all that Leo knows, and if it doesn't work, we just pull out. Both of us have money coming in for the cookbook, and Leo can maybe put some of his toward a few small renovations so he has a stake in the place too. And, Ginny, maybe you could help with some ideas for that?"

"My dream job," she says, grinning. "And what about your feelings about Leo?" Ginny adds quickly.

"Yep. Dreams aside, this is emotionally complicated, Olive," says Kate, nodding.

"Maybe it is, maybe it isn't," I say, throwing my hands in the air. "It can't be more complicated than Mum and Dad."

Kate and Ginny and I keep talking for the next few hours,

analyzing the situation from every angle, until I start to form a full picture of what I'd be taking on.

The best of friends. An abundance of patience. Not a stifled yawn or a change of subject between them. And then the conversation turns back to Leo.

"Have you heard from him?"

"Of course," I say, heart squeezing in an entirely different way. Thinking of Leo alters my brain chemistry, despite everything. "Because he's Leo and he's thoughtful and he wants to know I'm okay."

On the train back from Mum's, I sent him a message with an abridged version of the story.

> **ME:** I was right. Mum confessed. Feeling pretty shocked & heading back to London to process. Thank you for everything. Olive x
>
> **LEO:** What can I do? Leo x
>
> **ME:** Nothing. I'll call you soon, I promise.
>
> **LEO:** Don't think about me. Lx

Later, as the train pulled into Euston station, he sent another message.

> **LEO:** But I am thinking about you. x

I need to call him, but I wanted to speak to him after I'd had time with the girls to regroup and figure out what I really want.

"What are you going to do?" says Ginny, her eyes rounding in sweet hope.

"How do you feel about him?" Kate asks.

The physical response is immediate; my cheeks flush, my stomach tightens, I feel breathless and filled with life at once. I close my eyes and see flashes of Leo. The twinkle in his eye. Chasing me up the hill on our bikes. Cherries. His hands on me in the pool. His freely expressed passion. For life. For food. For me.

"I am drawn to him . . . ," I say, one shoulder rising.

"A moth to a flame?" *Ginny.*

"No. It isn't all danger, danger. It's like sugar to cream," I say, laughing. "Like butter to bread."

"Like peanut butter to jam," says Ginny.

"Like a hot dog in your bun, more like," says Kate.

"We fit," I say, simply. "I've enjoyed doing the book with him. Once we found our groove it was great."

"That's so good," Kate says.

"He finished all the recipes. Oh god, that reminds me," I say, glancing back through the balcony doors into the house. "My suitcase that got returned. There's a manuscript in there. I need to go through it. I need to get this fucking book done!"

"We'll leave you to it, honey," says Ginny, standing up immediately.

"Thank you," I say.

After the girls leave, I open up my suitcase, smiling at the dresses and bikinis and all the lost, nervous thoughts that went into packing for this trip. And then I pull out the bound manuscript, opening immediately to the first page, when something falls out.

I look down at the floor and there's an envelope.

On the front, it says *To Olive.*

Dad. It's from Dad.

34

Dearest Olive,

The nurse is writing this for me because my hand is not working very well. It seems my time is come. Don't worry, I am not scared.

I wish you so much happiness in life, Olive. I wish you fall in love. I wish you work hard and enjoy what you do. I wish you all that you deserve. Which, in your old dad's opinion, is the whole world.

I want you to finish my book. I have made some notes for you in there. Ask the estate solicitor for it. I will speak to him in the next hour and tell him my wish. I hope the publisher agrees.

Olive. I do not know what comes next. But I do know that I am not sad. That you were the greatest gift of my life, and I am thinking only of you and holding your hand in my heart. And that makes me very happy.

I love you too much.

And I'm sorry for the parts I got wrong.

Dad

35

A WEEK HAS PASSED since that letter opened my heart fully to the grief I'd been holding at bay. I handed in my notice at *The London Post*. I hadn't yet decided what to do with Nicky's but I knew it was time to move on from that at least. My heart was not in the feature TEN DELICIOUS (AND SURPRISING!) WAYS TO USE PICKLED HERRING.

When I was ready, I finished the draft pages of Tuscany and Liguria. I did it with Dad's annotated manuscript next to me, skipping through to the notes he'd made.

Sicily—Oranges, pistachios, and/or aubergine. Sicilian food a product of its immense, diverse history. Have sardines! Try the orange cake. You'll find it all over, but there used to be a good one in Taormina.

I shake my head in amazement. Somehow, it feels like Dad had been quietly guiding me.

Tuscany—Wild boar is good but tomatoes are better. Nothing else! Please say something with Chiara's tomatoes. I want

to help her. Farm is a century old and sells some obscure va-
rieties. Tomato salads, tomato bread soup, panzanella.

And here too, Leo and I had organically found the path my
father laid out for us. The notes on Liguria are less specific, but
when I read his scrawled handwriting, I smile to myself.

Liguria—Was thinking about beans, but basil a good option.

Oh boy, I cannot wait to show that note to Leo. *Basil a good
option*!

Leo.

I sit and write with an open heart, not shying away from
treacly memories of cut oranges shared in the sea. Pushing my
cynicism to the side and allowing the love I have for food, for
Italy, for my father, to run from my heart down my veins to my
fingers and onto the page. At times I feel like he is beside me, holding my hand, like in the old photo with the gelato. An apparition
in sepia with white teeth, a tan, and obscenely short swimming
trunks.

I talk to Dad often now. He is around me. He is beaming,
proud, and happy.

The publisher chased me yesterday, and today I will send
her the final version as soon as Leo has okayed it. I am sending Leo the drafts as they are done, and he is sending me his feedback.

LEO: Sicily is done in my opinion. Feel like Tuscany
should have a reference to cherries in the swimming
pool

ME: STOP IT
LEO: I'm trying, Olive

I roll my eyes at his message.

LEO: Liguria is like a childhood dream. Wonderful.
ME: In Gucci and Dolce and Gabbana.
LEO: I want to see you, Olive. When you're ready
ME: I'm ready

That afternoon I receive a message on the manuscript. The subject reads:

FROM: SLOANE BOOKS
RE: COPY EDITS.

The publisher has accepted our final draft. The book is finished.

I check my watch. He will be here soon.

I DON'T WANT to fuss over what I cook. I make focaccia. I make stew with beans and Italian sausage. I make dark chocolate mousse. Everything is easy to execute and allows me time to dress.

I am aching to see him after two weeks apart. Almost as long as we'd ever been together, in fact.

I am jittery and giddy at every sound that could be a knock on my door. I take time with drying my hair, shaving my legs, and painting my toenails. I pull on a simple black dress. I stay barefoot as I finish the dinner.

And then, when eight rolls around, the doorbell rings.

Seeing Leo again takes my breath away. He bites his lip, grinning as he stands in the doorway looking me up and down.

"Well, hey," he says.

He's casual. Sneakers, jeans, shirt open a little at the neck.

"Are you a sight for sore eyes," he says, this time a little nervously. I watch him ball his hands together before I put him out of his misery.

"Come in, stranger," I say, holding out a hand. "It's getting cold out."

Leo takes my hand and I close the door. We stand for a minute staring at each other, with misty round eyes, before Leo tugs me roughly in for a hug. It's so fucking nice to be in his arms, I collapse into his body.

"It's weird seeing you in London," he says, finally pulling back. "Though I've been picturing it every day. You at Spitalfields. Wondering if you would like a Brick Lane bagel. Wanting to show you this amazing market in South London."

He rolls his eyes and laughs at his admission, and I smile back at him, wondering how it is possible to feel such love for someone I've only known for half a summer.

"I missed trying to make you smile," he quips, rubbing his fingers across my knuckles.

He studies my room. Eyes on the old sofa, the small television tucked away among my bookshelves. "You have a lot of cookbooks," he says, grinning, as he finally pulls away and shrugs off his jacket. I hang it over a chair.

"Everyone buys me cooking gadgets and cookbooks. It's all I ever get," I say, smiling. "Well, that and red lipstick."

Leo smiles. "I'm looking forward to meeting *everyone*," he says. "Ginny and Kate seem like a right laugh. Do they still call me—"

"Hot Chef?" I ask, folding my arms. "No. You're just Leo now. You're no longer being objectified."

"Damn," he says, shaking his head. "That was quick."

Leo looks at me and tips his head to the side. "What did you cook?"

"Come on," I say, leading him to my kitchen table, a small four-seater with mismatched chairs.

He sits across from me, and we eat. Leo is pleasantly surprised by how good of a cook I am.

I tell him about my mother, my time in Yorkshire. And he tells me about what's been happening at Nicky's and a trip to see the football he's planned with his friends.

"I don't know any of your world in London," I say, with some trepidation.

Leo shrugs. "You will," he says. "If you want to."

I look down at the plate of beans and sausages and I take a deep breath.

"Don't hold me in suspense any longer, Olive," he says. "I need to know where your head is at."

"With the restaurant?" I ask carefully.

"No," he says, pulling back, his face screwed up in offense. "No. Not about that. About you and me. *Us.*"

I lean forward and I squeeze his hand. "Sorry. *Sorry.*"

"The restaurant is important, but like I said in Tuscany, I have a plan B." He leans in, and his face is so serious my eyes search his for what might be coming. "There is no plan B when it comes to you. There is only you."

I feel a flush of pleasure run from my toes to the top of my head and I squeeze Leo's hand again. *I am falling in love with this man.* How can it be? How do I deserve it?

"You want to know how I'm feeling about you?"

"I have been thinking about you every moment since you left me at the airport. I need to know. Are we going to try?"

"Leo," I say, looking up to the ceiling and then back down at him, and I laugh gently. "The heart wants what the heart wants. And mine wants *you*."

36

I REACH UP AND put my hand on the flicking sign that says NICKY'S, my mouth breaking into a warm smile. My eyes dart to the bar across the street, Temp, the one Ginny, Kate, and I were at when I started this crazy journey. Stuck to the window is a notice of foreclosure. *I win, Leo.*

I shake my head, my nerves starting to rise.

"This is going to have to come down," I murmur, tapping the sign one last time.

I take a steadying breath and push the door open.

I hear sounds coming from the back office and take a moment to myself as I peer into the kitchen and see the framed photo of me, right next to the clock.

Then I walk to the bar and run my hand along it, turning to the dining room, and I am filled with not sadness, but excitement.

"Olive?" I turn, and Leo has emerged from the kitchen just as he did that very first time I came in here weeks ago.

"You look good," I say, taking in his sharp sweatshirt over brushed-cotton pants, rolled up, with black trainers. "I'm getting used to seeing you in damp, wet London attire."

"Well, *you* . . . look beautiful," he says, and I melt. I have made some effort, it's true. Hair blow-dried; a cobalt-blue dress with a diamond cutout on the bodice, a flirty skirt, with just two finely crossed straps on the back.

"Well, yes," I say haughtily, though I can feel the crimson blush on my cheeks giving me away.

"Come. Let me show you around properly," he says, and I follow, a wry smile on my face as he holds out his hand to guide me. Without hesitation I take it. It is a desperately tender feeling, the warmth of my hand in his.

"I blacked out the windows," Leo replies, pointing over his shoulders to the huge windows at the front of the restaurant, which are covered with black garbage bags and electrical tape. "Just trying to re-create a little evening dining experience for you so you can try the set menu."

"But first, a look around?"

He nods, taking me through to the back kitchen, with the same layout and large walk-ins. Those walk-ins into which I would sneak to steal ice cream and the small chocolates that went out with the coffee. The office where Mum would sit, poring over invoices and "the books." The little photo album stuffed with my reviews. Our family photos still prominent between actors and football players on the wall of guest photos on the way to the restrooms.

A family restaurant. With family memories. Ready, I think, to start new ones.

Leo doesn't know that I'm ready to do this. I haven't told him yet; there is still one thing to consider.

"Something smells really good," I say, nodding to the lone set table in the middle of the room.

"Right, take a seat, then. *London's toughest ex-critic.* And allow me to put my whole self on a fucking plate and serve it up to you," he says, laughing.

"You're very brave," I say. "But don't worry, I'm sure I'll love it."

"Liar," he says, guiding me to the table.

Leo lights the candle and then disappears into the kitchen, returning moments later with two bowls, and a bottle of wine under his arm. I stand up and take the bottle from him, turning it to see the label.

"The Spumante from the ferry?" I say, surprised.

"I ordered a case," he says, "so it was ready and waiting."

"Waiting?"

"For you," he says. "For you, Olive."

It makes me blush, and I cannot control the urge to kiss him. I put the bottle down and remove both of the bowls from Leo's hands and place them on the table.

Then I reach my arms around his neck and wait until I see him smile and his eyes start to sparkle. "Worth the wait, though," he says.

I kiss him, softly, on the mouth. He puts his hands on my back, gently moving them to my waist, where he holds me firm, pulling me into him.

I pull back. "Whoa there," I say. "I plan on eating first."

Leo adjusts his trousers and laughs. "This meal is going to be excruciating in more ways than one," he says.

"We have stuff to talk about." I nod, sliding into my seat. I peel the foil back on the Spumante. "Doesn't mean I don't want to jump you."

I pop the cork, with a brow raised for comic effect, and we both tuck into the soup.

"You can't serve these bubbles with this soup," I say, after almost inhaling the entire bowl in minutes.

"I love how you eat." Leo laughs. "But can you start by saying something nice?" he says, cautioning me.

"Sorry," I say, shaking my head. "It's divine. It's even sweeter than the soup you made for me at Chiara's. I love it."

"Thank you," he says, putting down his spoon.

He looks at me, puts his hands in his hair.

"Olive, I want you to know two things. Firstly, I sent my CV to a bunch of places, and I got some offers. One of them is pretty exciting. It's at DeLuca's on Shaftesbury Avenue. I would love that job, okay?"

I nod. He's giving me a guilt-free out.

"But the other thing is, if you're considering it . . . If you might want to give this a go . . . I have some money. It isn't a lot, but it's enough to have some ownership of the business."

"Leo," I say, "I already spoke to the bank."

He nods, looking down at his soup. "I get it."

"No, I mean, I already spoke to them about *you*. Property rights aside, if you invest the money from the book. It's a decent amount. I can get you in for a healthy share in the value of the business."

Leo's head snaps up. "What?"

"The restaurant isn't worth much as a business for sale," I say. "The turnover is too terrible. It's a bargain. Most of the value is in the property, which would remain mine. We'd lease off me, so to speak."

"What, so we'd be partners?"

"Can you get that money together?" I say, reaching into my bag and handing him a folder with all the financial details.

"So, it would be mine too?" he says.

"Yes. It would be ours," I say.

"Are you . . . are you sure?"

"Why should I take all the financial risk?" I say with a grin.

"Fuck," he says, shaking his head. "Fuck DeLuca's. Olive. Are you really sure?"

I take a deep breath, and I nod. "Yes," I say, wiping my mouth with the paper napkin. "It's time for a fresh start for us both, Leo."

"Okay," he says, folding his arms.

"But I'm nervous. I want to make sure we have time away from here, that this is our work, and that we love it, but that we nurture the side of our lives that isn't inside these walls. I want to make sure I'm not overwhelmed by you because you're the chef. You need to listen to me, and to take my concerns seriously. You're not the star of the show."

Leo knows better than to laugh. He nods, a genuine smile on his face.

"And if I tell you one day I want out, you need to listen to that."

"I will," he says. "And I have a few conditions too."

I snap my head up and smile at him. "You do?"

"It's going to be hard," he says. "And at times it might feel overwhelming. And I'm going to need you to accept that we won't get everything right."

"You're worried I'm going to be too tough to work with?" I say, my eyes flicking to the ceiling.

"Something like that," he says, laughing. "Go easy on me, okay?"

"Only if you keep to my exacting standards," I say, and Leo

laughs. "But seriously, Leo, I'm opening my heart to this, and all the anxieties that come with it. We're in it together, okay?"

Leo nods. "I am so fucking happy, I can't . . ." He looks at me, square in the eye. "I would have been happy if you'd sold it too."

"Liar," I say. "But I know you would have accepted it."

Leo stands up and points to a large folder sitting on the bar. It's heavy and canvas, an architect's folder. "I have some plans. Based on your feedback."

"What is this?" I say, seeing Ginny's firm's initials in the corner of the folder.

"It's the new interior ideas." He moves his finger across the plans, pointing to each of the features. "The focus is on vibrant, classical Italian dining. With the big-ass bar still in place."

"No, I mean . . . you spoke to Ginny?" I say.

"It was a happy accident," he says. "I called her firm, they're literally around the corner. Anyway, I asked them to put together some preliminary ideas for me. So that I could engage them if we got the investor excited."

"They put you through to Ginny?"

"Yes," he says. "It was a pretty awkward conversation, as far as they go."

"That fucker never told me," I say, laughing.

"Well, she's very professional," he says. "And also, she said she would do it as a favor to help you . . . what did she say? Hmm. That's right . . . 'come to your senses and follow your destiny.'"

"That sounds like Ginny." I laugh.

Leo turns a page and taps the plans, showing a rough design of the menu. A single, elegant page. "PASTA @ NICKY'S. Polished and elevated Italian food."

"Deconstructed Scotch egg tagliatelle?" I say, grinning. Tagliatelle with Italian sausage, egg, and pecorino sauce, topped with garlic breadcrumbs. I'm not sold, but as with everything, Leo and I will find a perfect compromise.

"There's room to talk," he says, laughing. "I figured I'd start in the clouds and we could meet somewhere in the middle."

I feel Leo's hand on the back of my neck as he leans in to kiss me, just behind the ear. I feel a tingle down my spine as his hot breath hits my neck, and I have to clench down on my bottom lip to contain my moan.

"I miss you when you're not beside me," I say, leaning back into him as he puts his arms around me, pulling me into an embrace so I feel his whole body pressed into the back of me.

"I can't believe we're doing this," he says, kissing me on the neck again. "I want to take you into the kitchen and ravish you."

"Where all the best love affairs begin," I say, turning and jumping up and wrapping my legs around his waist as he kisses me and leads me, slowly and deliberately, to the kitchen.

Epilogue

LEO AND I have hiked for two hours to get here, but we are finally standing at the top of Etna, near the third crater. The smell is unreal—rotten eggs—and the heat of the sun at this high altitude burns my face.

"You couldn't do it in the fucking ocean?" Leo says, panting as he follows me on the goat path. "This is so dramatic. So Olive."

"Come on," I say, "hurry up and we can get back down the hill and go to dinner."

Leo finally meets me by a mass of hardened lava rock, and he hands me the backpack with the urn inside.

"It's a good idea, though," he says, turning to see the bay of Catania behind us, the cliffs of Taormina in the distance.

"I know. I have this vision that he'll slowly make his way down into the lush farms and vineyards and one day I'll drink some wine that grew in Soil of Dad," I say, smiling. And then I think about the words and add, "It sounded more romantic in my head."

I carefully unscrew the lid of the urn and place it on a rock, his ashes decanted already from the plastic bag, and I slide my letter to Dad into the metal barrel.

"Pass me the lighter," I say to Leo, who is ready with the silver Zippo.

I roll my thumb across the flint and it bursts into flame, and we both watch as my letter burns into the ash with my dad.

"Now he knows," I say, throwing my hands around Leo and kissing him on the mouth.

With a deep breath I hold a handful of Dad's ashes out and allow it to fly from my hand and downwind toward the central crater.

"Go on," I say to Leo, and he nods, grabs a handful, and does the same.

After we finish, we make our way down the mountain, back to our rental car. In the back seat sits a box of early copies of the printed book. The inside cover has a photo of my dad and me, the one from Rocco's, and I wrote a foreword explaining how the book was finished and what it meant. It was soppy and sentimental, and honest. I'm proud of it.

"What did the letter say?" Leo asks, as he puts his key into the ignition. "You don't have to tell me, but I was wondering."

"Oh, it just thanked him for being such a wonderful dad. And said not to worry, he would always be my dad," I say with a shrug.

"Perfect," he says.

"And that I thought he should know we've renovated Nicky's and how much it needed it."

Leo smiles, turning the ignition. "Sounds like you covered everything."

"And . . . ," I say, leaning across to kiss Leo on the cheek. "That

I've been dating his sous chef for a year. And that I think getting Leo to come to Italy with me, forcing us to finish the book so that I fell in love with him and came back to the restaurant . . . I think this might have been Dad's plan all along."

Leo gives a knowing grin and then turns to face me.

"I love you," he says.

"You better," I reply.

Acknowledgments

Always, a heartfelt thank-you to my agent, Hattie, and my editor, Tara, at Penguin Random House. Thanks for continuing to stick with me, even when I'm not sure of myself!

This book is really a love letter to Italy, and I want to talk about some of my time there. It can seem like a bit of a cliché to say that Italians love food, but Italians *love* their food. It is an inescapable truth!

I first visited in the late nineties and have a lifelong memory of climbing a hill in Florence and watching the sunset from a patch of grass with a bottle of wine, thinking I might have been in the most beautiful place on earth. I took my mum back there a decade or so later; the spot had been developed, but the view was still just as magical.

Rome, though not featured in the book, is my favorite city on earth. On one of several visits, I was lucky enough to travel with a friend, Carolyn, who had gotten a long list of local hotspots, and we ate like queens for a week. The tip I got from an Italian friend, Andrea (who also edited the Italian in this book), was to stay in Monti—and it was the perfect spot. On my first night we ate at La Taverna dei Fori Imperiali. We were late, the kitchen was almost closed, but the owner gave us a small table anyway. He told us to just sit and he would bring some food, and to just say stop when we were full. It was a great way to eat in Italy and something I continue to do when I visit. "Bring me whatever you recommend." So far it has worked wonders. I've never been given the leftover chicken.

The last time I went to Rome, I was pregnant with my daughter Billie. What a great place to be constantly hungry. I think I ate gelato three times a day!

I also had the fortune of spending a week in Catania while I was drafting this novel. I was picked up at the airport by a lovely man in a perfectly tailored suit named Salvatore, who spent nearly twenty minutes explaining how to make the perfect carbonara. He also bragged about a WhatsApp group that he has with some of the local fishermen and showed me the videos he gets every morning from the market.

I ate at so many great places in Sicily, and as a woman traveling alone, I have to express my gratitude for the hospitality I was shown in every place I ate. Trattoria U Fucularu was a standout— a family-run place with the most divine prawn and pistachio pasta and the first serving of caponata I ever tried.

Gambino Winery was also a highlight—it's in an incredible position at around nine hundred meters up the side of Mount Etna, overlooking the sea. I arrived there with six other travelers: Two friends from Dorset—lovely men in their seventies. A couple from Arizona. And a wonderful newlywed couple who were having a COVID-delayed honeymoon. (Big shout-out to Emma, who was a rom-com reader; she bought a copy of *The Summer Job* while we were driving there.)

I have ordered several cases of wine from Gambino since I left Sicily. I fell in love with their most delicious rosé: Tifeo Rosato. If you have the means, get online and order yourself a case for the summer.

Antonia's hotel in the book unfortunately doesn't exist, but its position is the same as the hotel I did stay in. I love that spot—near the fish market, which is a wild place to go and explore day or night.

Thanks so much for reading my book. I continue to feel amazed and blessed that I get to do this for a living. I hope you enjoyed visiting Italy in this book. Go and make some fresh pasta! It's so much easier than you think.

Love, Lizzy x

Keep reading for an exciting excerpt from

The Summer Job

by Lizzy Dent

· · · · ·

"My perfect summer read! Sure to be one of the sweetest,
funniest, and sexiest books of the year."
—Emily Henry, #1 *New York Times* bestselling author

· · · · ·

What if you could be someone else . . .

just for the summer?

1

May

Y OU HERE FOR a wedding?" the driver asks, his cheery eyes focused on me and not on the tiny track we're careering up.

"No, no," I reply, as my fingers begin to ache from all the seat clenching they're having to do. He's got to be doing at least seventy.

"Aye, you're not dressed for a wedding," he agrees.

I look down at my shirt, self-consciousness pushing away fear for a moment. I'd bought a white silk shirt for sixty percent off from T.J. Maxx, but several hours into my journey I'd remembered that white silk shirts were only for rich people or anyone who liked doing laundry. The deal clincher for me, when buying clothing, is whether it will come out of the dryer like it's been ironed.

The car takes a sharp turn and the single lane thins to a ribbon before the woods clear completely and we drive through a simple iron gate fixed to two old stone pillars. Vast lawns rise slowly upward, and along the approach, rows of towering trees stretch their branches across to meet in a tunnel of crooked wood and leaves. Everything is sepia in the fog.

Ahead, the house comes into view, though in truth it looks more like a small castle. A gray-and-sandstone mother ship, with pointed turrets flanking the sides and an enormous staircase leading from the circular drive to the entrance. It's far grander than I'd imagined, but strangely bleak. I text Tim immediately.

I'm in a fucking gothic novel.

I'm pleased with my tone. Funny, irreverent, mysterious. I think about calling him to elaborate but I'm not entirely sure he'd get the joke. Tim isn't exactly well-read.

The car tires skid, jolting me back to the reality of the speeding vehicle. We are momentarily stuck as the tires spin hopelessly in the mud and the driver revs the engine. He switches gears and we thrust forward.

"Round the back there's a short road to the stables and cottages. And then a small car park," I say, double-checking the instructions on my phone.

"Staff entrance?" he questions, with a single raised eyebrow.

"Yup," I say, nodding, then stare wistfully out the window.

The back of the house is just as grand as but arguably more beautiful than the front. The ground drops away from a pebbled courtyard and rose garden down to a river, which I can hear but not see. The stables sit about a hundred meters to the side of the house, and the car pulls to a halt between them and a trio of small stone cottages. I look at the house, which is barely in view through a small grove of oaks.

The largest of the three cottages has woodsmoke rising in pleasing spirals from the squat chimney, and there's a small slate-and-silver sign on the wooden door that I can just make out. STAFF ONLY.

"This is it," I say, getting out and handing the driver two hundred pounds in Scottish notes, trying not to wince as I say good-bye to all the money I had left in the world. "Thanks for the ride. Who knew you could get to the west coast in under one and a half hours from Inverness? It must be a world record."

He looks inordinately proud.

There are about a dozen cars in the car park: a white van; some four-wheel drives; a few of those big, black, expensive-looking SUVs; and a couple of golf carts—but still no humans. A dog barks once, far in the distance, the sound echoing ominously around the estate.

I feel my anxiety blossom into full nerves. This is it. The literal end of the road, and potentially the craziest thing I've done since walking out on that stupid West End play. Right before my first line.

"Hope you enjoy Scotland, lass," the driver says, then takes off with a screech of tires on gravel.

I knock a few times on the wooden door. For late spring, it's far colder than I'd imagined, and my thin trench coat is proving a nonsense kind of cover-up for this weather.

My phone beeps and it's Tim.

What do you mean? 😕

I chuckle. He's so predictable.

There is still no sign of anyone. Crossing my arms to try to brace myself against the icy breeze, I look around the courtyard for some sign of life. I can hear the horses scuffing at the hay-covered stone floor in the barn, and I can sense the smell of mossy earth. I lean forward to look through the small window of the end cottage, and a small motion light springs on, blinding me to my surroundings.

"Heather?"

I jump at the voice behind me—deep, with a thick but soft Scottish accent. I hold my hand up to my face and try to make out the figure emerging from behind the white van. He is tall, dressed in chef's whites underneath a dark coat that is open and flapping in the wind, with a dark woolen beanie pulled down over his forehead. *Tall, mysterious, and can poach an egg.* I am instantly intrigued.

"Hello! Yes, I am. That's me," I say, saluting him like a general, my nerves apparently turning me into a comedy idiot.

"We need you to start right away," he says nervously, pulling up the collar on his coat.

"Right this minute?" I reply, desperate for a hot cup of tea and a shower.

"Our emergency cover fell into the river while taking a tinkle," booms a posh English accent, as a much older, shorter man in a dark suit with a bulging belly arrives, dragging one of those fancy bellhop trollies behind him. The light shines onto his reddish face, which is heavily lined but jolly. "Hospitalized with exposure."

"Double exposure," I reply with a giggle—I can't resist—and he shoots me a wicked grin.

"I'm William. But everyone calls me Bill. And this is James, here to welcome you on behalf of the kitchen," he continues, glancing down at my bag. "Well, I won't need the trolley. You travel light. Goodness gracious me. You should have seen last night's late arrival—poor night porter had to make a dozen trips up and down the stairs. *And* he's got a dicky leg."

"I don't like having more than I can manage on my own," I say, smiling at him.

"Well, I hope you brought some wellies," he says, glancing down at my shoes.

"No. I'll need to get some. And a coat. Didn't anyone notify Scotland it's May, for God's sake?" I say, clutching at my arms.

"Northerly. They're bitter, even in summer," says Bill as he sticks the key into the lock of the cottage, and it makes a heavy *thunk* as he turns it. He pushes the door open, but instead of showing me in, he pops my suitcase just inside and pulls the door shut. "Couldn't grow a Pinot in this windchill, eh?"

I stutter, then scramble for a quick reply. "Yes. Certainly it needs to be warmer. Except when there's a frost. You also sometimes need frost." He's staring at me, so obviously I continue my verbal drivel. "For the grapes, because sometimes they need frost. To make the wine, er, better."

"We need you to start tonight," James says again, cutting through the chatter. He and his tense shoulders are looking back toward the main house as if he's left a pan of hot fat on full.

I start to feel a little panicked. "I'm not dressed," is all I can think to say. "I thought there would be some kind of formal orientation first? Watch one of those *welcome to the company* films. Spend hours getting your email set up? Meet the boss? Go for a welcome drink?"

"My kinda girl," Bill chortles again.

"We've got you a uniform." James furrows his heavy brow my way, then turns sharply away to do more brooding.

Bill turns to me with an apologetic smile. "I'm sorry, this is all very sudden. But I'm sure you'll take to it just fine, with your incredible experience. Oh, don't look so sheepish—I was the one who hired you, remember? I've seen your CV."

"Right. Of course. Okay, let's go," I say as confidently as I can. No need to discuss my CV in front of James, or anyone.

Bill jumps into the nearest golf cart and turns on the ignition. James offers an impatient smile and nods toward the passenger seat.

"Cheers," I say as he jumps on a little platform on the back and hangs on.

"If James is edgy, it's because he needs to go over the menu with you, like, *now,*" Bill whispers.

I'm going to have to be careful with everything I say. Play the new girl. With the number of jobs I've had, that's one thing I can do.

We pull up at the entrance to the kitchen, and as the heavy modern door is pushed open, the light and noise spill out onto the courtyard, and suddenly a new set of senses comes fiercely alive.

The back kitchen is buzzing. There are three chefs in whites preparing for the evening service. Piles of small new potatoes are being scrubbed, and another chef has a great sheet of tiny herbs, which are being forensically picked through with what look like tweezers. There is a kind of rhythmical chorus as knives hit wood, pans slam on granite, and my block heels *clip-clop* across the stone floor.

"Hi, Chef," says the youngest-looking of them. He's covered in blood splatters and holding a comically large butchering knife. James nods in approval at the young lad, who blushes and smiles shyly back at him. It's a cute exchange, and I warm a little to James.

Smells of lemon zest and rich, dark chocolate fill my nose as we pass the pastry counter. Then the sting of onions hits my eyes as we duck under a low doorway into the preparation area. There are two rows of stainless-steel cooking surfaces and large ovens, and another serious-looking young chef, her dark hair stuffed into a hairnet, is standing over a huge pot, carefully spooning in what seems to be an enormous ladle full of tiny lobsters.

"Oh my god, baby lobsters," I whisper, aghast, but Bill has suddenly disappeared out through the swinging door into the restaurant. There's a glimpse of a dark, candlelit room with accents of deep red and tartan.

"Langoustines, three minutes, fifteen seconds. Rolling boil," the chef says to herself as she starts a small timer. *Langoustines.* I blush at my stupidity and take a deep breath. *I won't last five minutes if I don't keep my mouth shut.*

"Heather?" James calls to me from the service area, where he is sorting through scribbled sheets of paper.

"Hey. Jamie for short, is it?"

"James, actually," he says abruptly, before glancing at the floor. "Are you ready?"

"Sure," I reply, painting on a face full of efficiency and confidence.

He waves a piece of paper at me. "We've matches for the langoustine and hot-smoked salmon, but not the beetroot and pickled cabbage. We also need a pairing for the blade steak. I would have gone for a Cabernet, but there's the spring greens and turnip foam to consider in the balance. What do you think?"

James puts the paper down and looks up at me, and for the first time I see his full face in the light. He's definitely a looker, if you like that kind of accidentally handsome, full-lipped, furrowed-brow, forgot-to-shave-for-a-week kind of thing, which I most certainly do. Dark hair, chestnut eyes, and cheeks flushed from the heat of the kitchen. And in those starched chef's whites too. I try hard not to stare.

Okay. I'm definitely staring.

Still staring.

"Heather?"

I shake myself out of my daze and back to the job at hand.

"Do you have any ideas what we could pair them with?"

"What do you usually pair them with?" I ask, hoping for a shortcut.

"The menu changes all the time, with the season, so this is a new dish, I'm afraid. There's normally something new needs pairing every day. As I said, we often pair the blade steak with the Cabernet, but I think the turnip—"

"*The menu changes all the time?*" I gulp.

James takes a breath. "Sorry. I know this is a lot to take in. Before each service we sit and discuss the pairings for the degustation menu. The sommelier and me. Then I run it past Chef."

"Chef? I thought you were the chef."

"No," he says with a shy smile. "Russell Brooks, our new executive chef, will check over everything tonight. It has to be right first time," he says, somewhat apologetically.

"Russell Brooks." I smile. "Sounds like an electrical appliance."

My gag hangs in the air for a moment, then withers and dies.

"He's got two Michelin stars," James says, his eyes wide.

"Oh yes," I say quickly.

Two Michelin stars? That doesn't make sense. I thought this place was meant to be stuck in the Dark Ages. I glance around the kitchen and realize the whole setup does look rather too grand. "Of course I know who he is. Everyone knows Russell Brook."

"Brooks," he corrects.

"Yes." I nod quickly. "Two Michelin stars."

"Do you want a little time to familiarize yourself? I can give you thirty minutes, and then we have to get the draft ready for Chef." He offers me the menu.

I study James's face for a moment. I can't tell if he is desperately begging for my help or angry that I'm not helping already. One thing is for sure: He is waiting for me to take control, and up until this point I've been trying to delay the inevitable. Time to bite the bullet.

"Where do you keep the wine list? And the wine? I'll need to see the cellar and maybe do some sampling," I say, reaching for the food menu. Christ, it's complicated! This place is fancy as fuck. What the hell is smoked sea bacon? "What did you say I need to match, again?"

"The guinea fowl, the crab, the beetroot, and the blade steak," replies James, the raised vein on the side of his neck dissipating somewhat. "The new wine list is here," he says, dumping a large black leather folder into my arms. "And the cellar is out back, the way you came in, and down the stone stairs by the Deepfreeze. I can show you?"

"No need. I'll be half an hour," I say, nodding in determination, deciding the quiet of the wine cellar will be the safest place to panic. *New wine list?*

"One sec. Anis?" he calls to the baby-lobster boiler, who frowns at the disruption. She is carefully pouring deep-green oil into a blender with all the steady seriousness of an open-heart surgeon. "Once you've finished the dill emulsion, make a tasting plate for Heather," James commands.

"Yes, Chef." She scowls and heads to the refrigerator.

And with that, James nods and almost smiles, before going

back through to the kitchen. I breathe out for a moment, before remembering the clock is ticking and I have very little time to spare.

I walk quickly back through the preparation area and make my way down the gloriously romantic stone stairs to the cellar. I fish around for a light switch just as another bloody sensor light flicks on, but this time it's a warm, dull-yellow glow. My eyes adjust and, for a moment, I marvel at the space before me.

The cellar stretches out into the darkness, but it isn't only wine down here. Large rounds of cheese are stacked on modern steel shelving, and huge legs of cured ham and bacon hang from stainless-steel hooks in the ceiling. And beyond that, more cheese. God, I love cheese.

But there's no time to dither. I pull out my phone and lay the enormous wine list and the menu out on the shelf in front of me. Shit! This was certainly not the wine list I'd printed out from the website. The one I had stuffed in my bag back at the cottage had a dozen or so reds and whites, in varying degrees of cheap and less cheap.

The plan up until now—if you could call it a plan—was a crash course with my brand-new copy of *Wine for Newbies* and Sir Google as my tutors later this evening. Surface knowledge. A bluffable amount. Enough to blag my way through the summer at a crappy hotel in the middle of nowhere. Only the crusty, ramshackle, shithole Scottish hotel has not materialized, and instead I find myself in a fine-dining, luxury boutique property. This place is in need of a world-class sommelier to decipher the brand-new twenty-page wine list. Which I am definitely not.

It's time to call for help.

It's time to call the *real* Heather.

KERSTIN WEIDINGER

About the Author

LIZZY DENT is the author of *The Summer Job*, *The Setup*, and *The Sweetest Revenge*. She (mis)spent her early twenties working in Scotland in hospitality, and after years traveling the world making music TV for MTV and Channel 4, and creating digital content for Cartoon Network, the BBC, and ITV, she turned to writing. She now lives in Austria with her family.

CONNECT ONLINE

LizzyDent.com
🐦 DentLizzy
📷 Lizzy.Dent

About the Author